ICE

Lyn Gardner

Edited by Bron T.
Cover by Robin Ludwig Design Inc.
http://www.gobookcoverdesign.com

Library of Congress Number: 2014933409

ISBN 13: 978-1519261144

ISBN-10: 1519261144

Disclaimer: This is a work of fiction. Names, characters, businesses, places, events and incidents are either the products of the author's imagination or used in a fictitious manner. Any resemblance to actual persons, living or dead, or actual events is purely coincidental.

DEDICATION

To Tanya
May you rest in peace, and know that
when He called you home, tears fell around the world.

ACKNOWLEDGMENTS

I'd like to thank the readers of my fan fiction for insisting that
I could write. Thank you for the compliments, for the pokes,
for the prods, for the threats and for the laughs. Without you,
this would not have happened. I am forever in your debt.

PROLOGUE

After spending the last two hours standing in a cramped, filthy kitchen, as soon as Maggie Campbell exited the dilapidated house on the east side of London, she welcomed the feel of the cool night air on her face. Pausing for a moment to breathe in the dampness, when she saw that her long-legged partner was almost to the car, she mumbled to herself, "Oh, no you don't."

The silence of the night was broken by the sound of her sensible, low-heeled pumps on the walk as she ran after Blake. Finally catching up to her near the curb, Detective Inspector Maggie Campbell grabbed the other woman's arm and spun her around.

"What the hell is your problem?" Campbell shouted, glaring up at the woman.

Raising an eyebrow, Detective Inspector Alex Blake yanked her arm out of Campbell's grasp. Without saying a word, she reached into her pocket, pulled out her cigarettes and calmly lit one. Allowing the smoke to slowly exit her nose, she said, "Excuse me?"

Taking a step closer, Campbell growled, "What exactly do you call what you just did in there?"

"I call it, doing my job," Blake said.

"Your job? Your *job*! You're a police officer, not some sort of fucking vigilante, for Christ's sake! What you did was inappropriate and unprofessional! Do you have *any* idea how many rules you just broke?"

With a smirk, Blake replied, "I didn't break any, darling, I just bent a few."

Gritting her teeth at the sound of the endearment, Maggie said, "You threatened his bloody life!"

Alex Blake's temper began to simmer. Partnered with Campbell for only two weeks, it hadn't taken long for her to realize that her approach to a kidnapping investigation clashed with Campbell's, but they had both managed to work through their differences…at least, until now.

Swallowing back her anger, Alex thought twice before saying another word. Looking around, she could see that there was still at least a dozen police officers roaming about. Not wanting any of them to hear what she had to say, she leaned her five-foot ten-inch frame in Campbell's direction.

Setting her jaw, Blake growled, "I made him talk, and he told us what we needed to know. The boy is safe, and as far as I'm concerned, that's all that matters."

"So, acting like some sort of maniac is your idea of how to properly question a suspect?"

Crossing her arms, Blake said, "It worked, didn't it?"

"It's not the way it's supposed to be done!" Campbell said, clenching her fists. "We have rules to follow, and regulations to adhere to, or did you skip that part of the training?"

Dropping her cigarette on the grass, Blake pulverized what remained with the toe of her boot until it disappeared into the soil. Barely managing to hold on to her temper, she decided to walk away. It was her only option. If not, she knew that she'd say something she'd regret. Casting a steely glare in Campbell's direction, she said, "This conversation is over."

Turning on her heel, Alex began to walk away, but her momentum was stopped when Campbell grabbed her by the arm again.

"No, it's not!" Campbell yelled. "For two weeks I've had to put up with your bullshit. I've kept my mouth shut out of respect for the job that we were trying to do, and for the little boy who we were trying to find, but now that he's safe, I'm going to have my say!"

Invading the other officer's space, Campbell pointed her finger in Alex's face. "You're a lousy cop, Blake. You're a bully with a warrant card, and you don't know the first bloody thing about being a *good* detective. You're impulsive and insolent, and if someone gets in your way, you steamroll over them like they weren't even there!"

"I do what it takes," Alex replied through clenched teeth.

"No, you do what you *think* it takes, but I've got news for you, being a Detective Inspector takes more than muscle and threats. It takes intelligence, intuition and *tact*. It takes skill to examine the evidence, follow the rules and apprehend the suspect. It does *not* take the promise of dishing out bodily harm, such as cutting a man's dick off and ramming it down his throat!"

Well past simmering, Alex's temper was now at a rolling boil. Furrowing her brow, she yelled, "He talked, didn't he?"

"Yes, he did, but if you had allowed me to question him properly, using the bloody rules that we're *supposed* to follow, I assure you, the results would have been exactly the same!"

With every syllable, their voices were getting louder, and the officers milling about had begun to take notice. With Campbell a full six inches shorter than her partner, at first the exchange seemed almost comical. Most of them couldn't hide their grins as the smaller woman scolded the towering Blake, but as more and more words were spewed, their grins began to fade.

"I didn't break any *fucking* rules, and if I did, so what? It's my file being filled with reprimands, not yours."

"Jesus Christ, this is not about you! Your actions speak for all of us, don't you see that? We're all out there working our arses off trying to make the public trust us, and you come along and piss on everything we've tried to accomplish without batting an eye. You're dangerous, and you give the rest of us a bad name. If it was up to me, you wouldn't even be on the force."

"Well, it's not up to you, is it, you haughty little cow!" Alex Blake bellowed. "And you're not the only one that's had to put up with *shit*, Campbell. I have no idea how anyone could be your partner for a day, let alone two bloody weeks! You are, by far, the biggest brown-nosed tart I've ever met. You're like the Chief's pet, for Christ's sake. Skipping after him as he goes for his coffee so you can give him all your ideas, looking like a bloody dog waiting for a treat! And if that's not enough, I've had to put up with you prancing around in your fucking power suits, jotting down your little notes and offering witnesses cute little smiles in hopes that they'll talk. I may be a bit rough, darling, but at least I'm not laughable."

Pointing her finger in Blake's face, Campbell yelled, "You're nothing but a thug!"

"Maybe so, but it's better than being an arse-licking bitch!"

The force of the slap that followed sent Alex Blake to her knees.

CHAPTER ONE

Three years later…

"You *cannot* be bloody serious!"

Chief Superintendent Clive Ramsey looked up from his desk and offered a weak smile to the man who had just barged into his office. Most would have been severely reprimanded for such a loud show of disrespect, but when it came to Chief Inspector Andrew Loveland, Clive Ramsey graded on a curve. They had been friends for years, and even though Clive had moved up the ranks a bit quicker than his counterpart, their friendship had always remained strong.

Motioning for Andrew to close the door and take a seat, Clive returned his attention to the papers on his desk, but when he heard the door slam and the metal blind thwack against the glass, he looked up and scowled.

Offering only a shrug of his shoulders as an apology for the noise, Andrew sat in the chair opposite his supervisor and glared back. Andrew Loveland wanted answers, and he wanted them now. Holding up the roster, he mentally counted to ten before he blurted, "Clive, this is a joke, right?"

"I'm afraid not, Andy," Ramsey said, leaning back in his chair.

"Have you forgotten about that fiasco three years ago?"

Wincing at the memory, Clive Ramsey ran his fingers through his wavy, gray hair. Taking a deep breath, he said, "I don't think *anyone* will ever forget—"

"Then why the hell are you doing this?" Andy said, tossing the paper on his chief's desk in disgust.

"It's only for two days—"

"I don't care if it's for two bloody minutes! Those two hate each other. You know it. I know it. Hell, everyone in this department knows it!"

Up until that moment, the two men had always managed to keep their friendship and their work relationship separate. However, staring back at the red-faced man, Clive Ramsey knew that he would soon have to pull rank if his friend didn't compose himself.

"Andy," he began calmly, believing his tone of voice would somehow cool the man's temper. "I am well aware how they feel about each other, but the Commissioner called me this morning. He needs two female officers for this assignment and—"

"We have other female officers—"

"I know that, Andrew."

"But what happens if they—"

Knowing where his friend was going, Clive held up his hand, stopping Andrew in mid-sentence. "Andy, three years is a long time. People forget, *and* people grow up. Since that time, they've both had—" Stopping abruptly when he noticed the other man's eyebrow arch, Clive quickly corrected himself. "Okay, so Blake's file has got a bit of paper in it, but Campbell's been exemplary, which gives me every reason to believe that for *two* days, they'll be able to put their differences aside."

"And if they don't?"

"Then they answer to the commissioner, and if they can't control their dislike for one another, they may very well lose their jobs."

"But they're two of our best."

"You're preaching to the choir, Andrew," Clive said, glancing at the papers on his desk, signifying in his own way that the discussion was over.

Resigned to the fact that this was going to happen, Andrew asked, "So, what's the assignment?"

"All I can tell you is that they'll be acting as escorts for a government witness."

Andy's annoyance level rose again. Having already been left out of the decision to have two of his officers utilized for the assignment, now his chief was offering breadcrumbs instead of answers. With a huff, he said, "Why so cryptic? The last time I checked those two work for me."

"Yes, they do, but *you* work for me, and *I* work for the commissioner. This is on a need-to-know basis, and as far as I'm concerned, this conversation is over."

Taking a deep breath, Andrew Loveland stood and walked to the door. "So, I guess you want me to tell them—right?"

"No, actually I had that…um…*honor* earlier today, before they left shift."

"They already know?"

Nodding his head, Clive replied, "Yes, and believe it or not, neither said a word about it."

***

Standing on her front porch, Maggie Campbell rubbed the bridge of her nose. While no headache yet existed, she knew that in a short time, one would start. Unlocking the door, she walked quietly into her house. Setting her handbag and jacket on a nearby chair, she waited for her boyfriend to appear.

At the age of thirty-two, Margaret Katherine Campbell had worked for the Metropolitan Police Service for eight years. Born and raised in Scotland, she was the daughter of an Air Force Group Captain, and her upbringing had been regimented and directed toward the military. However, during her years in university, she developed a passion for the law, and after graduation, she took a job at the Met. Like most, she started out as a Constable, but her drive and hard work enabled her to climb the ladder faster than her colleagues. With a penchant for following the rules and regulations, she crossed every 'T' and dotted every 'I' along the way, and in five short years, she reached the rank of Detective Inspector with only one demerit to her name. Although she longed to continue her education at night to obtain the law degree she so desperately wanted, the demands of her job *and* her boyfriend, more often than not, got in the way.

"You're late," Glenn Shaw growled as he came from the kitchen with a dish towel in his hand. "I had to start dinner myself."

Biting her lip, Maggie took a slow, easy breath before she began to speak. "I'm sorry, but the chief called me into his office about an assignment, and I couldn't very well tell him no, now could I?"

Scowling, Glenn asked, "What do you mean an assignment?"

"It's just two days. I'll be home Friday night."

Throwing the dish rag on the floor, he yelled, "What?"

With a sigh, Maggie picked up the towel. "Glenn, please don't start."

Snatching the green and white cloth from her hands, he wound it around his fist. Glaring at her, he said, "Have you forgotten that we have plans?"

"I'll be home *Friday* night," Maggie repeated, walking to the lounge.

"Tell them no," he said, stomping after her.

"Glenn, I can't do that, and you know it. It's my job."

"I want you to quit!"

"What?"

"You heard me. Quit that bloody job. It's not a career for a woman anyway!"

Up until that moment, Maggie had managed to keep her annoyance in check, but Glenn had just pushed the wrong button, and her Scottish temper flared.

"And what the hell are we supposed to live on—eh? Or have you miraculously solved all your business issues?"

As soon as the words left her mouth, Maggie winced. For months, she had refused to allow her frustrations to show. Hiding behind false smiles, she had moved through endless nights and weekends with him by her side, hoping that things would get better. They hadn't, and she had finally reached her breaking point.

"Fuck you, Maggie!" he yelled, throwing the towel in Maggie's face. Grabbing his jacket, he stormed out of the house, slamming the door so hard that the glass rattled in the frame.

Sitting on the arm of the sofa, she shook her head and muttered, "Shit!"

They had met three years earlier when they had both been invited to a mutual friend's wedding in St. Albans. With yet another failed relationship under her belt, Maggie had gone stag and Glenn, having not yet met the girl of dreams, had done the same. Seated together during the reception, they struck up a conversation, and before the evening was over, they had agreed to a date.

The son of a vicar, Glenn Shaw was as polite and well-mannered as they came. Having just started a small landscaping company on the outskirts of London, most of his time and energy was directed toward getting his business off the ground, but he always managed to find time for Maggie.

Dutiful and attentive, he took her out to dinner, to the cinema, and for short walks in the park, and eventually, they became lovers.

Over the next two years, their relationship grew, albeit slowly. As Maggie worked her way up the law enforcement ladder, Glenn spent his days trying to keep his business afloat. Although he had a degree in horticulture, he had very little business sense, and it wasn't long before he had made enough bad decisions, that his bank account began to suffer.

After weeks of hearing him moan about money troubles, Maggie graciously suggested that he move in with her until his business got back on track. Believing her offer to be only temporary, when Glenn showed up and announced that he had sold most of his belongings to pay the bills, Maggie's heart sank. Even though they had been lovers for quite some time, Maggie always thought of Glenn as more like a friend with benefits rather than a man with which to build a life. In her attempt to do the right thing, she had tried to help a friend and ended up with a partner she didn't want.

Taking a deep breath, Maggie walked into the kitchen and looked around. Thankful that Glenn's idea of making dinner was simply heating up yesterday's leftovers, she pulled the dried chicken from the oven, and debating only for a moment, dumped it into the rubbish bin. Turning off the cooker, she poured herself a small glass of wine, flicked off the kitchen light, and as she slowly climbed the stairs, a distant ache began to invade her brain.

As she expected, the bedroom was in shambles. Disregarding the mess, she removed her suit jacket, and hanging it in the wardrobe, she reached down and pulled out a small overnight bag. Gathering what clothes she would need for two days, she packed her toiletry case and placed everything neatly inside the carry-on before going into the bathroom and turning on the taps. As the water began to steam she stripped out of her clothes, and as she stepped under the hot spray of the shower, she let out a long, relaxing breath. Thirty minutes later, feeling better than she had in hours, she emerged from the bathroom, but as soon as she saw the state of the bedroom, her head began to pound again.

Throughout their courtship, Glenn had always been the perfect gentlemen, almost to the point of being old-fashioned, and as far as Maggie had been concerned, it had been a refreshing change. She enjoyed that he preferred taking her to quiet restaurants over noisy pubs for their dinner dates, and when he suggested visiting a neighborhood park for a walk, it hadn't been because he had wanted to join the football game being played. From opening doors and pulling out chairs, to paying for dinner and chastely kissing her goodnight, Glenn Shaw seemed to be a man born a hundred years too late. Unfortunately, men born in the early nineteen hundreds also had other beliefs, and that fact became all too clear a few weeks after Glenn unpacked his clothes and hung them in her wardrobe.

Suddenly, he was content to stay at home so she could prepare him dinner, and whenever Maggie suggested that they go out to eat, he balked. Although not a sports fanatic, Maggie always enjoyed meeting her friends at a local pub during football season to watch a game and drink a few pints. It had been a way to unwind and to catch up with all of her mates, but Glenn didn't want to unwind, and Glenn didn't drink. A devout teetotaler, he loathed anything to do with alcohol and cigarettes, and even though they had visited a few pubs while they had dated, once he had moved in with Maggie, he no longer saw the need. While they continued to go for short walks in the park, the trips to the cinema also ended. No matter which movie Maggie would choose, he would find something about the film that he found appalling to the point that even trying to rent a video became impossible. However, of all the things that Maggie hadn't known about Glenn, the one that absolutely floored her happened only a few days after he had placed his slippers under her bed. As far as Glenn Shaw was concerned, housework was women's work.

As she stood in her disheveled bedroom, she shook her head at the mess, and with a sigh, went about picking it all up. Gathering the dirty clothes that he had left strewn all over the room, she tossed them on the floor of the closet and then straightened the bed. Fluffing her pillow, she wearily climbed under the duvet, and letting out a slow breath, she thought about the assignment she had been given. Protecting a witness for a few days wouldn't be a problem, but knowing that she'd be working with Alex Blake again, caused Maggie's blood pressure to rise.

Entering the police academy two years apart, they hadn't met until they had both been assigned to a kidnapping case three years before. While Maggie had heard dozens of stories about the cocky, live-on-the-edge Detective Inspector, nothing could have prepared her for meeting Alexandra Blake. Tall, beautiful, and with short black hair that had a style all its own, Maggie's first thought was that Blake looked more like a runway model than an Inspector. Even though she had felt dwarfed by both the woman's height and her beauty, Maggie had been the consummate professional, and with a handshake, they had become partners on the case.

At first, they were like oil and water when it came to how they approached the case, but in only a few days Blake's pig-headedness and Campbell's professionalism began to complement the other. When Blake would rant and rave, Campbell would calmly read through the facts, and then reeling Blake in, they'd discuss the case again. Methodically, they'd go over everything, and as they did, more clues were uncovered, more witnesses were found, and the powers-that-be were impressed.

Blake's ability to walk the fine line between right and wrong grated on Maggie's sensibilities throughout the assignment, but Maggie put her personal feelings aside. For fourteen days she worked the case like she had been taught, and surprisingly, things went rather smoothly, but on the fifteenth day, everything went to shit.

It hadn't been her finest moment, and as Maggie stared at the ceiling and thought about that damp and dreary night so long ago, she blanched at the memory. She regretted the words that she had spoken, as well as the slap that had sent Blake to the ground, but Maggie had done what she had needed to do...at least that's what she told herself.

With a sigh, she leaned over and switched off the light. With the help of two paracetamol, her headache had dulled, and closing her eyes, she prayed that tomorrow would be a better day.

***

Yanking a sweater from its hanger, Alex tossed it on the bed, and then stormed across the room toward her dresser. Snatching some underwear from a drawer, she balled them up, and one by one, hurled them at the bed.

Alex Blake had worked for the Met since the age of twenty-two. Born and raised in Surrey, she had grown up among the rich and famous, and before she had reached the age of eighteen, two modeling agencies had offered her contracts. Tall, slender, with eyes the color of cinnamon and cheekbones to die for, she could have easily graced the covers of numerous magazines without a care in the world, but Alex did care. She cared too much. Sitting around the breakfast table discussing the world with her parents, she learned of the wrongs and rights. She saw the grainy photographs in newspapers and read the words, and they horrified her. Alex Blake didn't choose her career. It chose her. So turning her back on the glitz and glamour of monthly publications filled with makeup advertisements and emaciated models, after graduating university, Alex joined the Metropolitan Police Service.

It took her seven long years to reach the rank of Detective Inspector. While her sights had been set slightly higher, and she believed she would attain them in a shorter amount of time, something always stood in the way: her attitude.

Alex was a good cop. In fact, she was an excellent cop. When it came to aiding victims, Alex was as caring as a mother would be to her newborn, but when it came to the criminal element, she was not. Driven, stubborn, and willing to cross the line if need be, more than once, her desire to catch the felon overshadowed acceptable operating procedures. Her overzealousness resulted in formal reprimands being placed in her file on more than one occasion, and once, her inability to control her temper resulted in a two-week suspension. However, Alex had a saving grace, and she knew it. She had the uncanny ability to study a crime scene and memorize every single detail.

While her fellow officers would spend hours poring over photographs or return to the scene of the crime for just one more look, Alex could see it all in her head. A dustless spot on a table where once sat a picture frame, or bedroom slippers now under the bed instead of next to it, were sometimes missed in a photograph, but they were never missed in her mind's eye. On occasion, her unorthodox methods would send shivers down the spines of some, but her drive and attention to detail had earned her the respect of not only her peers, but also her supervisors. They had learned to accept her quick temper and sharp tongue, and so had her friends.

Having spent the last few minutes watching Alex stomp around the bedroom mumbling expletives under her breath as she looked for clothes, Paige Harrison smiled. "Has your clothing done something to offend you in some way?"

Glancing over her shoulder at the statuesque blonde standing in the doorway, Alex growled, "I've got two bloody days until my holiday starts, and they're sending me on a fucking babysitting trip!"

Before Paige had a chance to say a word, Alex's tirade continued. "I've got enough bleeding paperwork on my desk to keep me busy for months, but does that matter? No! No, they think my time will be better spent traveling to bum-fuck nowhere just so someone's nose doesn't run!"

"I thought you liked your job?"

"I love my job!" Alex barked. "I love investigations. I love the hunt. I love catching the bad guy, but I don't love babysitting. Hell, I don't even like kids!"

Trying her best to lighten the mood, Paige joked, "Yeah, I can't see you playing with dolls to pass the time, unless, of course, they're the blow-up type."

With a huff, Alex glared at her best friend. "For Christ's sake, Paige, it was just an analogy!"

Thinking back over the past fifteen years, Paige hid her grin as she mentally tried to count the number of times Alex had lost her temper. Deciding that she didn't have enough fingers and toes to keep track, Paige leaned against the door frame and waited for Alex to calm down.

They had met at university, and before the first semester had ended, they became the best of friends, and prior to the second one ending, they had become lovers. Although their career choices differed, both were passionate about what they wanted from life, and it was that passion which ignited their lust for one another…at least for a little while.

Spending much of their time helping each other study or cram for tests, when their work was done for the night, they'd put down their books and talk about their dreams. Young and invincible, they rattled on for hours about what they wanted from life, before falling into bed and making love through the night.

At first, it was a perfect co-existence. They gave and took from one another exactly what they needed. They shared love, laughter and a few tears, but as one year passed and then another, things began to change. Focused on her career, Alex spent much of her free time studying police procedures and investigative techniques, and when she wasn't reading, she was working out.

While the Metropolitan Police Service had its fair share of women, men were still in the majority. Believing that some would label her a member of the weaker sex, Alex decided to prove them wrong. Never considering herself a fitness freak, she nevertheless worked her body until it was honed. Between the miles she ran on a treadmill, the mountains she climbed on an elliptical, and the weights she lifted until she could bench press twice her own, she gave herself a rock-hard physique while still maintaining the curves that announced her gender.

At times, Paige joined her in the gym, trying her best to share Alex's interests, but that became increasingly difficult by their third year in school. Majoring in business, Paige's goal after graduation was to open a nightclub where the lesbian and gay community would feel welcome. Preferring to spend her free time visiting the numerous pubs and nightclubs in the city gathering ideas for her dream club, it was inevitable that their interests would eventually pull them apart.

One night, after Paige had come back from a night on the town, they sat and talked honestly about their relationship. They decided that they would always be friends, but their romance had come to an end. After making love one last time, they held each other close, both wondering where their lives would take them, and in the morning, they parted as friends. Neither ever regretted their decision, and over the years, they rejoiced in the other's accomplishments and love affairs, and offered comfort when things didn't go as planned.

Standing in Alex's bedroom, watching as her friend's face seemed to get redder by the minute, Paige decided to try to offer comfort.

"Maybe you should have taken me up on my suggestion to come to the club last night. It might have helped you unwind."

"Oh, that would have been a great fucking idea!" Alex yelled as she threw her backpack on the floor. "That's all I would have needed today! Go to work with a hangover. Great idea, Paige! Bloody marvelous!"

Taken aback by Alex's outburst, Paige tilted her head as she stared back at her. Crossing her arms, she waited patiently until Alex, in all her fury, returned to earth.

A few minutes passed before Alex finally looked up, and seeing the expression on Paige's face, her shoulder's fell. Realizing that she was being a prat, she walked over and kissed Paige lightly on the cheek.

"I'm sorry, babe. That was wrong. I didn't mean to take it out on you."

"It's only for two days, Alex," Paige said. "I don't see why you're so wound up about it."

Glancing at the bed in the corner, Alex sighed. "I wanted to be here for Sandy."

Smiling, Paige said, "Alex, I've already said that I'd stay and keep an eye on her. I promise not to leave the flat until you get back tomorrow night."

A weak grin appeared on Alex's face as she walked over and retrieved the backpack. With a loud sigh, she began stuffing it with the clothing that she had tossed on the bed.

Chuckling to herself as she watched Alex push the wadded up clothes in the black satchel, Paige asked, "Does this have anything to do with Campbell being assigned to the same case?"

"I don't give a toss about her! It's Sandy I'm worried about."

"I just remember the last time—"

"Paige, that was three years ago."

"Yeah, but you two didn't exactly get along, now did you?"

"I don't know how *anyone* can get along with her!" Alex said in a huff. "She's so by-the-book it's fucking unbelievable. She's got to have that bloody thing shoved up her ass, as much as she can quote it, chapter and verse, all the while prancing around in her sensible shoes and power suits like she's about to be made Chief or something!"

If there was one person on the planet that knew Alex Blake, it was Paige Harrison. She had seen all of Alex's moods through the years. She had seen her high on life and down on love. She had seen her smile wide when a case had been solved, and she had seen her cry like a baby when a victim had been found just a little too late. There wasn't much that Alex could hide from Paige, no matter how hard she tried, and right now, Alex was as transparent as glass.

"You like her, don't you?"

"What?" Alex blurted as she looked up. "Who?"

"You know *who*…Campbell."

"Paige, you're daft! She's a pain in the arse, and if she was any straighter, she'd be a fucking lightning rod!"

Paige's eyes went wide. Snickering, she said, "Oh, she must be gorgeous to get you this worked up."

"Fuck off, Paige," Alex said as she disappeared into the bathroom to gather her toiletries. Emerging a few minutes later, when Alex saw the knowing expression on Paige's face, her mood softened. Paige was right, and they both knew it. Preferring not to talk about the woman who she would be spending the next two days with, Alex quickly changed the subject.

"You're going to take care of Sandy for me, right? I mean, don't leave her alone or anything, and don't forget the doctor's number is on the fridge."

Rolling her eyes, Paige said, "Alex, I know where the phone number is, and I already said that I wouldn't go anywhere until you get home. She'll be fine. I promise."

Seeing Alex pull yet another sweater from her wardrobe, along with a long, black leather coat, Paige asked, "What the hell are you doing? It's not that cold outside."

"I was told to bring a warm coat and pack for cold weather," Alex replied, stomping out of the room.

"Where are you going anyway?" Paige called out as she walked to the corner of the bedroom and knelt by the small bed on the floor.

"I've got no fucking idea!" Alex yelled back from the lounge.

Grinning, Paige leaned over and patted the head of a very pregnant five-pound Yorkshire terrier named Sandy. Giggling as the dog returned her affection with a few quick kisses, Paige whispered to the black and tan ball of fur, "Your mum is a complete nutter, but one thing's for sure, she loves you more than anything else in the world." Pausing for a moment, she remembered Alex's tirade when Detective Inspector Campbell's name had been mentioned. Smiling to herself, Paige leaned over to place a kiss on Sandy's head. "At least, I think she does."

Once again, the little dog anointed Paige's face with lick after lick of love, before putting her head down and covering her nose with a paw.

CHAPTER TWO

Walking through the concourse, Alex ran her fingers through her short black hair. As directed by her chief, she had taken a taxi to the airport, and once passing through security, she had been escorted down several corridors to a small lounge where she was instructed to sit and wait. Noticing the vending machines, she quickly ordered up a large black coffee, and since no one was around to tell her different, defiantly lit a cigarette. Although Alex was certain that smoking was not allowed, she inhaled the mentholated smoke and smiled, enjoying the fact that she was knowingly breaking a rule…just for the sake of breaking it.

It wasn't long before boredom set in, and with nothing but housekeeping and gardening magazines to read, she walked to the windows that ran along the length of the back wall of the room. Taking a seat, she mindlessly watched as the workers on the tarmac loaded and off-loaded luggage. About to have the last drag of her cigarette, Alex heard the door open, and glancing over her shoulder, she watched as Maggie Campbell walked into the room.

During the ride to the airport, Alex Blake had made herself a promise. She would not push buttons. She would not start an argument, cast a dirty look, or make a derogatory comment. However, defense mechanisms are just that: ways of preventing people from getting too close or from seeing the truth, and as far as Alex was concerned, she had no intention of allowing Campbell to do either. Alex had learned her lesson the hard way, and even though she thought Maggie was the most beautiful woman that she had ever laid eyes on, the woman was undeniably straight. End of subject. Time to push buttons.

Quickly giving her the once over, Alex held back a snicker. Matching the description that Alex had given Paige earlier that morning, Detective Inspector Maggie Campbell's choice in clothing defined the word nondescript. Wearing a dark-gray jacket with trousers to match, and a pair of black, ankle-high, featureless boots, the only bit of color *not* in the shade of mourning was the maroon cowl neck sweater that Campbell wore underneath the suit.

Curling her lip in disgust at the smell of cigarette smoke in the air, Maggie cast a dirty look in Blake's direction. Having enjoyed an occasional cigarette during her days at university, Maggie had never been offended by the smell, but smoking in public places was now against the law. She knew it, and so did Alex Blake.

Unable to hold back a smirk at the silent reprimand she was being given, Alex took one final drag before dropping the remainder of her cigarette into her half-empty coffee cup. Tossing it in a nearby rubbish container, she returned to her seat near the window. Glaring back at Maggie, Alex slowly blew the smoke above her head.

Despite being bothered by Blake's total disregard of the law, the dull throb between Maggie's temples was all the headache that she could handle at the moment. Simply shaking her head in disgust, she placed her coat and handbag on a nearby chair and headed to the vending machine to get a cup of tea. Pulling a bottle of over-the-counter painkillers from her pocket, she tapped out two, and as soon as her tea was cool enough to drink, she quickly washed them down. Closing her eyes for a moment as if hoping they would work instantaneously, when they didn't, she let out a long breath and pocketed the bottle. Refusing to look in Alex's direction, Maggie walked to the small seating area in the middle of the room, picked up a magazine and sat down.

Alex stopped just short of laughing out loud at the cold shoulder she was being given, but after three years, she had become somewhat used to it. Working in the same department, it was inevitable that they'd occasionally see each other during the morning meetings, or while refilling their coffee mugs, but in all that time, Maggie had never said a word, and Alex had been thankful for the silence. She regretted what she had said that fateful night, but every time she found herself wanting to apologize, Maggie would throw one of her patented condescending looks in Alex's direction. Without saying a word, Alex would walk away, all the while telling herself it was the way it had to be.

Sitting quietly by the window, Alex had observed Campbell take the medication. Deciding that it would be a very long two days if someone didn't at least try to make an effort, she rose to her feet and walked across the room. Sitting in a chair across from Campbell, Alex debated for a minute before politely asking, "Are you afraid of flying?"

Up until that moment, the only sound in the room had been the hum of the vending machine. Startled by the interruption, it took Maggie a few seconds before she finally managed to blurt, "No, of course not!"

Amused by Campbell's obvious indignation at her innocent question, Alex tried to explain. "I'm sorry. I just thought…well, I noticed you taking the painkillers, and I thought that maybe you didn't like to fly."

"I've got a bloody headache, if you must know," Maggie snapped back. "It's got nothing to do with flying, and it has absolutely nothing to do with *you!*"

Without waiting for a response, Maggie stared back at the magazine in her lap. Embarrassed by her own outburst, and shocked that she had felt the need to tell the woman that her headache wasn't due to anything Alex had done, Maggie began flipping through the magazine at breakneck speed.

A few minutes later, reaching the end of the boring periodical, Maggie tossed it aside. Casting a quick glance in Blake's direction, she breathed a sigh of relief, seeing that the woman was no longer paying her any attention.

With her eyes closed, Alex was leaning back in her chair seemingly oblivious to her surroundings *and* to her company. Her long legs, encased in black denim, were stretched across the coffee table, and as Maggie looked at the woman, she couldn't help but notice the knee-high leather boots that Alex was wearing. Glancing at her own pair of ankle-high, Maggie frowned. Although technically it had only been her superior's suggestion to wear her warmest winter clothes, as far as Maggie was concerned, it had been a directive. Unfortunately, she hadn't planned to spend the entire morning in a knock-down, drag-out fight with Glenn, but it was time well spent. She was now without a flat-mate *and* a boyfriend, and not having the time to hunt down her winter boots seemed a small price to pay for the luxury of being single again.

Turning her attention back to Alex, Maggie studied her for a moment. Alex Blake hadn't really changed much in the past three years. Her hair was still worn short, and her fondness for simplistic, yet stylish clothing was more than obvious. The straight-leg designer jeans and turtleneck jersey she wore appeared new, as the color of both had yet to be washed out by dozens of cleanings. However, in contrast, the fabric of the oxford shirt covering the black turtleneck was frayed a bit at the cuffs, and the once crisp, white Pima cotton had been softened by age.

Noticing that Alex was beginning to stir, Maggie was about to reach for another magazine when she heard the door behind her open. Glancing over her shoulder, she watched as a tall, balding man with wire-rimmed glasses walked into the room. Placing a large shopping bag on the floor, he removed his raincoat, and tossing it on a chair, he retrieved the bag and approached the Inspectors.

"My name is John Harper," he began, handing Maggie the bag. "You'll need to put these on."

Raising an eyebrow, Maggie glanced into the bag. Seeing that it contained what appeared to be old and ragged clothing, she looked up at Harper and said, "Excuse me?"

"I know you were told that you'd be escorting a witness today, but that's not entirely the case."

Taking a step closer to the man, Blake asked, "Who the hell are you?"

With a snort, he pulled out his identification, and flipping it open, he stated, "John Harper, Interpol."

"Interpol?" Alex asked.

"Like I was saying, you weren't exactly given all the facts," he said, slipping his identification back into his pocket.

Confused, Alex leaned over and looked into the bag. Seeing the clothing inside, she quickly added two and two.

"Christ, we're decoys, aren't we?" Alex said, trying to keep her temper in check.

Nodding, Harper said, "I'm afraid so. Normally, this type of thing would be handled by our own people, but we believe we might have a leak in our department, so we asked the Met for help. We have a woman in custody that we need to keep out of harm's way. In order to get her out of the country in one piece, I've arranged for three teams of officers to pose as the woman and her escort. Each team will leave here today on separate flights, all of which will be heading in different directions. You and DI Campbell will be one of those teams."

Accustomed to following orders, without saying a word, Maggie headed to the ladies' room to change her clothes, leaving Harper alone with Alex...and her temper.

Perturbed that her assignment had just been reduced to a ruse, Alex walked over and sat down. Defiantly crossing her arms, she groused, "Apparently Campbell fits this woman's description, but why me? I don't see why you can't get a constable to play *my* part!"

Frowning, Harper said, "Detective Inspector Blake, apparently you think this is a waste of your time?"

"Yes, I do. I would think someone in your position would know better than to waste the time of two Detective Inspectors on nothing but a bloody ruse."

Narrowing his eyes, he said, "Well, Inspector, I frankly don't give a damn what *you* think. You *will* escort DI Campbell through the airport and onto a small jet we have waiting, just as you've been ordered to do."

"So she gets on the plane, and I leave?" Alex asked, quickly sitting up in her chair.

Snickering at the DI's continual attempt to shorten her assignment, Harper shook his head. "No. You and DI Campbell will take a rather long flight, land at a small airport, change planes, and *then* you will return to London."

"But—"

"That's final, Blake, and I think it wise that you shut your mouth and do your job! I may not be your direct supervisor, but trust me, I have his number."

Knowing that she was very close to stepping over the proverbial line again, Alex did as instructed and remained quiet until she heard the door to the ladies' room open. Glancing over her shoulder, Alex couldn't help but grin at the sight of her fellow Inspector.

Campbell's gray power suit and maroon sweater had been replaced by an ill-fitting black wool skirt and a baby blue twin set, and draped around her neck was a garish paisley scarf. Her polished ankle-high boots had been exchanged for a pair of scuffed black slip-ons, and to complete the ensemble, over her arm she was carrying a dowdy black cloth coat which had seen better days.

As soon as Maggie came back into the room, she glared at Blake as if daring her to say a word, but the other detective remained mute, although the grin Alex was wearing said it all.

"You'll need to cover your hair with that scarf, I'm afraid," Harper ordered. "And I'll need your mobiles."

Forgetting the Interpol agent's scolding tone a moment earlier, Alex blurted, "What? Why?"

Scowling, Harper took a deep breath and held out his hand. Eyeing the obstinate police officer, he said, "Those signals can be traced. You'll get them back when you return to London."

Having finally grasped the concept that it was pointless to argue with the man, Alex reached into her pocket and handed him her shiny piece of state-of-the-art technology, with Campbell following suit immediately. While he quickly slipped Maggie's mobile into his pocket, he examined the other high-end phone for several seconds before grinning at Alex and dropping it in his pocket. As the two women stood in silence, Harper gave them their instructions.

A short time later, following their orders, they left the room and walked down several long corridors before re-entering the bustling airport concourse through an unmarked door. As instructed, Alex kept her hand wrapped around Campbell's bicep as she guided her to the departure gates. Acting the part of someone older and frail, with her face partially hidden by the drape of the scarf, Maggie kept her head bowed and her voice silent as dozens of people hurried by.

Their hearts were pounding as the women made their way through the airport. The knowledge that an attempt could be made on their lives was frightfully real, so when they finally reached the gate, both let out a sigh of relief. Ushered through another door by a waiting police officer, they walked down the stairs and exited the building.

Assuming it would be hours before she could feed her nicotine habit again, as soon as they were standing outside, Alex pulled Maggie to an abrupt halt. Quickly fumbling to light a cigarette, Alex refused to acknowledge the evil look she was being given. A minute later, she tugged at Maggie's arm, and silently they walked across the tarmac to a small corporate jet.

At five-foot-four, when Maggie boarded the small jet she had no issue with the low ceiling height; however, Alex wasn't so lucky. More interested in the interior of the plane than the lack of headroom, she immediately bumped her head against the ceiling.

"Fuck," Alex mumbled, rubbing her head.

Paying no attention to the expletive Alex had blurted, Maggie shrugged out of her coat.

As Alex tried to struggle out of hers, she noticed an attractive flight attendant walking from the cockpit.

"I'll hang them up for you if you'd like?" she said, holding out her hand.

Smiling at the attractive redhead, Alex placed her coat in the woman's outstretched hand.

"Thanks. I'm Alex Blake…and you are?"

Having been a flight attendant for several years, Jane Connors grinned at the look being thrown her way. Over the course of the past decade, she had been hit on by dozens of men, it was part of the job, but there had only been a few occasions when a woman had tried to catch her eye. Noticing that the detective's fingers had lingered a little too long when the coat had exchanged hands, Jane was confident that if she was interested in joining the Mile High Club with Alex Blake, it would happen. Unfortunately for Alex, Jane Connors wasn't interested.

Unable to prevent a small snort of amusement from escaping, Jane stared back at the beautiful woman with the dark, smiling eyes. "My name's Jane...and I'm happily married. Now, why don't you two take a seat. It'll be a few minutes before we're ready to leave."

Confused, but indifferent at the flight attendant's cryptic reply, Maggie walked down the aisle and took a seat. Seconds later, bowing her head to prevent another run-in with the low ceiling, Alex casually strolled up the row and sunk her long, lanky body into a seat. Within minutes, they were rumbling down the runway en route to their unknown destination.

***

The bitter Arctic wind blew ferociously across the snowy tundra as the dropping pressure forced masses of air to swirl and push through the darkened winter skies. A sliver of sunlight still visible on the icy horizon faded behind the gusts and eddies that whipped snow into the air as the storm began to build. Squinting against the flurry of ice in the air, a polar bear made a mournful sound as she called to her cubs, and two white-coated bodies lifted their noses toward Heaven. Mirroring their mother, they sniffed. Too young to know the scent, two pairs of dark eyes looked back at their tense mother. Her snout in the air, she continued to sniff. She knew the scent. It was the scent of danger.

The mammals of the Arctic Circle weren't the only warm-blooded creatures paying attention to the danger looming in the Northern Hemisphere. Meteorologists, climatologists and atmospheric scientists from all over the world were on the phone, on the fax and on their computers. Debating, assuming, postulating, predicting and at times guessing, they bantered back and forth as data from satellites filled their computer screens with images curious and possibly deadly.

They knew that problems would be born from what lurked high above the clouds. A few fenders would no doubt be bent, and some would lose a day at work for traveling would be precarious, but if their predictions were correct, a small part of the world would simply stop. There would be no venturing out the morning after to stock up on forgotten supplies, and mountains would not be visited by skiers with smiling faces and knit caps. People would be far too busy doing other things, like staying alive. The average neighborhood roof isn't built to withstand the weight of the snow the blizzard could bring, and homes not having a set of stairs leading up to their front door, would be lost behind dunes of white, several feet tall. Parked cars would be consumed, fire hydrants would be buried, and electricity and cable would be iffy at best.

Of course, there was still time for things to change. Upper troughs and ever-changing winds could easily alter courses, but warnings were issued, nonetheless. As always, some took heed, running to their favorite market to fill their cart with the essentials, topping off their gas tanks and making sure they had plenty of videos to watch, while others scoffed and turned their backs. They had enough to last a day or even two. They were fools.

There had been another storm that some had labeled perfect, but this one…this one was more than perfect. If the pieces of the puzzle slipped into place as many believed they would, this storm wouldn't be perfect. It would be God.

***

Shortly after takeoff, Jane walked down the aisle. Stopping near Maggie, she offered a soft smile as she asked, "Would you like a drink, Detective Inspector?"

On duty, and her throat now sore and scratchy, Maggie quietly replied, "Just water please."

"And how about you, Alex?" Jane asked, grinning at the smiling officer to her right.

Noticing how Campbell looked up when the question had been asked, Alex said, "I know you can't tell us *where* we're going, but can you at least tell us how much time we have before we land?"

"Oh, several hours, I'm afraid."

Without missing a beat, Alex said, "I'll take a scotch."

Seeing Campbell's expression change from one of interest to one of contempt, Alex quickly added, "On second thought, make it a double."

"Double it is," Jane said with a wink.

"Oh, before you go. Can you give me a hand with this entertainment unit? It doesn't seem to be working," Alex said, pointing to the small digital screen to her right.

Frowning, Jane said, "That's because it's turned off. We're not allowed to tell you where you're going, and those units have destination and directional settings. I'm sorry."

"Can I at least listen to some music?"

"No, I'm afraid it's all connected, but we have quite a few magazines around. Shall I bring you one?"

With a sigh, Alex nodded her head. "Sure, but bring me all you've got."

CHAPTER THREE

Having already broken the rule about drinking on duty, Alex decided to break another. With nothing but time on her hands and scotch in her belly, it wasn't long before she reclined her seat and fell asleep. At times, the flight became bumpy, and she stirred at the turbulence, but shifting in her seat and mindless of Campbell sitting across the row, Alex returned to her dreams without a care in the world.

Six hours later, she opened her eyes and the first thing she noticed was that Campbell's seat was empty. Shrugging at the discovery, Alex yawned. In need of the bathroom, she lowered her footrest, but before she could stand, Jane appeared and knelt by Alex's seat.

"I think your partner is ill," she said in a hushed tone.

Still wiping the sleep out of her eyes, Alex stared back. It took her several seconds before she finally realized who Jane was talking about.

"Campbell is *not* my partner. We're just working together for today and today *only*," Alex growled back. "And she's just afraid of flying, but she's too bloody proud to admit it."

A bit surprised at Alex's harsh response, Jane stood up, and as she was walking away, she said quietly, "Well, I just thought you should know."

As she watched the shapely flight attendant walk up the aisle, Alex let out a long sigh. A victim of air sickness a few times in her life, most of which had been caused by the amount of alcohol she had consumed, Alex suddenly found herself becoming sympathetic to Campbell's predicament. Taking a deep breath, she climbed out of her seat and strolled down the aisle. Just as she got to the restroom, the door swung open and Campbell emerged.

Shocked by the woman's ghostly appearance, Alex asked, "Are you okay?"

Trying to pay Blake as little attention as possible, Maggie walked around the woman blocking her path.

"I'm fine," she muttered.

"Hey," Alex said, grabbing Campbell's arm to stop her escape. "You look a bit pasty, that's all."

Achy, sweating, and feeling if her head was about to explode, Maggie yanked her arm out of Blake's grasp. "If I want your concern, I'll bloody well ask for it. Now leave me the hell alone!"

Startled by the woman's outburst, Alex watched as Campbell slowly made her way to her seat, carefully holding onto several seat backs as she weaved her way down the aisle.

***

An hour later the plane landed on a sparsely lit runway in the middle of nowhere, and as soon as the exit door was opened, Campbell rushed from the small jet.

Walking to the exit, Blake took her coat from Jane and asked, "So what now?"

"Well, this is as far as we take you."

"What? Harper said we'd be back in London by tomorrow!"

"Relax," Jane said with a grin. "They've made arrangements for another plane to fly you back. There's apparently a rather nasty storm brewing, so we've been told to refuel as quickly as possible and get out of here."

"I don't understand. Why can't we just go back with you?"

"Because we're heading in another direction, I'm afraid," Jane said. Walking to the cabin door, she pointed at a hangar in the distance. "Inside, there's an office to the left. The people in there will get you back to civilization."

Exiting the plane, Alex quickly lit a cigarette, and hunching her shoulders at the frigid air cutting its way through her coat, she trotted across the tarmac. Pausing near the door for one more quick drag, she flicked the butt to the ground, and then headed to the office with purpose in her step. The sooner she found Campbell, the sooner they could board a plane and get back to London.

Walking inside, she was surprised to see that the only person in the room was a man sitting behind a desk working at a computer. Gnawing on the stub of his cigar as he studied what was on his screen, he looked up for a moment to acknowledge her arrival with a simple nod before returning his eyes to the monitor.

"Where's Campbell?" she said.

"Your partner's in the restroom," he said, gesturing to a door across the way.

"She is *not* my partner," Alex mumbled under her breath as she glanced around the room. Noticing a coffeemaker on a small table, she walked over and poured herself a cup. Turning back around, she studied the man at the desk. Looking to be in his mid-forties, the green jacket he wore appeared to be of military issue; however, all the insignia had been removed.

"So what happens now?" she asked.

"Well, you were supposed to leave immediately, but there's a massive storm coming in, so we need to check a few more things before deciding whether you'll be leaving tonight, or in a few weeks."

"*A few weeks*!" she shouted.

Nodding his head, he removed the chewed cigar from his mouth. "Like I said, it's a mother of a storm."

Running her fingers through her hair, she said, "Look, I've got responsibilities back in London, and I *cannot* stay here!"

"I understand, love, but if we *can* get you out of here, it's going to be one hell of a ride, and I don't think your partner's up for it."

"What the hell are you talking about?"

"She came in and headed straight for the bathroom. Between you and me, she looked like shit."

***

The illness that was slowly creeping into Maggie's body had begun to take its toll, and even though she had been told that she could change back into her own clothes on the plane, she hadn't been able to find the strength. Still dressed in her frumpy disguise, Maggie sat on the floor of the tiny bathroom as she tried to open the safety cap of the painkillers. Hearing someone knock at the door, she sighed. "I'll be out in a minute."

"You've been in there for almost fifteen, now open the bloody door," Blake said.

"Just wait your turn, okay?"

Already furious that they may be stranded in the desolate airport for a few weeks, Alex Blake's temper boiled over. "Campbell, either you open this bloody door or by God, I'll kick it in!"

Too tired to argue, Maggie paused for only a moment before crawling over and unlocking the door. Sliding back to the corner of the bathroom, she rested her head against the cool tile wall and let out a long breath.

After hearing the latch being thrown, Alex mentally counted to ten before opening the door. Stunned to see Maggie sitting on the floor, it only took a second for Alex to realize that the woman was ill. Although the room was cool, Maggie's forehead and upper lip glistened with perspiration, and her face had turned ghostly pale.

Kneeling by Maggie's side, Alex asked, "What's wrong?"

"Nothing, just give me a minute," Maggie said in a hoarse whisper.

"That's crap and you know it," Alex snapped. Cupping Campbell's chin in her hand, Alex turned her face so she could see her clearly, and when she felt the heat radiating from Maggie's skin, Alex said, "You've got a fever."

"Yeah, I know. I think it's the flu. It was going around the department last week."

With a sigh of relief, Alex stood up and stared at the woman on the floor. "Oh, is that all."

"What?"

"I thought it was something serious."

Seeing that Alex was about to leave, Maggie swallowed hard. "Blake...wait."

Turning around, Alex said, "Why?"

"I need to get to a hospital."

With a snort of disgust, Alex shook her head. "A bit over dramatic, don't you think?"

Defeated, Maggie shook her head. "I'll die if I don't get to one."

"What the hell are you talking about?"

"Can't you just trust me?"

"Look, you don't know this, but there's a storm coming in. The guy outside said we might be here for weeks."

"No!" Maggie cried out. "We can't be. I can't...I won't..."

Seeing that Campbell appeared on the verge of hysterics, Alex angrily grabbed her by the arm and pulled her off the floor.

"What the fuck is going on, Campbell? Tell me, or I'm walking out that door, and you're on your own."

Maggie pulled away and walked slowly to the sink. Turning on the tap, she soaked some paper towels with cold water and held them against her forehead. Uncomfortable with the fact that she was about to confess a weakness to Blake, she let out a long breath before turning around. Refusing to look the woman in the eye, Maggie said, "Ever since I was a kid, whenever I got really sick, like with the flu or something, I'd end up getting a…a high fever."

Tilting her head as she processed the information, Alex asked, "How high?"

"High enough to put me in the hospital."

When Blake didn't respond, Maggie raised her eyes, and seeing Blake's expression, it was clear that the Detective Inspector was waiting for something more. Taking a ragged breath, Maggie said, "High enough to kill me."

When she had walked into the bathroom, the only thing Alex had allowed herself to feel for Campbell was contempt, but seeing the worried look in the green eyes staring back at her, Alex's disdain disappeared. Without saying a word, she left the room.

Believing that the insolent officer was refusing to help, tears sprang to Maggie's eyes, but then the door opened and Alex walked back inside.

Placing the bag containing Maggie's belongings on the floor, she said, "Change your clothes." Seeing Campbell's puzzled expression, Alex added, "I've got to convince them to get us out of here, and when I do, you've got to be ready. Okay?"

Nodding her head, Maggie said softly, "Thank you."

"Don't thank me yet, darling," Alex said, offering the woman a weak smile before walking out and closing the door behind her.

In four quick strides, Alex was standing in front of the man at the desk. "I need to see the pilot."

"There's no point in that now."

Narrowing her eyes, Alex asked, "What do you mean?"

"The decision's been made. We're grounded."

"No!"

"Sorry, but—"

"Where's the pilot?"

"Look, I know—"

"I said, *where's the bloody pilot!*" Alex barked.

Taking a deep breath, the man stared at the woman who was glaring back at him. Deciding that he wasn't paid enough to deal with the likes of her, he gestured toward a door at the opposite side of the office.

"He's through there."

Turning on her heel, Alex stormed across the room. Without wasting time to knock, she pushed open the door with such force that it slammed against the inside wall. Startled by the noise, the man sitting behind the desk in the small office jumped, and the coffee mug he had been holding emptied into his lap.

"Jesus Christ!" he hollered as he got to his feet. "What the hell do you think you're doing barging in here like that?"

"We need to get out of here," Alex said, ignoring the fact that the front of his trousers were now covered in coffee.

Scowling back at her, he said, "Sorry, honey, no can do."

"Yes, you can, and by God, you will."

Flicking the coffee from his hand, he picked up a stack of papers and shoved them in Alex's face. "Do you see these? These are weather reports, and every bleeding one of them shows three nasty storms heading our way. They're coming from almost every direction, and in another hour, they'll be here. The only thing we can do is hunker down and ride them out. We've got plenty of food and water to make it through—"

"Do you have a doctor?" Alex blurted, grabbing the papers from his hand and tossing them on the desk.

Thrown off by her question, he eyed her up and down. "You sick?"

"No, but Campbell is."

"How sick?"

Pausing for a moment, Alex said, "She's got a fever, and if we don't get her to a hospital, she'll die."

Befuddled, his eyes narrowed. "What the hell are you talking about?"

"Look, I don't know the specifics, but she says that it'll kill her if it goes untreated, and I believe her."

Sitting on the edge of the desk, he crossed his arms. "Well, that makes one of us."

"You don't know her, but I do. She's as by-the-book as they come, and she wouldn't lie...not about something like this. I'm begging you, if there is any chance that we can make it to a hospital, we've got to try."

Taking a deep breath, he rubbed his chin as he debated on what to do. Glancing at Alex again, he paused for a moment before rising to his feet. Deciding to question Maggie himself, he walked out of the room without saying a word, but came to an abrupt halt when he saw her standing just outside the bathroom door. He had seen her only a few minutes earlier when she had come into the hangar, and at the time he had noticed that she appeared ill, but now she looked cadaverous. Watching her sway slightly as she held onto the door frame for support, he no longer needed to ask any questions...because she was the color of death.

Without acknowledging Alex as he went back to his chair, his eyes darted back and forth between the weather reports scattered across his desk. Turning to his computer, he began tapping away on the keyboard, mumbling every once and a while at the images flickering on his screen.

Minutes ticked by as Alex stood in silence watching the thick-waisted pilot study the weather reports until finally, he looked up and nodded his head. Standing, he grabbed his jacket and said, "I'll get the checklist done, and you get her ready. We don't have a lot of time, so don't dilly dally…and if you believe in God, you'd best start praying."

***

He sat in his bedroom sipping a beer, intently watching the images on the three monitors spread across his desk. Lighting another cigarette, he glanced at the window to make sure it was open; his parents didn't like him to smoke in their house. Most his age would have moved into their own homes by now, but he wasn't like most. He had no interest in leaving for greener pastures. These were green enough. They fed him. They housed him. They loved him. He loved them back.

They knew of his addiction and tried their best to look the other way. There really wasn't any harm in it. Police weren't going to knock on the door because of the Internet sites he surfed. They were legal; put there by people with the same affliction that had caused him to rush home from work that day. He just had to see her again. He had to see *them* again.

It had started three days prior, and when he saw her for the first time he couldn't look away. She was large and subtle as she slowly moved in front of his eyes. She was hypnotic, and he had named her Andrea.

Smiling to himself at the names he had given them, he took another sip of his beer and turned his attention to the center screen. This one he called Gabrielle. Although more voluptuous than Andrea, it wasn't Gabrielle's full-figure that had caught his eye; it was her muscles and her strength. He could tell that she would be a force to be reckoned with, and his excitement grew.

His eyes moved to the monitor on the right, and he studied the image on the screen. Aloof and wild, he had named the last one Valerie.

His thoughts were interrupted by his mother calling up the stairs. Wishing him a good evening, she asked that he not stay up too late, and easily, he replied that he wouldn't, but he had lied. Such was the life of a weather geek.

Andrea had appeared a few days before. A low-pressure system which had formed over the Pacific Ocean, she had gathered strength and moisture before slowly, seductively moving east-north-east. She had been stalled by a high-pressure system that had formed over the Great Plains, and remaining cradled in the clouds, she churned, patiently waiting for Gabrielle to arrive.

A massive cold front over two thousand miles long, Gabrielle had swept over the Labrador Sea, hungrily consuming moisture and cold as she continued to move west. Well aware of her track, the National Weather Service in the United States, as well as the Meteorological Service of Canada had issued their severe weather warnings, and he had read them both, wondering if his forecast would match that of the experts. On his way home from work that night, listening to his favorite twenty-four-hour weather station, his chest swelled with pride. He was right. There were three.

Valerie was a nasty bitch that had begun to form over the Arctic Ocean that very morning. Another low-pressure system, she carried with her tremendous winds and frigid, polar temperatures. Meandering south, sucking up every ounce of moisture and wind as she went, she was slowly creeping toward Gabrielle and Andrea with a purpose. Destruction.

A shiver ran down his spine as he thought about the power of Mother Nature. Any one of the storms could easily wreak havoc with just the precipitation that they held in their clouds, but together they were going to be cataclysmic.

Picking up his calculator, he read the data flashing on the monitors, and after entering a few numbers, he sat back in his chair. Fifty-seven minutes.

CHAPTER FOUR

Slowed by the fever, it had taken Maggie every ounce of energy she had to change into her own clothes and emerge from the bathroom. Pausing to catch her breath, she closed her eyes and leaned against the door in hopes that the room would stop spinning. She felt surrounded by a thick fog, its murkiness pressing the life out of her as she fought to stay awake and aware. Time seemed to stand still, mired in the muck of pain and aches, she had no idea how long they had been at the airstrip, but for Maggie, it seemed like an eternity. At the sound of footsteps approaching, Maggie slowly opened her eyes. When she saw the smile on Blake's face, she silently thanked God that her partner that day was the headstrong and defiant Detective Inspector Alexandra Blake.

"We've got to get to the plane before they change their mind," Alex said as she walked past. "Let me use the loo and then we'll go."

After emptying her bladder and washing her hands, Alex stared at herself in the mirror. While she hated the fact that she had been partnered with Campbell, she couldn't just stand idly by and watch the woman suffer, or possibly even die. Although she wasn't convinced that a simple fever could kill the healthy police officer, the terrified look in Campbell's eyes had won her over.

Glancing at the medicine cabinet, Alex pulled at the corner and examined the contents filling the shelves. Noticing a bottle of aspirin, she pocketed the painkillers, flicked off the light and walked out. Finding Maggie still standing where she had left her, Alex took her by the arm and led her out of the warm building, and into the beginnings of a blizzard.

Snow had already begun to dust the ground, and as they stood in the shadows getting adjusted to the dim lighting, the arctic wind cut through their coats like a knife. Seeing the pilot walking away from a small Cessna parked on the airstrip, Alex tugged on Maggie's arm and guided her silently to the plane.

Opening the door, Alex moved the co-pilot seat out of the way, and after tossing in her backpack, she did the same with the shopping bag and Maggie's carry-on. As she was about to climb inside, she asked, "Do you need help getting in?"

"No...no, I can do it," Maggie said. "I'm fine."

Even though the woman looked frightfully ill, Alex didn't try to argue. Scampering inside, she tossed her backpack and Maggie's belongings behind the seat, but when she saw Maggie struggling to climb onboard, she rolled her eyes at the woman's stubbornness. Extending her hand, she said, "Take it. You've never struck me as a stupid person, so don't start now. Okay?"

Offering Alex the weakest of grins, Maggie grabbed her hand, and seconds later Alex was pulling the door closed behind her. With the help of the gusting wind, Maggie's fever had cooled a bit, but by the time she had settled in her seat, she was sweating again. Opening her coat, she welcomed the feel of the chilly cabin air, and when the pilot's door opened and a rush of wind entered, she breathed it in. Seconds later, a burly man with a large, bushy gray mustache climbed into the front seat.

Turning on the interior lighting, he glanced over his shoulder. "Name's George Busby," he said. Pausing for a moment to look at his sick passenger, he asked, "Your partner tells me that you're ill and in need of a hospital. Is that true?"

In a ragged whisper, Maggie replied, "Yes, sir."

More than once while he had walked around the plane doing his pre-flight checklist, he had found himself questioning his decision. He was paid to follow orders, and his orders had been to stay on the ground, but the look of gratitude on the woman's face was undeniable. He was her savior...and they both knew it.

"Right then," he began, glancing back and forth between his two passengers. "I should let you know a few things before we take off. First, this airstrip...this *place* is in the middle of nowhere for a reason. It's here because it's covert, and the location is only known by a few organizations and governments. Also, my orders were to stay put until the storm passes, and I'm about to break those orders, but in doing so, I will not destroy the integrity of this airstrip. Therefore, I'm going to follow the original flight plan issued for your return journey. It doesn't take us to a major city, where I'm sure there'd be a hospital, but I have radioed ahead to the airfield where we'll be landing, and requested that they have a doctor meet us when we get there. Will that work for you?"

Knowing that the question was directed at her, Maggie said, "Yes, sir. That will work."

Keeping his focus on Maggie, he continued, "I told your partner earlier that there are three storms in the area. The one to our west, I'm not worried about. I can easily outrun it, but the other two might give us a few problems. It's going to take us about three hours to get where we're going, and the flight is not going to be comfortable. I've flown in this shit before, and it's doable, but I want you to know that once we're in the air, there's no turning back."

Pausing for a moment, Maggie asked, "I understand, but if you're saying that we can't make it—"

"Honey, if I didn't think we could make it, we wouldn't be sitting in this plane," he interrupted. "I just need you to know that it's going to be rough. Okay?"

"Yes, sir. I understand."

Studying the ill woman for a few more seconds, he finally glanced at Alex and nodded his head. Turning back around, he started the engine of the Cessna.

"Buckle up," he said loudly, trying to be heard over the roar of the propeller. "And there are some barf bags on the back of the seats. Trust me, you're going to need them."

***

George Busby had always considered himself a good pilot. Having flown for over thirty years, he had experienced blizzards, monsoons and sandstorms. He had flown without the help of radar and radio, and on one moonlit summer night, he had brought his plane down on its belly when the landing gear had failed. He had survived it all with nary a scratch, but as he reached over and tried the radio again, he began to believe that his luck had finally run out. Not long after takeoff, the radio had gone silent, and now, two hours later, it was all he could do to keep control of the Cessna in the ever-increasing wind. Although not yet enveloped by the winter tempest which was closing in on them from all sides, the little plane had been pummeled by opposing wind currents throughout the flight.

Between rolling side-to-side, and feeling as if they were driving down a rutted dirt road, the small craft had bounced, dipped and tilted more than a dozen times. And while Alex had not yet needed to use an airbag, twice she had winced as she heard Maggie heave into the plastic-lined paper sack. Worried that she hadn't seen Maggie move in over twenty minutes, Alex reached over and placed her hand on the woman's forehead, and instantly, Maggie jerked away.

"Relax, I'm just checking," Alex said, checking her temperature. "Christ, you're hot."

Welcoming the feel of Blake's cold hand on her head, Maggie said, "I know."

"Have you taken anything?"

"No, I'm out."

Reaching into her jacket pocket, Alex opened the stolen bottle of painkillers. Quickly putting two in her hand, she handed them to Maggie. "Here, take these."

"Where did you—"

"Don't ask," Alex said with a guilty grin. Opening her backpack, she pulled out a bottle of water and placed it in Maggie's lap. "You'll need this."

"I can't. It's yours," Maggie said, trying to give her back the bottle.

Shaking her head, Alex said, "I'm fine, Campbell. You need it more than I do."

Too weak to argue, Maggie quickly swallowed the pills. Taking a few more sips of water to ease the pain in her throat, she slowly capped the bottle. "How long...do you know?"

Shaking her head, Alex turned to the pilot, and shouting over the hum of the engine, she asked, "Hey, how long before we get there?"

Turning partially in his seat to answer, when the plane suddenly dropped, Busby's large, knobby hands gripped the yoke as he fought to correct the problem. Like a roller coaster, the Cessna dipped and rose, and then, without warning, the air grew quiet as the engine shut off.

"Shit!" he muttered as his hands flew across the instruments, trying desperately to restart the engine.

"Oh, Christ," Alex blurted, casting a quick look at the wide-eyed woman sitting to her right.

"We've got a problem," he said as the plane continued to glide downward. "I can't get it started...so we might have to land a little sooner than we had planned."

"What? *Where*?" Alex exclaimed.

"There's a place not far from here...had a fire a few years back...burned down a lot of trees. It should be large enough."

"And if it's not?" Alex yelled back.

"Honey, we don't have a choice."

Returning his attention to the matter at hand, Busby quickly began to make the plane ready for an emergency landing. Shutting off the fuel to reduce the risk of a fire, he adjusted the flaps to slow their speed, and banking slightly, he headed the Cessna into the wind to slow it down even more. Fighting against the currents jostling the plane, he gripped the yoke with determination.

Within seconds after Busby's announcement, Maggie bowed her head and began to pray. Alex saw her make the sign of the cross, and even though she could see that Maggie's lips were moving, Alex didn't strain to listen. She knew that the words Maggie was whispering were only meant for God's ears.

Alex also said a quick prayer, but she was smart enough to know that they needed more than just prayers. They needed a shitload of luck. If they survived the landing, they would still have to contend with the cold and the blackness of night, so she began to study the inside of the cabin as if it were a crime scene. As fast as she could, she committed everything she could see to memory, assuming once the plane landed the minimal interior lightning would go out and leave them fumbling in the dark.

"We've only got a few minutes, so listen closely. Okay?" Busby yelled.

Startled from her thoughts, Alex looked toward the cockpit. "Yeah, go ahead."

"I've got to keep the landing gear up...it's safer that way...but they've already had three or four good snowfalls up here this year, so we've probably got a base of two or three feet, which should help soften our landing."

"Okay."

"Just north of where we're going to land are cabins...fishing cabins. They'll be empty at this time of the year, but they'll protect us from the storm."

"North, you say?" Alex asked.

"Here," he answered as he pulled a large silver watch from his wrist. "You hold onto this until we land. It's got a compass."

He looked over his shoulder as he handed Alex the watch and their eyes met. She could see his terror, and he could see her guilt.

Taking it from his hand, she said, "Look, I'm sorry for insisting—"

"No need to apologize," he said, turning back around as he continued to struggle with the yoke. "If I didn't think we could make it, we would never have left the airstrip."

"But—"

"No buts, honey. When we get out of this, you owe me a beer."

"I'll buy you a whole bloody crate," Alex replied, slipping the watch on her wrist. Glancing over at Maggie, Alex suddenly realized that the woman hadn't spoken a word since the engine had failed.

Reaching over, she pushed Maggie back into her seat and tugged at the seat belt to make sure it was fastened. Taking the bottle of water from its resting spot in Maggie's lap, Alex said with a weak smile, "I'll give it back once we land. Okay?"

"I've killed us all," Maggie said in a whisper.

Giving her hand a squeeze, Alex waited until Maggie's eyes met hers. "You haven't killed us. We're going to be fine. I promise."

"I know you don't like me very much, but I want you to know that I hope you survive. I really do."

Confused, Alex said, "What…you've got a death wish?"

Shaking her head, Maggie's expression turned sad. "You don't understand. Even if I live through the landing, without a hospital, I'm still dead."

In all the commotion, Alex had forgotten the reason why they were on the stalled airplane in the first place, and Maggie's words hit her in the stomach like a balled fist. Up until that moment, Alex had refused to think about dying. Steadfast in making mental preparations for when they landed, she hadn't prepared herself for Maggie's imminent death, and tears appeared in Alex's eyes. There were no words to be said; no assurances that all would be well and warm and safe because the only thing that Maggie needed to survive, Alex knew she couldn't give her, and she was gutted.

Breaking the silence, Busby yelled to brace for landing, and sitting back in her seat, Alex pulled the seatbelt as tight as it would go. Watching as the plane broke through the clouds, she held her breath, and as the altimeter wound down toward zero, Alex gathered her thoughts. There was no time for regrets or prayers. She was going to live. She refused to accept anything else.

Feverish and weak, Maggie was transfixed by the large snowflakes now bouncing off the windshield. In her mind, she saw them as white puffs of cotton, cloaking the world and all its hardness in a cocoon of cushiony softness, and she breathed easy. There was no need to worry anymore. No need to be afraid of something so soft and so pure. They were the fabric of His robe, and He would protect her. He would take her into his arms and carry her to the heavens where she would be forever safe. Maggie closed her eyes and said good-bye to the world.

The storms had begun to battle, and as they fought for position, the clouds shifted and streams of moonlight split the darkness. It only took George a few moments to get his bearings, and peering through the windshield, he searched the countryside for the burned-out section of forest. Spotting a large patch of whiteness against the dark, he managed to bank the plane slightly north and let out a sigh of relief. They were going to make it.

The quiet of their glide was suddenly interrupted by something scratching against the skin of the plane. A small screech, followed by a scrape, and then a ding, followed by a bang, and an eerie melody of impending doom began to fill the cabin. The women stiffened immediately, but Busby did not.

With over thirty years of flying under his belt, he knew the procedures, and he had followed every one of them. He had shut off the fuel, slowed the plane as much as he could, and he kept the landing gear raised so that it wouldn't snag against a branch or boulder and send them somersaulting to their deaths. The scratching sound was simply tree tops rubbing the underbelly of the plane as he flew over the pines, but when he cleared the last and saw the stumps of trees scattered across his landing path, he swallowed hard. His eyes darted right and left, and seeing a section void of tree trunks, he steered toward it. For a moment, he smiled, but then something dark and imposing filled the windscreen and under his breath, he muttered, "Shit."

With a loud crash, the branch smashed into the windscreen, shattering the glass and sending it flying into the night. Snow and harsh winter wind rushed in as Busby fought to correct the plane's direction, but it was too late. While most of the trees in the clearing had been burned to the ground, those that had lived for hundreds of years had been too thick to turn to ash so easily. As the plane touched down, a tall, charred trunk stood its ground and ripped the right wing from the fuselage as if it had been made of paper, and the impact sent the Cessna spinning across the snow.

Forced to close her eyes against the sting of the wind, Alex felt as if she was on a carnival ride that had spun wildly out of control. Tossed back and forth in her seat like a ragdoll, it was all she could do to keep herself from passing out as the plane continued to screech and spin. It seemed like an eternity to her, but it had taken less than a minute for the plane to travel the length of the clearing, and nose first, it smashed into a stand of trees. The impact drove Alex forward in her seat, and as her head hit the back of Busby's seat, concussion sent her into darkness.

CHAPTER FIVE

Running down the hallway, he pushed open the double doors with a bang and every head in the room looked up. Scanning the room until he saw the man he had left in charge, John Harper stormed over and bellowed, "What the hell is going on?"

"Busby took off."

"What? His orders were to stay on the ground!"

"Yeah, well, apparently he didn't listen."

"Where are they?"

"That's why I called you," the man said, pointing to a blinking light on his console. "They went down."

"Christ," Harper groaned, seeing the emergency locator transmitter signal flashing on the screen. "Do you know where?"

"Right smack-dab in the middle of the storm of the century."

"Can we get to them? Send a team in on snowmobiles, or even on foot?"

"No way. All the reports that we're getting say that the temps are dropping, and when those three storms finally become one, it's going to be hell."

Seeing the expression on Harper's face, the man touched his sleeve and whispered, "I'm sorry, John, but they're gone. Even if they survived the crash, there's no way they can make it through that storm."

"But what if—"

"John, trust me, they're gone."

***

Gradually, the darkness dissolved as the bitter temperature brought Alex Blake back to the land of the living. Swallowing several times to rid herself of the metallic taste in her mouth, she ran her tongue over her lip and felt the split at the corner. Licking away the blood, Alex slowly opened her eyes. Adjusting to the lack of light, as well as to the pain now throbbing in her head, she carefully reached up and felt her left temple. Wincing at the stickiness she discovered, she closed her eyes and took a moment to gather her thoughts. In her mind, she could still hear the terrible sounds of the crash, but everything else was just a swirl of images. Unsure of her injuries, Alex took a few deep breaths before she tried to move.

As if doing slow-motion aerobics, she carefully tilted her head from side to side, and then shrugged her shoulders and lifted her arms. Grateful that she only felt the dull ache from bruised muscles, her confidence grew. Shifting to find the buckle of her seatbelt, her movements were brought to an abrupt halt when a knife-like pain shot through her right thigh.

"Fuck!" she screamed as bolts of pain ran down her leg. "*Fuck*!"

Afraid to move, she sat like a statue until the pain eased. Outside, the snow-covered ground reflected the minimal moonlight which had managed to find its way through the clouds, but inside the plane, it was eerily dark. Unable to see Busby or Campbell, and believing that her screams would have caused a response if they were still alive, Alex's heart sunk. She was alone.

Finding the courage to move again, she ran her hand over her right thigh, trying to find the injury that had taken her breath away, and when she did, she hissed at the discovery. Poking through her black denim jeans at mid-thigh was a shard of steel.

"Shit," she muttered, carefully running her fingers along the spire. "Shit. Shit. *Shit!*"

Feeling her heart begin to race, Alex rested her head against the seat and forced herself to calm down. Panic was the last thing she needed to do. Allowing her mind to return to the minutes before the crash, images of the contents of the airplane filled her brain, and the slightest of grins appeared on her face. Gingerly leaning forward to reach the back of the pilot's seat, she ran her hand along the edge until she found the long flashlight clamped to the side. Pulling it free, she pushed the soft rubber button and blinked at the brightness as the LED light came to life.

Preparing for the worst, Alex shined the light downward and grimaced at the twisted piece of metal covered in blood she saw protruding from her thigh. Debating on how she was going to hold onto the sharp, slippery steel, she reached into her pocket for her leather gloves. It was only the slightest of movements, so when another lightning bolt of pain shot through her leg, Alex was stunned. Crying out, her voice echoed in the cabin as she fought back tears.

"Jesus Christ!"

Taking several deep breaths to prevent herself from passing out, Alex swallowed the saliva building in her mouth and tentatively reached under her thigh. She prayed that she would be wrong, but when her fingers traced the fragment of steel protruding from the seat cushion before it entered her leg, Alex swallowed hard. She was impaled.

"Oh, fuck me," she muttered.

Mentally weighing her options, and knowing that there was only one, Alex decided to face one demon at a time. The first was finding out if anyone else was alive. The second would be freeing herself from the shrapnel piercing her leg.

Taking a deep breath, she aimed the flashlight at the cockpit, hoping that George Busby had survived, but he hadn't. Lying across the center console with his neck at a deadly angle, he stared back at her with empty eyes. Paling at the sight, Alex swallowed hard and then reluctantly shined the light in Maggie's direction.

Still buckled in her seat, Maggie was hunched over, and with her face completely hidden behind her hair, Alex had no idea if the woman was alive or dead. Careful not to move her leg, she reached over and pressed her fingers against Maggie's neck. When she felt the thumping of a pulse, a fresh dose of adrenaline burst through Alex's veins. Knowing that she needed to free herself before she could tend to Maggie, she flashed the light around the cabin. Seeing the shopping bag lodged between the seats, Alex searched until she found the paisley scarf, and placing it within reach, she removed her belt. Folding the leather strap several times before placing it in her mouth, she closed her eyes, took a deep breath, and pushed herself off the seat.

The belt muffled her screams, but nothing could stop the tears from rolling down her face as spasms of pain radiated up and down her leg. Whimpering in the icy solitude of the cramped cabin, it took several minutes before Alex was calm enough to shine the light toward her seat. Using the end of the flashlight, she bent the bloody spike protruding from the seat to the floor, and wrapping the scarf around her thigh to stop the flow of blood, she pulled it tight.

Settling back into her seat, she was about to wake up Maggie when she felt the plane shift ever so slightly. Hearing the groan of the fuselage as it rubbed against something outside, Alex frowned. She knew they had landed. She remembered the hard thump as the belly of the plane touched down and the whirling spin as it skidded across the field...or was it a field? Realizing that they could have easily exited the forest and ended up on the side of a mountain, or precariously perched at the edge of a cliff, her heart began to pound.

Unlocking her door, Alex carefully pushed it open and shined the light around. Seeing snow-covered earth as far as her eye could see, a small grin appeared on her face, but it disappeared almost as quickly. Another loud groan filled the air as the fuselage strained against something unknown and the plane shifted again.

Baffled, she climbed out and slowly put pressure on her injured leg. Discovering that the pain was now dull and quite manageable, she walked carefully around the wreckage searching for the source of the noise. Following the sound with the LED beam, Alex found her answer. The tail of the plane was submerged in water.

"Fuck me!"

No sooner had the words left her mouth when something crackled under her feet. Shining the light on the ground, and seeing nothing but snow, Alex shuffled her feet, and feeling the ice beneath them, the color drained from her face. Swallowing hard, she carefully retraced her steps, holding her breath as the frozen water cracked and strained with every step she took. Reaching the cabin door, she flashed the light toward the nose of the plane, and seeing it buried in a small stand of spindly trees, Alex couldn't help but smile.

Land was only a few feet away. Taking a long, calming breath, she carefully climbed back into the plane.

As if working on a criminal case, Alex methodically sorted the facts. The pilot had told them to head north, so shining the flashlight on her wrist, she checked the compass displayed on the heavy silver watch to get her bearings. Relieved that north was in the direction of the trees rather than the lake, Alex began to make ready for the trip. Within seconds, she found Campbell's carry-on lodged under a seat and the half-filled bottle of water she had placed in the holder on the door, but her backpack was nowhere in sight. Scratching her head, Alex was about to give up when she spied it wedged under the pilot's slumped body.

"Shit," Alex said under her breath, staring at the lifeless form. Taking a few moments to get up the nerve to disturb the dead, she gently extracted the backpack from under his shoulders. Grimacing as he slipped further between the seats, she reached over and closed his eyes. "I'm sorry, George. I'm so, so sorry."

Settling back into her seat, she hunched her shoulders as a gust of wind and snow whipped through the plane. Fighting off the chill, she emptied the bag containing Maggie's disguise and began tearing apart the black wool skirt. Using the first strip as a bandage, she wrapped it around her head to stop the flow of blood still trickling down her face, and wincing, she pulled it tight. What was left of the skirt, she quickly fashioned into two scarves, and after covering her head with one, she set the other aside.

Leaning over, she placed her hand on Maggie's shoulder. "Campbell, wake up," she said firmly. When Maggie didn't move, Alex began to shake her gently. "Campbell, you've got to wake up. We need to get out of here."

After several attempts, Alex was on the verge of slapping the woman into consciousness when she heard Maggie begin to moan.

Grinning slightly, Alex said, "Campbell...come on, darling, you need to wake up."

"Don't call me that," Maggie mumbled as the fog in her head faded away. Leaning slowly back in her seat, she moved her head from side to side to work out the stiffness before finally opening her eyes.

"How do you feel?" Alex asked. "Is anything broken?"

"I don't know. I don't think so," Maggie replied as she slowly moved in her seat.

"Good, because we need to get out of here, and we need to do it right now."

"What are you talking about?"

"We landed on a lake...or a pond...or some other fucking piece of frozen water, but the point is, we've broken through the ice, and we need to get our arses out of here before the plane sinks."

Achy and feverish, Maggie had resigned herself to the fact that she was going to die. With a sigh, she said, "You go...I'll stay."

"Not on your life, darling," Alex snapped, grabbing their luggage and tossing it out the door. "Now, either you get out of here on your own, or I'll pull you out. Your choice!"

"Please, just let me—"

Grabbing Maggie's chin, Alex forced their eyes to meet. "I'm only going to say this once, so listen carefully. I will *not* leave you here! You got that? The pilot told us to travel north, and that's exactly what *we* are going to do."

"The pilot—"

"He's dead, so it's just you and me. Now, come on, get out of that seat and let's go."

"I'm going to die regardless," Maggie explained. "I'll only slow you down."

"Jesus Christ! I don't know what kind of life you've got...maybe it's shit...I don't know, but you are *not* dying on my fucking watch! Now get out of this bloody plane *right now!*" Carefully climbing outside, Alex waited as Campbell began to shift across the seats to the open door.

Grimacing in the darkness, Maggie closed her eyes for a few seconds to allow the pain to pass. She had no clue as to the extent of her injury, but as she felt warm blood leak from her body, she knew that she'd be in God's hands soon. Pulling her coat tightly around herself, Maggie climbed out of the plane and allowed Blake to guide her north.

***

They methodically plodded through the forest for over an hour, trying their best to brace themselves against the wind that whipped through the pines, but it was impossible. The squalls of winter's fury had become so strong that both were knocked to their knees more than once. Ice and snow pelted their faces until they were raw and chafed, and fingers and feet protected by gloves and boots simply didn't have a chance against the rawness of Mother Nature at her fiercest.

If there was one word in the English language that described Alex Blake, it was tenacious. When she set her mind to do something, it would be done. From graduating with honors, to tracking down criminals in the bowels of London, most of her achievements could be directly attributed to just one thing...her stubbornness. Tell her no, and she would find the yes. Tell her impossible, and she would prove you wrong. So, as Alex trudged through the snow, she knew that death was trying to wrap its icy tentacles around her, but she had other things on her mind. Fuck death.

Alex stopped and glanced over her shoulder, watching as Maggie struggled to follow in her footsteps. Slogging through the ever-deepening snow, Alex had slowed her strides in order for the shorter woman to keep up, but as each minute passed, the snow grew deeper and Maggie was falling farther and farther behind.

The frigid temperature helped to keep Maggie's fever in check, but just barely. She was rapidly reaching the point of exhaustion, and after stumbling several times, Maggie knew that her life's blood now flowed freely from the wound on her side.

Looking to the north, Alex peered through the darkness, and shielding her eyes from the unrelenting snow, she shined the flashlight through the trees. Up ahead she could see a clearing, and set back into the opening was something boxy and dark. Narrowing her eyes, Alex strained to make out what it was, and sprinting toward it, her heart began to pound with excitement. Mindless of the distance she was putting between her and Campbell, Alex high-stepped it through drifts until the cabin came into view. Grinning, she spun around to shout out her discovery, only to find that Campbell had been swallowed up by the storm.

"Shit!" Alex said, realizing her mistake. Retracing her steps, she darted back through the trees in a panic. Finally seeing a dark heap in the snow, she ran to Campbell and dropped to her knees.

"Come on, you need to get up," she said, wiping the snow from Maggie's face. "Campbell, there's a cabin up ahead. Come on, woman, you need to get up."

"Please...I can't. Just leave me...please, just leave me," Maggie whimpered. Ravaged by fever, exhaustion and blood loss, her will to live had disappeared. The snow felt good against her heated skin, and all Maggie wanted to do was sleep. Just sleep.

"No fucking way!" Alex shouted into the wind. Grabbing Maggie, she pulled her to her feet, and wrapping her arm around her waist, Alex growled, "Start walking, Campbell, or by God, I'll carry you!"

Praying that she could make it to the cabin, if only to save the life of the woman trying to save hers, Maggie tried to take another step, but her knees buckled instantly. Without missing a beat, Alex bent down and pulled her to her feet again. Leaning into the fevered Inspector, she laid Maggie over her shoulder, and taking a deep breath, Alex stood straight. Slowly, she lumbered through the snow carrying an unconscious woman over her left shoulder and a carry-on bag and knapsack over her right.

***

By the time Alex reached the porch of the deserted cabin, her muscles were screaming for relief. Their sanctuary was only a small flight of stairs away, but she was exhausted. Deciding to give herself a minute to catch her breath, she lowered Maggie gently to the ground, and then climbed the steps and wearily walked to the door. Seeing the padlock barring the entrance, Alex's shoulders fell. "Oh, you have got to be bloody kidding me!"

Thinking for a second, she looked to her left and right, and then stomped around the porch, checking every window and door, but even the meager storage shed attached to the back of the cabin had a shiny lock hanging from a hasp. Whoever owned the cabin had done their due diligence. It was locked up tighter than a vault.

As each padlock came into view, Alex's fear and desperation began to grow. Their situation had become all too clear. They had survived a plane crash, and had struggled through a blizzard to find protection from the storm, but if she couldn't find a way to get inside, they would both freeze to death. It was just that simple.

Returning to the front door, Alex pounded her fist against it in anger. Swearing into the wind as she felt tears well in her eyes, her aggravation grew into rage. Unleashing her fury on the padlocked entrance, and mindless of the pain in her leg, she slammed her body against it again and again until finally, defeated, she crumpled to the porch. Seconds grew into minutes as Alex sat there, lightly tapping her head against the door in frustration as she racked her brain for a solution. When she realized that there wasn't one, her temper erupted. Alexandra Blake did not like to lose.

"No!" she shouted, scrambling to her feet. *"I will not fucking die this way!"*

Infuriated, Alex marched around the porch one more time, pulling at every lock with her frozen fingers, and checking the tops of all the windows and doors for a hidden key. Even though the small shed at the back of the house wouldn't have given them much protection, she nonetheless rammed her shoulder against the door, her instinct to survive stronger than it had ever been, but the lock was far too strong, and Alex had grown far too weak. Dejected, she slowly returned to the front of the cabin, and sniffling back a tear, she limped down the steps to retrieve the woman she had left in the snow. With her last ounce of energy, Alex carried Maggie to the porch, and slumping to the floor, she pulled her near. Propping the flashlight between them, Alex aimed it at the small overhang above their heads. She had no idea how long the batteries would last, but knowing that permanent darkness would come soon enough, she welcomed the muted light reflecting down on them.

Up until that moment, Alex had never thought about her own death. If she had been ill or weak, perhaps it would have entered her mind before now, but healthy and young, death had always seemed so distant and foreign. As she sat on the porch slowly freezing to death, Alex couldn't help but ponder her demise. Would it be warm and peaceful? When the cloak of the grim reaper covered her, would a bright light suddenly appear to guide her to Heaven? Would she struggle with her last breath or simply slip into the afterlife with the ease that comes from faith? Would Maggie die first? Jolted by her last thought, she shook her head at the flood of macabre questions. Pushing them away, Alex turned her attention to their executioner…the storm.

As her hope of survival faded away, her senses grew keen. Even though she had walked through a forest for over an hour, Alex hadn't noticed the fragrance of pine in the air until just then. It reminded her of the wreath she had hung on the door to her flat at Christmas, and the tree, tall and proud, she had admired in her parent's lounge six weeks earlier. A smile appeared on her face as she remembered Christmas day with her family, and then it disappeared just as fast when she realized that it had been her last.

With a sigh, Alex closed her eyes, and as if on cue, the wind slowed. The night grew silent for a moment, almost peaceful, but then the symphony of the storm began to build again. Ice and snow pinged and skittered across the porch as the wind grew strong, and in the distance she could hear the faint strain and crack of branches losing their fight against the torrents of air crashing their way through the timbers. The cacophony was deafening.

A brutal gust of wind whipped across the porch, and Alex's eyes flew open. Squinting against the sting of it, she tugged Maggie closer, trying to share what little warmth she had left, but it was pointless. She could see that the snow had begun to creep over them like a white plague, and its goal was simple. Steal their remaining heat and turn them to ice.

Taking a ragged breath, Alex's eyes filled with tears as she looked at the woman in her arms. She had always longed to hold Maggie close, and now she would hold her for eternity.

Noticing a delicate gold chain around Maggie's neck, Alex pulled it from underneath her sweater. Smiling softly at the tiny gold cross dangling from the intertwined links, Alex began to pray. There was nothing else to do.

CHAPTER SIX

A tear rolled down Alex's cheek. Nearing total exhaustion, she knew that when she finally closed her eyes, she would never open them again. A kaleidoscope of images and thoughts invaded her mind. Allowing herself to accept the inevitable, she took a deep breath and made peace with God.

Lightly kissing the top of Maggie's head, Alex took a deep breath and slowly let the air empty from her lungs. Her head nodded forward as she allowed sleep to take hold, but then a thought popped into her head. Opening her eyes, she glanced at the religious symbol around her partner's neck.

"Son of a bitch," Alex said, staring at the tiny cross. "*Son of a bitch!*"

Propping Maggie's lifeless form against the wall of the cabin, Alex struggled to her feet. Calling on every molecule of strength and adrenaline she had left, she forced herself to take one step and then another…and then another. Traipsing through the drifts of snow now piled on the porch, she stopped in front of the door to the storage shed. Staring at the white crucifix hanging above it, Alex swallowed hard as she removed it from its hanger. Holding her breath, she said a prayer and flipped it over.

"Thank you, God!" she cried out, seeing a key sticking out of a slot carved in the back. "Thank you. Thank you. *Thank you!*"

Pulling the key from its hiding spot, she gave the crucifix a quick kiss, placed it back on the nail above the door and rushed to the front of the cabin. Stepping around Maggie's slumped body, Alex placed the flashlight on the porch, tugged off her gloves and began fumbling with the lock. More than once the key almost fell from her frozen fingers, but finally, she found the keyway and the padlock sprung open with ease. Unfortunately, the door did not.

Shocked, she grabbed the flashlight, and seeing that ice had formed in the cracks around the door's edges, she began ramming her body against it. Her leg was pounding and her shoulder ached, but it didn't matter. Determined, she continued until the door gave way, and she stumbled into the cabin triumphant.

"Yes!" she hissed, shining the flashlight here and there. Quickly taking note of her surroundings, she went back to the porch to get her partner.

"In you go," she groaned as she grabbed Campbell by the lapels of her coat and dragged her through the doorway.

Struggling and swearing, Alex didn't stop until Maggie was lying in front of the stone fireplace that practically filled one wall of the cabin. Standing straight, she shined the flashlight around the room again, and getting her bearings, Alex got to work.

Although the firebox was void of wood, she reached up, opened the damper, and with purpose in her step, headed to the dining area on the other side of the room. Picking up one of the Windsor-style chairs, she raised it above her head and slammed it to the floor, shattering it instantly. Gathering what remained, Alex strode to the fireplace with kindling in hand, and taking a book from the mantle, she began ripping out the pages and stuffing them around the spokes and rungs. Searching her pockets for her cigarette lighter, she tried and failed several times to work the mechanism. Wincing at the sting in her frozen fingertips, she warmed them with her breath and tried again. Smiling at the sight of the small yellow flame dancing at the end of the lighter, she held it against the pages of the book and watched as the paper slowly began to burn and char.

With her adrenaline now pumping, Alex quickly stood up and immediately wished that she hadn't when the room began to spin around her. Grabbing for the mantle, she closed her eyes and prayed that it would pass. Hungry, dehydrated and well past the point of exhaustion, Alex was running on empty. There was only one problem. Alex was too stubborn to admit it. She wasn't ready to rest, at least not yet.

"Five more minutes, I just need five more minutes," she said aloud. "God, please…just five more minutes."

When she opened her eyes again and found her dizziness gone, Alex wasted no time. Retrieving a blanket that had been draped over the back of a nearby chair, she returned to Maggie's side and within minutes, the woman's snow-covered coat had been replaced by a warm, albeit dusty blanket. Pausing to catch her breath, she studied Maggie in the firelight. Pulling the scarf from Maggie's head, Alex combed her fingers through the woman's hair, and then checked her fever. Thankful that it seemed to have eased, she tucked the blanket tightly around Maggie and sunk to the floor. Pulling the scarf from her head, Alex's shoulders slumped as she let out a long breath. Seconds later, sleep took hold.

***

Alex had no idea how long she had slept, but when she opened her eyes, her teeth were chattering and the fire had dwindled down to almost nothing. Although her leather coat was providing her some warmth, her jeans were soaked through and her boots, while knee-high, had never laid claim to being waterproof. Shaking off a chill, she crawled over and placed her hand on Maggie's forehead. Noting that the woman's forehead was still warm, but definitely not hot, Alex said glibly, "So much for death by fever."

Getting to her feet, Alex winced as a bolt of pain shot down her leg. Grabbing her wounded thigh, she held her breath until the ache dulled, and then she slowly made her way to the dining area. Turning another chair into firewood, after she stoked the hearth with the spindles of oak, she decided her next priority was to get them both out of their wet clothes. Glancing around the room for her knapsack, her brow furrowed. "Where the hell is it?"

Scratching her head, Alex glanced at the door, and realizing what she had done, she rushed outside and began searching the snow-covered porch. At last, finding both her knapsack and Campbell's cloth carry-on near the stairs, she dusted them off and went to sit by the fire. Emptying the contents of both, she groaned. Snow had made its way inside, and all their clothes were now frozen into solid blocks of fabric.

"Not one of your finer moments, Alexandra," she said, holding up a pair of her ice-cubed knickers. Dropping them to the floor with a thud, she grabbed the flashlight and said, "Okay, time for Plan B."

Frowning when the LED bulb dimmed immediately, she switched it off and made her way to the kitchen. When she had first scanned the room, she had noticed a hurricane lamp on the counter, and picking it up, she listened as the oil sloshed in its belly. Alex adjusted the wick, raised the glass and within seconds, the kitchen was filled with a dim, shimmering light.

Crossing her fingers that the owners of the cabin had left behind some clothes, Alex headed down the hallway leading to the back of the cabin, the rough sawn flooring squeaking under her feet as she went. Coming to the first door, she peeked inside and smiled at the conveniences that the bathroom contained. Walking over, she worked the pitcher-pump handle over the tub, but when no water appeared, she simply shrugged her shoulders. "Melted snow it is, then."

Continuing to the next room, Alex looked inside and sighed. While the room contained metal frames of bunk beds, each had been stripped of their mattresses, pillows and blankets. Taking a deep breath, she headed to the last door at the end of the hall, and saying a quick prayer, Alex stepped inside the room.

Grinning at the sight of the quilt-covered bed, she was about to pull off the patchwork spread when she spied a large trunk at the foot of the bed. Placing the lamp on the floor, Alex opened the latches of the trunk and raised the lid. Her smile grew wide when she saw the stacks of clothing sealed in plastic bags, and quickly grabbing a few, she tossed them on the bed. As she was about to shrug out of her coat, Alex noticed the stone fireplace that filled one wall, and cocking her head to the side, she began replaying in her head what she had just seen.

"Talk it out, Blake," she muttered. "There's enough room here to sleep seven or eight, and two enormous fireplaces. You're not going to come up for a fishing trip and then spend the entire week chopping wood. So where the hell is it?"

Grabbing the oil lamp, she strode up the hallway, and exchanged it for the flashlight. Pounding it against the palm of her hand until the light grew bright; she headed back outside into the storm.

Steadying herself against the gale-force winds, Alex fought her way down the stairs, and struggling through the drifts as the ice and snow pelted her face, she trudged toward the side of the cabin. Turning the corner, she aimed the flashlight into the darkness and when she saw an unusually tall drift of snow a few feet away, she exclaimed, "Bingo!"

Sweeping her arm across the tarp to clear away the snow, she found the cord near the bottom and worked out the knots. Pulling back the canvas, she wasted no time in filling her arms, and even though her thigh still ached, Alex pushed past the pain until she had stacked enough firewood in the cabin to last them the night.

After placing some logs on the fire, Alex carried an armful down the hall, and a few minutes later, with the help of the pages from yet another paperback, the hearth in the bedroom began to glow with warmth. Although desperate to get out of her wet clothes, her mind returned to Maggie, and Alex let out a sigh. She was freezing, but Maggie was sick.

Wearily, she limped up the hallway and knelt by Maggie's side. One quick check of the woman's temperature told Alex that the fever had come back. Realizing that Maggie's prophecy of her own death might very well come true, Alex began to try to shake her awake. She had questions that only Maggie could answer.

"Campbell...Campbell, you need to wake up. Come on, woman, open your eyes."

Jostling Maggie as hard as she dared, Alex was quickly running out of ideas, and after several minutes, totally exasperated, Alex sat back and frowned. "How in the hell am I supposed to wake you up?"

Glancing at the kitchen, Alex spied the red and white curtain under the sink. Smiling, she walked over and pushed it aside. Rummaging through the aerosol cans and assorted cleaners, she pulled out a plastic pail and behind it, she found her answer. Taking the bottle, she returned to Maggie's side, and pulling her into her lap, Alex opened the cap and held the ammonia under Maggie's nose.

It took only a few seconds for the fumes to find their way, and when they did, they shocked Maggie into consciousness with a jolt. Coughing and sputtering at the vile smell, she opened her eyes for the first time in hours.

"Okay, that's better," Alex said, putting the bottle aside. Gently lowering Maggie to the floor, Alex asked, "Campbell, can you hear me?"

When she didn't answer, Alex grabbed the lapels of Maggie's suit jacket and shouted, "Campbell, God damn it, wake up!"

Wincing, Maggie mumbled, "I'm awake. I'm awake."

Fearing the fever would send Maggie back into unconsciousness before she got the answers she needed, when Alex began to speak, her voice was loud, clear and demanding.

"I need to know what the doctors did in the hospital when you got sick."

"What?" Maggie said in a breath, fighting to stay away from the darkness shrouding her brain.

"In the hospital, when you got sick. What did the doctors do to fight the fever?"

"I don't know."

"Oh, Christ," Alex growled as her anger began to build. "Campbell, come on. I'm trying to save your life here, now think! What the hell did they do?"

Taking a few ragged breaths, Maggie said, "I...I was on an IV..."

"Great," Alex said, rolling her eyes. "What else?"

"Medicine...drugs...to lower the fever..."

Remembering the bottle of aspirin she had stolen from the airport bathroom, a faint grin appeared on Alex's face. "Okay, that's good. What else?"

"I don't remember..."

Grabbing the ammonia, Alex removed the cap. Shoving it under Campbell's nose, she allowed the potent fumes to bring the woman, once again, back to reality. Choking on the pungent odor, Maggie opened her eyes and looked up at the woman staring down at her. Alex's expression said it all. She was worried.

Alex had long ago committed Maggie's face to memory. She knew that the color of her skin was the warmest of ivories and when Maggie smiled, the smallest of dimples appeared on her cheeks. She knew that the tiniest of laugh lines existed at the corners of her eyes, and in those green eyes, which Alex adored so much, were flecks of gold swimming amidst the emerald. It was a face that had kept her awake many a night. It was one that had caused her to dream marvelous dreams, but now those dreams had turned into a nightmare. Dark circles had formed under Maggie's eyes, and with her skin appearing almost bloodless, it looked as if she was wearing a death mask made of the whitest of porcelains. Alex swallowed hard at the sight, and the truth finally hit home. If she couldn't find a way to keep the fever in check, Maggie Campbell was going to die.

Alex's eyes filled with concern, and leaning in close, she said quietly, "I'm trying to save your life. Please, Maggie, I'm begging you. Try to think. Was there anything else?"

As she felt sleep beckoning to her, Maggie remembered a time when she was a child, and a fever had racked her small body almost to the point of seizure. Her father had held her under a cold shower until the medics had arrived. She remembered the sting of the IVs as they were inserted, and voices of men shouting at her to wake up, telling her to hold on, assuring her that she'd be okay…and then she was cold.

"Maggie, please…try to think," Alex pleaded. "Come on, darling. I don't want you to die."

Doing her best to focus on the Alex's face, Maggie managed one more word before blacking out again. "Ice."

The word echoed in Alex's head, and glancing toward the front door, she thought about her options. Knowing that she didn't have the strength to drag Maggie outside, she wasted no time in retrieving the bucket from under the sink and heading back out into the storm.

***

Alex was exhausted. Drained of every ounce of energy she had, she had lost track of time as she continued to sit by Maggie's side, swapping warm scraps of fabric with snow-coated ones and placing them across the woman's fevered brow. Placing her hand repeatedly on Maggie's forehead, Alex prayed that the fever would ease, and finally, it did. Taking a ragged breath, she struggled to her feet, and going outside to fill the pail with more snow, she bolted the door and then slowly and painfully limped down the hall to the bedroom.

Her head was pounding from a wound that she had yet to see, and her leg ached from hip to foot. Rapidly running out of steam, it was all she could do to grab a few bags of clothes from the bed before she slumped to the floor in front of the fireplace. Placing the pail close enough to the fire so the snow would melt, Alex pulled off her shoes and socks, and let out a sigh of relief. Even though her feet felt like ice, she couldn't see any sign of frostbite. Stretching her legs, she allowed the heat of the fire to slowly warm her feet, waiting as long as it took until she could finally wiggle her toes without pain. Untying the paisley scarf from around her thigh, she fought her way out of her wet jeans and examined the damage left by the steel spire that had pierced her.

Swallowing back the saliva building in her mouth, Alex dipped the scarf into the bucket of slush and wiped away the blood coating her leg. Pleased to discover that the gash on the front was small, it only took her a few minutes before she was satisfied it was clean, but when she tried to see the entry wound on the back of her leg, she wasn't so lucky. No matter how she twisted or turned, it was impossible to see. With no other options, she blindly cleaned the wound, tied the scarf around her leg and hoped for the best. After tugging on a pair of blue sweatpants, she tossed her shirt and bra aside and quickly replaced them with an oversized flannel shirt. Placing her boots by the fire to dry, she covered her feet with a pair of thick gray and orange socks that were so soft they made her smile. She was finally warm.

She rested her head on the bed for only a moment to gather her thoughts, but that was all it took. Alex wouldn't wake up for another three hours.

CHAPTER SEVEN

Startled from her dreams by the sound of distant whimpers and unintelligible moans, Alex's eyes popped open. Scrambling to her feet, she hobbled up the hallway just in time to see Maggie's hand narrowly miss the coffee table as she flailed about with fever.

"Shit!" Alex said, rushing to her side. Pushing the furniture out of the way, she placed her hand on Maggie's forehead and winced. The fever had turned deadly and Alex's heart began to race.

"Well, I hoped that it wasn't going to have to come to this," Alex said, pulling Maggie into her arms. "But it looks like it's time to go play in the snow."

With a grunt and a groan, Alex struggled to her feet. Getting to the door, she managed to throw the lock, and the storm did the rest. The force of the wind pushed the door open, and as it swung back and hit the wall, Alex stepped out into the blizzard.

Somewhere far above the clouds the sun had finally made an appearance, but the storm had swallowed up its brilliance, and the day was almost as dark as night. Squinting through the snow and wind to find the stairs, Alex misjudged the first and yelped as she and Maggie tumbled down the steps. Landing with a soft thud, it took only a few seconds for Alex to get to her knees, and mindless of the ache in her leg, she began sweeping snow over Maggie. Covering her up to her neck in the white powder, Alex prayed that her amateurish attempt to rein in the fever would work.

For three years, Alex had succeeded in building walls around her heart so her feelings for Maggie Campbell would remain hidden, but the bricks and mortar were now starting to crumble. Wearing only a flannel shirt, sweatpants and socks, Alex was shivering uncontrollably, but she couldn't bring herself to go back inside for her boots or coat. Fearing that if she left Maggie for a moment, she would die, Alex remained by her side, replacing the snow each time a gust of wind blew it away.

After several minutes, Alex saw Maggie's eyes flutter open. "Hey there," she said, leaning closer so Maggie could hear her through the wind.

Shivering, Maggie focused on the voice, and waiting until her vision cleared, she looked up at Alex.

"I'm...I'm...cold," she said through chattering teeth.

Grinning, Alex held out her hand. "Yeah. Me too. What say we get you inside?"

"Please," Maggie replied weakly as Alex helped her to her feet.

Maggie managed to climb the stairs on her own, but by the time she reached the door, her strength was gone. Feeling her knees begin to buckle, she reached out to steady herself, and then found herself being swept off the porch into Alex's arms.

"Put me down," she groused half-heartedly.

"Not on your life."

"I can walk."

"Yeah, like a drunken sailor," Alex said, carrying her into the house. Wincing as she kicked the door closed, she plodded to the bedroom and placed Maggie on the floor in front of the fireplace.

"How you doing?" Alex asked, quickly pulling off her snow-covered socks and replacing them with another pair from the trunk.

"I'm...I'm okay."

"Yeah?"

"I'm thirsty."

"Hold on, I'll get you some water."

Leaving the room for a moment, she came back carrying the partially filled bottle of water from the plane. "Here, but drink it slowly," Alex said, handing her the bottle.

Hoping that it would ease the pain in her throat, Maggie greedily gulped the water for a few seconds before Alex pulled it away.

"I told you to take it slowly. I don't want you throwing it all back up," she scolded. Eyeing Maggie for a moment, Alex gave her the bottle again. "Small sips, all right?"

"Okay."

Waiting until Maggie took a few more sips, Alex said, "We really need to get you out of those wet clothes."

"What's the point?" Maggie said with a sigh.

Sitting back on her haunches, Alex scratched her head. "Why do you want to die?"

"I...I don't, but there's nothing you can do for me and we both know it. I'm in God's hands now," Maggie said in a weak and raspy voice.

"Well, God can't have you until I'm done with you," Alex said, grabbing Maggie by the lapels of her suit jacket and pulling her into a sitting position. Quickly unbuttoning the jacket, Alex pushed it from her shoulders and lowered her back to the floor. Cupping Maggie's chin in her hand, she said, "I'm not going to let you die. Do you understand that?

You're too young. You're too strong, and...and you're too *damn* beautiful for me to allow that to happen."

"I thought you hated me," Maggie whispered.

Shaking her head, Alex frowned. "When you're feeling better, you and I can have a long, philosophical discussion about our differences, but I don't think now is the time, do you? We need to get you out of those wet clothes and into a warm bed before you pass out again."

Feeling no need to wait for an answer, Alex was about to remove Maggie's sweater when she noticed blood on the material. Seeing an even larger stain on Maggie's gray trousers, Alex held her breath as she lifted the hem of the sweater. Hissing at the sight of the gash as it came into view, Alex asked, "Did you know about this?"

"Yeah, it must have happened when we crashed."

"Why didn't you tell me?" Alex asked, but before Maggie could respond, Alex answered her own question. "Never mind, I forgot. God's hands, right?"

"I didn't want to slow you down. I thought if it was bad...I would just—"

"Jesus! You're a piece of work. Do you know that?" Alex growled as she stood up and snatched up the bucket still sitting by the fireplace. Storming from the room, she yelled over her shoulder, "I'm going to try to find something to clean that up. Do me a favor and don't *die* before I get back!"

Maggie couldn't fault Alex for being angry. If their roles had been reversed, she would have been equally confused over someone's nonchalant acceptance of their own death, but Alex didn't know all the facts, and Maggie did.

More than once in her life, she had ended up in the hospital when one of the most common of illnesses resulted in a fever that over-the-counter medication could not control. Influenza was her enemy, and Maggie knew it. She always took all the precautions, and every year she was first in line for her vaccination against the newest strain, but it didn't guarantee that another strain wouldn't get through, and this year, one had. Maggie knew that her fever would go from tepid to torrid and back again over the next few days before eventually taking a turn for the worse, and this time, it would be worse. This time there were no doctors to save her. This time would be the last time.

Alex's first stop had been the bathroom in her hunt for something to use as a bandage, but after checking the small closet and medicine cabinet, and finding them both stripped bare, she rushed to the kitchen. Pulling open every drawer and door, her annoyance began to build. They were all empty. Everything was gone.

"Damn it!" she said, pounding her fist on the counter. "Why lock this fucking place up like a bloody bank when there's nothing here that anyone would want?" Angrily grabbing the bucket, she went outside and filled it with snow.

"Who were you talking to?" Maggie asked quietly as she heard Alex shuffle back into the room.

Placing the pail near the fireplace, Alex took a pillow from the bed, removed the case and began tearing it into strips. "Tell me this, Detective Inspector Campbell," she said as she attacked the cotton covering. "Why lock up a cabin like it contained a million treasures, when there's nothing here?"

"What?"

Sitting on the floor, Alex pulled over the bucket and dropped a few strips of cloth inside. "There were padlocks on everything when we got here, but every bloody closet, drawer *and* cabinet are completely empty."

"There's no food?"

"No food, no dishes, no pots, no pans...nothing. It just doesn't make any sense, if you ask me." Lifting the edge of the sweater, Alex said, "Sorry, but this is going to be a bit cold, I'm afraid."

Wincing at the iciness of the cloth, Maggie said, "Maybe...maybe they hid it."

"What?" Alex asked, tossing the bloody piece of fabric into the fire as she grabbed another.

"We're both assuming we're miles from anywhere, right?"

"Yeah."

"Why would anyone travel with all that stuff—"

"That's exactly what I mean," Alex said as she continued to dab carefully at the bloody gash.

"Well, then maybe they hid it, so if someone broke in and didn't find anything, they'd just leave."

"Good point, but this place isn't that big," Alex said, throwing the bloody remnant into the fire. Wringing out another piece of cloth, Alex was about to press it to the wound when she looked up and saw that Maggie's face had gone gray.

"What's wrong?"

Wincing at the taste of bile growing in her throat, Maggie rolled to her side as she feebly replied, "I think I'm going to be sick."

"Shit," Alex said, quickly grabbing a wastebasket near the bed. "Here use this."

In seconds, Maggie's stomach emptied, and as she continued to heave, Alex sat behind her, intuitively rubbing her back until the sickness had passed. Finally, Maggie pushed the wastebasket away and rolled to her back. Sweating and pale, she said weakly, "I'm sorry. I guess I drank too much."

"That's okay. Lessons learned, but keep trying to drink more. You're going to get dehydrated, if you aren't already."

"What about you? You said there wasn't any food, and if there isn't any water—"

"Don't worry about me. I'll melt some snow. I'll be fine," Alex said. "And speaking of snow, we need to get you out of these wet clothes."

"All right," Maggie said, struggling to sit up.

"Whoa," Alex said, placing her hand on Maggie's shoulder. "You need to stay still. Every time you move, this cut opens back up, so just sip that water, and I'll do the rest."

Moving to Maggie's feet, Alex pulled off her shoes and socks. Smiling at the light pink nail polish on the Detective Inspector's toes, she began rubbing her feet to warm them up.

Noticing the strip of black wool wrapped around Alex's head, Maggie asked, "What happened to your head?"

Looking up, Alex said, "Oh, I must have bumped it when we landed."

"Is it bad?"

"I haven't had time to look at it."

Pulling her foot out of Alex's hand, Maggie said, "You need to take care of yourself. Don't worry about me."

Glaring at the ill woman, Alex snatched back Maggie's foot. "I'll take care of myself once I make sure that you're warm and dry, and since you are in no shape to argue, don't!"

After a few minutes, satisfied that the blood had returned to Maggie's feet, Alex looked up and asked, "How you doing up there?"

"I feel warm," Maggie said quietly, turning her face away from the fireplace.

Crawling to sit by her side, Alex placed her hand on her forehead. "You're getting hot again."

"Yeah, I know."

Picking up the bucket, Alex said, "Let me go fill this back up, and I'll get you a cold cloth. Be right back."

Having traveled the hallway several times, Alex knew where every single squeak lived in the old wooden floor, and approaching the one that annoyed her the most, she stepped over the small carpet outside the bathroom door without thinking twice. Quickly returning to the porch, she refilled the bucket and then headed back to the bedroom, but as she was about to step over the small remnant of carpet again, she came to a sudden stop. Tilting her head to one side, she thought for a moment, and taking four steps backward, she looked at the rug in front of the fireplace in the lounge. It made perfect sense that the living area and bedroom would have area rugs, but as Alex glanced down the hall at the mismatched scrap of carpeting, she could only think of one reason a rug would be placed in that particular spot. Walking over to it, she lifted up the frayed piece of matting and a smile appeared on her face. Cut into the floor was a small hatch complete with a black iron handle mortised into the wood.

The hinges creaked as Alex lifted the heavy wood panel, and wrinkling her nose at the musty, earthen smell rising from the darkness, she dangled the oil lamp into the opening. Seeing a ladder bolted to the side, she took a deep breath and climbed down into the subterranean room. Reaching the bottom, Alex turned up the wick on the lamp and her eyes widened at the sight of the treasures that the owners of the cabin had been trying to hide. The walls of the root cellar were lined with shelves, and on each were the supplies that she and Maggie would need in order to survive.

Canning jars filled with fruits and vegetables lined one shelf, while the next held dozens of freeze-dried food in foil packages. Glass containers marked sugar, coffee, tea, and dried milk were neatly lined up on another, and piled on the floor were clear plastic totes containing the missing pots, pans, toiletries and towels.

Noticing several bottles standing proud toward the back of one shelf, Alex walked over and read the labels. Grinning, she shrugged her shoulders. Scotch wasn't her favorite, but it would definitely do in a pinch.

Feeling as if she had just hit the lottery, Alex debated on what to open first, but when she saw several cases of bottled water stacked in the corner, she made up her mind in an instant. Tearing open one of the boxes, she pulled out a bottle, quickly drank it down and paused for only a moment before opening another. With her thirst finally quenched, she carried a case to the ladder, but then something caught her eye. Reaching up, she pulled a white metal case from the top shelf. Seeing the large red cross painted on the lid, she exclaimed, "Yes!"

With the first-aid kit firmly in her grasp, a few minutes later Alex strode into the bedroom and happily announced, "Hey, you were right!"

Hearing no response, she knelt down and placed her hand on Maggie's forehead.

"Damn," Alex said with a sigh. The fever had come back, and once again, it was out of control.

***

"You're wrong!"

"Mr. Campbell, I understand how you must feel—"

"You don't understand anything!" Douglas Campbell barked. "How dare you walk into my house and tell me that my daughter is dead without having any proof!"

"Sir, I can assure you—"

"Do you have proof?" Campbell screamed back.

"Sir—"

"Do you?"

John Harper had always considered himself a lucky man. He had worked for Interpol for over fifteen years, and in that time, he had never had to tell a parent that their child had died, but his luck had just run out. Even though Maggie Campbell and Alexandra Blake had not been his agents, he had felt it his duty to inform their parents of their demise. Having already broken the news to the officers' superiors at the Met the night before, he had traveled to Scotland on a red-eye flight to face the first of two sets of parents whom he would be visiting that day. He had prepared himself for tears and sadness. He had not prepared himself for anger.

"Mr. Campbell, I'm sorry I can't give you the proof that you're asking for, but please understand. I wouldn't be here if there was any chance that she was still alive."

Setting his jaw, Douglas Campbell sat on the arm of the sofa and glared at the man. Crossing his arms, he calmly said, "You said she was in a plane crash. How can you not have proof?"

Letting out a long breath, and relieved that the distraught parent had curbed his anger, John Harper walked over and sat in a chair opposite Campbell.

"Their plane went down in the middle of a blizzard. We can't get to it."

"A blizzard?" Campbell said, mulling over the information. "Are you talking about the one over North America?"

"Yes, sir."

"My daughter is a Detective Inspector with the Metropolitan Police Service. She works in London. What the hell was she doing on a plane over Canada?"

"My agency needed some decoys for a very simple mission, and your daughter and another Met officer were assigned the case."

"Decoys? Are you telling me that you put my daughter in danger?"

"No, sir, not at all. The mission was already over, but for some reason, they didn't stay at the airport where they landed. The pilot disobeyed orders and tried to fly them out, and that's when the plane went down."

"That doesn't make sense. I was in the Air Force. Pilots are trained to follow orders or…or people die."

"We're still trying to piece together why ours went against direct orders. He has a lot of years under his belt, and he's never done anything like this before." Seeing the confused look on Campbell's face, John Harper added, "Sir, perhaps...perhaps you might be able to help us with that."

"What do you mean?"

"We've had limited communication with the airstrip due to the storm, but what information we have received leads us to believe that one of the officers was sick, and that's why our pilot went against orders."

"Sick?"

"Yes, sir," Harper said, nodding his head. "We're not sure which one it was, or even the extent of her illness, but I was hoping that you might be able to tell us if your daughter had any kind of condition that we weren't aware of."

"A condition?"

"Yes. The Met assures me that both officers passed their yearly physicals with flying colors, but...but if there was anything else—"

Harper's words died in his throat as he saw all the color drain from Campbell's face. Watching as the man buried his head in his hands and began to weep, Harper had his answer. Although he didn't know the specifics, by the wails of anguish coming from Douglas Campbell, John Harper now knew that he had spoken the truth. Whether it was from the crash, from the cold, or from some unknown illness, Margaret Campbell was dead...without a doubt.

CHAPTER EIGHT

Naively believing that Maggie's fever wouldn't return, when it had, it had done so with a vengeance. Within minutes of returning to the bedroom, Alex was forced to carry Maggie back into the blizzard. Twenty minutes later, covered in snow and shivering, Alex returned to the bedroom with Maggie in her arms.

Pulling a pair of scissors from the first-aid kit, Alex said, "I'm going to cut off your clothes."

"What? No," Maggie replied weakly.

"They're covered in blood, and I need to get you into bed. I'm sorry, but we're both freezing, and I can't help myself until I help you."

"I'm not asking you to."

"When are you going to understand that I'm not going to let you die?" Alex said as she began cutting through the gray tweed trousers. Reaching for the bottle of water, she placed it into Maggie's hand. "Drink this."

"What's the point? I'm just going to throw it back up."

Shaking her head, Alex let out a sigh. "Not if you take small sips. Now stop arguing and start drinking. That's an order."

"You don't outrank me."

The smallest of grins appeared on Alex's face, and leaning over, she looked directly into Maggie's eyes. "I will if you die, and I know how much that would piss you off, so take a sip...or start calling me ma'am."

***

A short time later, wearing only her underwear, Maggie lay quietly under the quilt while Alex tended to the gash on her side. In and out of fever for the past several hours, she hadn't paid much attention to Alex's appearance until now, and as she took another sip of water, Maggie was finding it hard not to stare. Between the strip of black cloth tied around her forehead and the streaks of dried blood running down the side of her face, Alex Blake looked like some sort of crazed warrior.

"You need to do something about that cut on your head," Maggie said.

"I will," Alex said without looking up.

"Promise me."

Stopping what she was doing, Alex looked up. About to respond with a flippant reply, when she saw the concerned look on Maggie's face, she thought better of it. "I promise. As soon as I'm done with this, I'll take care of it."

"Thank you."

"You're welcome," Alex said. Thinking for a moment, she added, "Can I ask you a question?"

"Sure."

"What's wrong with you?"

Seeing the slightest hint of amusement cross Maggie's face, Alex softly chuckled. "I mean about the fevers. Why do they get so high?"

"I don't know."

"Surely the doctors have some sort of explanation."

"Not really," Maggie said, taking another sip of water. "I've been to dozens of them, but they never could find anything conclusive. Most believe that it's just a genetic glitch...something to do with my hypothalamus."

"Your hypo...what?"

"It's in the brain. It controls body temperature. Most times, if I get a low-grade fever, over-the-counter medication will take care of it, but if I get a fairly nasty virus, that's when my body goes into overdrive trying to fight it, and it just doesn't know when to quit."

"So the fever just keeps going up?"

"Yeah," Maggie said, quickly flinching when Alex touched a sensitive spot.

"Christ, sorry...did I hurt you?"

"No, it's just a bit tender, that's all."

"Well, I'm almost done. Just a few more minutes and you can rest."

"Where'd you find the first-aid kit?"

"In the basement."

"The basement?"

"Well, it's more like a small root cellar. There's a trap door under the rug in the hallway. I found it earlier when I went to get more snow, but when I tried to tell you about it, you had already passed out."

"Oh."

"And we don't have to worry about food or water anymore either. There's plenty," Alex said, reaching for the bandages.

When Maggie didn't respond, Alex looked up and saw that she had fallen asleep. Placing her hand on Maggie's forehead, when she found it warm, but not hot, Alex finished bandaging the wound, and then crept from the room.

***

After leaving the bedroom, Alex divided her time between bringing in more firewood, filling the bathtub with snow, and checking on Maggie. With the blizzard showing no signs of letting up, and not wanting to waste a minute of daylight, she traveled back and forth from the wood pile to replenish their supply. Stopping when the stacks of firewood by both hearths had reached her hips, she grabbed the bucket and began carrying snow into the bathroom. Praying that once melted, it would provide enough cold water to keep Maggie's temperature in check, Alex refused to give into her exhaustion, hunger or pain until the snow was piled high above the rim of the claw-footed tub.

Once satisfied that she had prepared herself for anything that the next twenty-four hours had in store for her, she climbed down into the cellar to bring up supplies. Concentrating on only the totes that held the towels, linens and toiletries, after four trips, she rewarded herself with an entire jar of canned peaches. Finally, after nearly three hours, she followed through on her promise to Maggie. Stripping out of her wet clothes, Alex washed herself with icy water, tended to her injuries, put on some dry clothes and then wearily shuffled to the bedroom. After making sure that Maggie's temperature had yet to rise to the point of being deadly, she hobbled back to the front room, and after tossing a log on the fire, Alex slumped near the sofa and stared into the flames.

Watching as they flickered and danced over the logs, Alex replayed the events of the past two days in her mind. Glancing at her wrist, she removed the watch that the pilot had given her, and flipping it over, her eyes filled with tears.

By the heartfelt words inscribed on the back, she knew that somewhere he had a loving wife whose heart would no doubt be broken when she heard the news. The tears rolled down her cheeks as she remembered his anger when the coffee had spilled in his lap, and the self-assured smile that he had flashed her just before taking off. He seemed so strong then. So invincible with his barrel chest and leather bomber jacket, the confidence he exuded had been infectious, but now he was gone. And the dead eyes that had stared back at her from the cockpit would haunt her forever. Resting her head on the couch, she cried herself to sleep.

***

Alex woke to the sound of screaming. With her muscles aching from sitting on the cold, hard floor, it took a few seconds before she managed to get to her feet. Wincing as she put weight on her injured leg, she pushed past the pain and shuffled to the bedroom. Seeing Maggie thrashing about on the bed, Alex knew in an instant what was happening. While the words that Maggie was speaking were garbled, the message they were sending was loud and clear. Maggie's fever had returned.

Wasting no time, Alex threw back the quilt, gathered Maggie in her arms and rushed her to the bathroom. Disheartened to see that the snow which had taken over an hour to pile high had turned into only a few inches of water, she nevertheless, lowered Maggie into the cold puddle. Draping a wet towel over Maggie's head, Alex hurried from the room for the bucket. Returning a few minutes later, she emptied more snow into the tub and then limped back outside for more.

It wasn't until Alex's fourth trip that Maggie began to shiver, and as her eyes opened, she weakly stuttered, "Pl...Please...no...no...more."

Hearing her voice, Alex grinned. "Hey there. How you feeling?"

"I'm cold," Maggie whimpered, trying to get away from the icy water that surrounded her.

Touching Maggie's arm to still her movements, Alex said, "Okay. Let me get some towels, and I'll get you out of there."

Retrieving three towels from one of the totes, Alex tossed two on the bed and hurried to the bathroom with the last in her hand. Up until that moment, the fact that the woman who Alex found incredibly attractive was wearing nothing but underwear hadn't been an issue, but the white fabric of Maggie's bra and knickers had become almost translucent because of the water. Swallowing hard, it was all she could do to keep her eyes off of Maggie's finer features as she helped her from the tub. Wrapping her in the towel, Alex guided her slowly to the bedroom, and lowering her to the carpet in front of the fireplace, covered her with the remaining towels.

Taking a bottle of water from the nightstand, Alex placed it in Maggie's hand. "Here, you should drink some of this."

Seeing that the liquid in the bottle was cloudy, Maggie shook her head and pushed it away. "No, it's dirty."

Smiling, Alex put the bottle back into Maggie's hand. "No, it's not. I put some aspirin in it a while ago. I thought it would be easier than you trying to swallow pills. Now drink up, but remember to take it slow."

"I will," Maggie replied. Clear-headed for the first time in several hours, as she sipped the water, she looked around the room. Except for the wall which held the fireplace, all the others were covered in smooth, rounded logs stacked from floor to ceiling. High above her head, she could see large timbers running to and fro. Although she had no idea the amount of snow on the roof, by the girth of the lumber, it was obvious that the cabin was built to withstand the fiercest of winters.

Taking another drink, Maggie ran her tongue over her cracked lips, trying to replace the moisture that her fever had sucked away. Noticing what she was doing, Alex opened the first-aid kit and handed Maggie a small container.

"Here, try this. It should help."

"What is it?"

"Balm for your lips."

"Oh," Maggie replied weakly.

When Maggie didn't make a move to open the small jar, Alex asked, "Would you rather I do it?"

"Please," Maggie said, placing the container back into Alex's hand. "Can you?"

"Not a problem."

Unscrewing the cap, Alex put some on her finger and then gently rubbed it across Maggie's parted lips. Although Alex was trying to keep her eyes focused on the task at hand, when she glanced up and her eyes met Maggie's, she felt her body react. Silently chastising herself for the thoughts which flashed through her mind, Alex put the jar aside and reached for the bandages. Lifting the corner of the towel, she removed the waterlogged dressing, and in silence, tended to the wound.

"You're not who I thought you were," Maggie said in a whisper as Alex pressed the adhesive tape in place.

"How so?"

"You seem so different. Not as…hard…coarse, as I remember."

Alex couldn't help but smile. It was rare that she had ever allowed any of her work colleagues to see her softer side, especially the colleague lying in front of her, but keeping up her stern and serious act twenty-four-seven was impossible.

Tossing the old bandage into the flames, Alex looked into Maggie's eyes and when she spoke, her tone was soft. "I'm a passionate woman, Campbell. I'm passionate about putting men behind bars that kidnap little boys for reasons that make me lose my lunch. I'm passionate about catching the men who rape women, and do more damage to their souls than they ever could do to their bodies. And I'm passionate about wanting to hunt down every man and woman who bring drugs into our country, turning our youth into addicts before they're old enough to vote. So yeah, I suppose I appear hard, but it's the woman I need to be in order to do my job."

"And what about when you're not working?" Maggie asked. "What kind of woman are you then?"

Maggie watched in amazement as Alex's entire persona seemed to change. In an instant, the intensity that had been etched into her forehead disappeared, and her eyes twinkled with amusement.

"I'm a woman who adores a five-pound Yorkshire terrier named Sandy, who, by now, has given birth to her puppies and is most likely driving my best friend crazy," Alex said with a wide smile. "I'm a woman who loves her family and all that entails, and I'm a woman who's content to sit in a darkened room at night and listen to the sounds of the street, thinking about the day that's passed so I can clear away the cobwebs and focus on tomorrow." A loud pop from the fireplace startled Alex, and blushing slightly, she said, "Sorry…got a little deep there."

"No, not at all," Maggie said. Shocked at how wrong she was about the woman sitting by her side, she asked, "So, you mentioned a dog and family, what about a boyfriend or a husband?"

"Not my flavor," Alex said as she stood and walked to the trunk.

"What do you mean?"

Returning with a blue flannel shirt and a pair of boxer shorts, Alex sat on the floor and said, "I'm gay."

"You're gay?" Maggie repeated in shock.

The stunned look on Maggie's face instantly ignited Alex's temper, and setting her jaw, she growled back, "Is that a problem?"

Shaking her head, Maggie said, "No...no. I just didn't think...I mean...you don't look like—"

"A dyke?"

"That's not...that's not what I meant," Maggie stammered, rubbing her forehead, "I guess I just assumed...I mean, you're a beautiful woman, and I thought that you'd be...um...straight."

Having had the same hesitant, fumbling response from so many other straight people in her life, Alex was about to unleash a torrent of angry words, but when she saw that Maggie was shivering, she reined in her anger.

"You need to get out of those wet things," Alex stated, placing the clothes on the floor. "And now that you know I'm a lesbian, I'm sure you'd be more comfortable putting these on *without* my help."

"You don't make me uncomfortable," Maggie argued weakly.

"Sure I do," Alex said sadly as she stood and walked to the door. "I'll be back in a few minutes to help you get into bed."

Mumbling expletives under her breath until she reached the kitchen, Alex poured some scotch into a coffee cup, lit a cigarette and tried her best to calm down. She hated being judged because of her sexuality, and seeing the shocked look on Maggie's face had cut her to the core. Waiting for the length of time it took to smoke two cigarettes, Alex returned to the bedroom with a scowl on her face.

"You ready?" she asked, walking to the bed to pull back the quilt. When Maggie didn't answer, Alex looked in her direction and noticed she was still lying under the towels. "Why haven't you changed?"

"I tried, but…but I couldn't do it. I…I don't have the strength," Maggie said in a hoarse whisper.

Alex's shoulders fell. In her anger, she had forgotten that Maggie was seriously ill, and she had left her on the floor covered in wet towels for over fifteen minutes.

"Christ, I'm sorry," Alex said, rushing to her side. "I can be quite the stupid shit at times."

"That's okay, so can I."

"Would you like me to help you?"

"Please," Maggie said as another shiver ran through her body.

Trying her best to keep Maggie's privacy intact, Alex reached under the towel, pulled the wet knickers down her legs and replaced them with a pair of boxers in a matter of seconds. Crawling to Maggie's side, Alex leaned over her and said, "Put your arms around my neck, and I'll pull you up."

Doing as instructed, seconds later Maggie was sitting up with her face buried in Alex's shoulder, waiting for the pain in her side to subside. Without saying a word, Alex unclasped the damp bra, and tossing it aside, she quickly pulled the flannel shirt over Maggie's cold skin. After fastening every button, Alex gently helped Maggie into bed.

Before she was able to cover her with the quilt, Maggie had already passed out. Alex quietly left the bedroom, and foregoing food or water, headed to the sofa and stretched out across the cushions. Taking a deep breath, before her lungs emptied, she fell into a deep, peaceful sleep. She had no way of knowing that in less than four hours, she would once again wake to the sounds of unintelligible words muttered by a woman on the verge of death.

CHAPTER NINE

Standing in the library lost in his thoughts, John Harper looked up as the man came back into the room. Although they had only just met, it seemed to Harper that Alexandra Blake's father had aged a decade in a matter of minutes.

"Is your wife all right?"

"Seeing that you just told her that her daughter is dead, do you really need to ask that question?" Gregory Blake said as he strode to the liquor cabinet. "I need a drink. Would you like one?"

"No, thank you."

"Well, that's too bad," Gregory said sternly, forcing a glass in Harper's hand. "I don't like to drink alone. It's much too easy to get drunk. Since I have to call my sons to tell them that their sister is…is gone, and then start making arrangements for…for Alexandra's funeral, I prefer to remain sober. I'm sure you understand."

"Yes, sir," John said, taking a sip of the whisky.

"Sit," Blake said, motioning to a chair in the room as he sat behind his desk.

Taking a seat, Harper remained quiet and watched as Gregory Blake struggled to hold onto his emotions. It was clear that the man was trying to be strong, but the look in his eyes said it all. He was devastated.

A few minutes passed in silence until finally, John Harper rose to his feet. "Perhaps I should leave now."

"I'll need some information before you go," Gregory said in a whisper. "The funeral home will need to know where to go…where to go to get my daughter."

"I'm sorry, Mr. Blake, but…but we haven't found her yet."

Looking up from his glass, Blake said, "Excuse me?"

Déjà vu. The feeling that occurs when you believe that you've witnessed or experienced the current situation once before, and it was the feeling now washing over John Harper. Taking a deep breath, he sat back down and looked over at Gregory Blake. "Your daughter and another officer were on an airplane that went down in a storm. We haven't yet been able to make it to the crash site to retrieve their…to bring them home."

"Then how do you know they're dead?" Blake asked, studying the man across the way. "And what do you mean a storm? The UK has been clear all week."

"They were assisting Interpol on a small mission, and their flight took them into Canada."

Gregory Blake paled. He had watched the news just that morning, and terms like *storm of the century* and *the blizzard to end all blizzards* had been bandied about on almost every station. Weather maps flashed red as forecasters predicted temperatures well below freezing and winds well above gale force. At the time, it seemed unimportant. Although he had sympathized with those living thousands of miles away as he had sat sipping his coffee in his conservatory that morning, the tragic events unfolding on his television screen hadn't been personal…until now.

Getting up, he walked over and picked up a silver-framed photograph of his daughter. Running his finger over the glass, a hundred memories flooded his mind. Her birth, her first steps, and her first day at school. Her enthusiasm when she had joined the Met and her excitement when she had solved her first case. But most of all, he remembered her strength. No task had ever been too tough for her, and he couldn't remember Alex once admitting defeat. It wasn't in her nature. It wasn't in her genes...and it certainly wasn't in his.

Carefully returning the frame to the bookcase, he turned around and stared at John Harper. "Pardon my impertinence, but I don't believe you."

Confused, Harper said, "Excuse me?"

"Unless you can give me absolute proof that Alexandra is dead, then she isn't," Blake stated firmly as he went back to his desk and sat down. "Now, when will you be able to get to them?"

"Um...I'm sorry to say that we won't be able to get anywhere near the crash site for weeks."

"Weeks!"

"The storm—"

"I know all about the bloody storm!" Blake shouted. "It's all over the airwaves, for God's sake, but that's not an answer to my question. That's an excuse!"

"Sir, you don't understand. Until the weather breaks, we can't risk sending someone—"

"You risked my daughter's life by sending her there, you bloody buffoon!" Blake screamed, getting to his feet.

John Harper had always considered himself an even-tempered man, and when he had made the decision to tell the families of Maggie Campbell and Alexandra Blake about their deaths, he knew it wouldn't be easy. However, he hadn't anticipated being called incompetent, and his composure slipped a notch...or perhaps two.

Rising to his feet, he glared at Gregory Blake. "Do you honestly believe that I would have allowed them to make that trip if I had thought for one instant that they would be in danger? I know how to do my job!"

"Well, as long as your job includes putting people in harm's way, then I'd say you're doing a bang-up job of it!"

"I'm not the one that convinced an agent to go against direct orders!" Harper barked back.

Blake opened his mouth to reply and then shut it just as quickly. Confused by Harper's outburst, he narrowed his eyes. "What did you say?"

Harper's shoulders fell as he realized his mistake, and letting out a long breath, he said, "I think I should leave."

"What do you mean that I wasn't the one that convinced an agent to go against orders?"

"It doesn't matter."

"Yes, it bloody well does. Now tell me the truth...please."

With a heavy sigh, Harper sat back down and took a sip of his drink. Unable to raise his eyes to meet those of Alexandra Blake's father, Harper stared at the floor as he began to talk.

"Due to the blizzard, communications with the rest of my people in Canada have been limited, but we've learned that the officer who was with your daughter was ill, and apparently her condition required a hospital. Your daughter convinced one of my most seasoned agents to go against orders and fly them out."

The sound of Gregory Blake's laughter filled the room, and stunned, Harper's head snapped up. "Are you all right, sir?"

"The poor bastard didn't stand a chance," Blake said as he continued to chuckle.

"Excuse me?"

"You obviously don't know my daughter very well."

"You're right, I don't. We only met the other day when I gave her the assignment."

Still wearing a wide smile, Blake got up and retrieved a book from a nearby shelf. Walking over, he dropped the dictionary in Harper's lap.

"Look up the word pigheaded in there, and you'll find a picture of my daughter," Blake said. "Alex is as stubborn as the day is long. Coupled with the fact that she would never stand idly by and watch somebody suffer tells me that your agent, orders or not, didn't have a choice."

"She's that hardheaded?"

"You have absolutely no idea," Gregory replied. Pulling over a nearby chair, he sat down next to Harper, and pausing a moment to get his thoughts in order, he said, "I'm a wealthy man, and if money is one of the reasons that you can't—"

"I assure you that it's not," John interrupted. "I promise you that as soon as the weather breaks, I'll fly a team in."

"Why can't they try it on foot? Surely those trained in rescue—"

"Sending anyone in on foot would only put more people in peril. The storm is still raging, and even after the snow stops falling, which I'm told won't be for another few days, we still have the wind to contend with, and the last radar forecast showed another smaller storm moving in. I'm afraid that we're just going to have to wait until the weather clears before sending in a search party."

"But by then it could be too late. I mean, they could manage to stay alive for a few days if the plane was intact. They'd be able to stay warm for a little while, but—" His words were cut off by the sound of a mobile phone ringing, and Gregory watched as Harper pulled one from his pocket.

Glancing at the screen, Harper rose to his feet. "I'm sorry, but I need to take this."

"Of course," Gregory said, emptying what was left in his glass in one swallow. "I'll pour myself another scotch."

Several minutes passed before John Harper walked back into the room, but when he did, the rather pensive look on his face, caused Gregory Blake to sit up in his chair. "You've heard something, haven't you?"

Without saying a word, Harper walked over and retrieved his drink from the end table. Taking a sip, he said, "I don't want you to get your hopes up."

"It's too late for that," Gregory answered anxiously. "Now, what is it?"

"We know where the plane is because of the transmitter on board. I've had my entire department studying every map and satellite photo they can get their hands on so when the time comes, we'll know what we're up against."

"And?"

"They've come across a map showing...showing a few cabins in the area where they crashed."

"Cabins!"

Hearing the exuberance in the man's voice, Harper said, "Please, I don't want you to read more into this than there is. The cabins are nearly three miles away from where the plane went down, and they would have had to find them in the dark, after walking for hours through a forest in a snowstorm."

"That doesn't mean they couldn't have done it."

"It's highly unlikely."

"Unlikely doesn't mean impossible."

Snorting at the man's determination, Harper said, "I see where your daughter gets her tenaciousness."

The comment brought a grin to Gregory's face. Motioning for Harper to sit down, Gregory said, "I know that you probably think me a fool to believe that my daughter is still alive, but I can't yet imagine her any other way. She's my little girl, and as long as there's a glimmer of hope, one minuscule chance that she could have survived and found shelter, then I must beg you that as soon as humanly possible you begin your search."

"Why would you think I wouldn't?"

"Because you believe you're looking for a body, and I believe you're not."

***

"Don't bother," Maggie said as she weakly tried to push away Alex's hand.

"The bandage is wet. I need to change it," Alex said, reaching for the soaked gauze.

"I said, don't bother," Maggie repeated, pulling the quilt over the bandage.

With a sigh, Alex said, "Why are you being like this?"

"I don't want you to waste your time on me. You need to take care of yourself."

"What makes you think I'm not?"

Through half-open eyes, Maggie looked back at her. "Because you look like shit."

Raising one eyebrow, the tiniest of grins appeared on Alex's face. Thinking for a moment, she said, "I'll attribute that remark to the fever."

"I'm serious. You're exhausted. You need to get some sleep."

"I'm fine, and when you sleep, I sleep."

"But fairly soon, I'm not going to wake up, so do yourself a favor and stop fighting a losing battle," Maggie said feebly.

"I don't think of it as a losing battle," Alex stated as she raised the bedspread and quickly removed the wet bandage. "And I refuse to sit back and just watch you die."

"You don't know what you're up against."

"Yes, I do," Alex said firmly, glaring at Maggie. "It's a fever, Campbell. A bloody fucking fever brought on by the flu. Your body goes into overdrive to fight it, and your fever spikes. I get that! But what you don't get is that what I'm doing is working. It's been almost two days since we crashed, and you're still here!"

"How long was I asleep this last time?"

"What?"

"How long was it before my fever spiked, and you had to carry me back into the bathroom?"

Shrugging her shoulders, Alex said, "I don't know. Maybe three or four hours. Why?"

"And the time before that?"

"I wasn't really keeping track. Maybe five or..." Alex stopped for a moment. "It's happening more often, isn't it?"

"Yes, and soon it won't come back down, no matter how much snow you pile on top of me."

"You don't know that!"

Struggling to keep her eyes open, Maggie replied, "Yes, I do, and since I don't know if I'm going to wake up again—"

"Stop staying that!"

Shutting her eyes for a moment, Maggie fought the urge to fall back into darkness. Taking a long, deep breath, her eyes fluttered open. "Please...I...I need to ask you a favor. Please...please just listen to me."

Steadfast in her belief that the woman would not die, Alex rolled her eyes at the sound of Maggie's whispered plea, and in a huff, crossed her arms. "Fine, what's the favor?"

"When it...when it happens, find someplace safe for me."

Confused, Alex wrinkled her brow. "What the hell are you talking about?"

"We're in a forest, right?"

"Yeah, out in the middle of nowhere as far as I can tell. Why?"

"I don't want...I don't want the animals to find me."

Alex's mouth dropped open, and looking toward the ceiling, she fought to restrain her temper. Taking a deep breath, she snapped, "Jesus Christ! You have got to stop—"

"Please, just promise me."

"You are not going to die!" Alex said, rising to her feet.

Teary-eyed and whimpering, Maggie begged again. "Please…just promise me…oh, please…my father…my father—"

Maggie's tears were Alex's undoing. In an instant, her anger disappeared and compassion took its place. Sitting on the edge of the bed, she took Maggie's hand and gave it a squeeze. "Sshhh…sshhh…it's okay. It's okay, Maggie."

"Just promise—"

Alex's eyes filled with tears, and in a ragged breath, replied, "I promise, Maggie. I promise the animals won't get to you."

***

Alex stared at the empty bottle of aspirin in her hand. She had managed over the past day to spoon-feed four bottles of aspirin-laced water to her unconscious patient, and between coughs and sputters, Maggie had swallowed it all, but now the over-the-counter medicine was gone. Alex hadn't beaten the odds; she had just prolonged their arrival.

While the cold baths had worked to cool Maggie's temperature, within a few hours of being placed back in the bed, her fever would rage again. Over the past twenty-four hours, Alex had carried the woman into the bathroom six more times, and each time it had taken Maggie longer to return to consciousness.

Grabbing the old, dusty blanket that had been draped over one of the chairs, Alex fingered the thick, woven fabric as her thoughts returned to the promise she had made to Maggie. Her eyes filling with tears, she tossed the blanket aside. Appalled that she had just allowed herself to think about how best to store Maggie's body, Alex threw the empty water bottle across the room.

Setting her jaw, Alex growled, "She is not going to die! You have never given up on anything in your life, and you're not going to start now. Now, think, Alex...think!"

All of a sudden, the sound of Maggie's moans came from the bedroom. In an instant, Alex was on her feet and running down the hall. Stopping in the doorway, her heart sank. Fighting invisible demons, Maggie flailed on the bed. Her body was covered in sweat, and her face had turned deadly white.

As she had done so many times before, Alex gathered Maggie in her arms and painfully limped to the bathroom. Mindless of the frigid water sloshing over the sides, Alex placed her inside, and when the woman didn't even flinch at the temperature, Alex rushed to get more snow. Bucket after bucket she carried through the cabin, but no matter how much snow Alex piled on her, Maggie remained motionless. Mindless that the socks on her feet were now covered in ice, and her own clothes were soaking wet, Alex refused to give up until the painful throbbing in her leg forced her to stop. Collapsing to the floor, she sat in a puddle of snowy slush and began to cry.

Staring at the floor, Alex sat there listening to the sound of Maggie's ragged breathing as it slowly grew fainter. Minutes ticked by, and even though she was shivering, Alex refused to move until finally the room grew quiet. It was over.

Choking back her tears, she looked up and when she saw Maggie's hazel-green eyes staring back at her, Alex's face lit up.

"Hey," she said, as she sniffled back what remained of her tears. Wiping her nose with the back of her hand, she grinned. "I thought for a minute, I'd lost you."

Exhausted and freezing, Maggie was unable to speak. Shivering in the water, she merely shook her head slightly to acknowledge what Alex had said.

Rising to her feet, Alex reached into the tub and lifted Maggie out, groaning as the strain caused her back to twinge and her leg to throb. Icy water dripped from Maggie's soaked clothes, drenching Alex in an instant, but Alex couldn't have cared less. Quickly returning to the bedroom, she placed Maggie on the floor, and even though she had always tried to allow the woman a certain amount of privacy, now was not the time.

Feeling as if she had just prevented death from claiming another victim, Alex practically ripped the wet clothes from Maggie's body, and disregarding the woman's nudity, placed her back in the bed and covered her with the quilt.

The room was warm, but under the blankets, Maggie shivered uncontrollably. As another chill trembled its way through her body, she stuttered, "I'm so…c—c—cold."

"I know," Alex whispered, tucking the blankets in around her. "I'm going to put some more logs on the fire and get something dry to wear. I'll be right back."

As Maggie watched in silence, Alex tossed more wood on the fire and then opened the trunk at the foot of the bed and rummaged inside.

"How you doing?" Alex asked, looking up as she pushed her sweatpants to the floor.

"I—I—I can't stop shaking."

Frowning at the response, Alex pulled a white t-shirt from the trunk. Turning her back to Maggie, she quickly changed her shirt.

Maggie knew that she should allow Alex some privacy, but as hard as she tried, she simply could not look away from the woman's well-muscled physique. Sinewy without being overt, it was clear that Alex took pride in her body, and at that particular moment, so did Maggie. However, when another shiver ran down her spine, Maggie groaned loudly as she pulled the blankets up to her nose.

Hanging the wet clothes near the fireplace, Alex walked to the bed. Without saying a word, she climbed under the covers, wrapping one strong arm around Maggie as she gently pulled her toward her. Fully expecting the ill woman to balk at her presence in the bed, when Maggie snuggled against her warmth, Alex let out the breath she had been holding.

"I'm scared," Maggie confessed as she continued to shake.

Rubbing her hand briskly over Maggie's back, Alex whispered, "So am I."

CHAPTER TEN

When she opened her eyes, Alex became aware of three things. Her nose was cold, her leg was throbbing, and she was holding a warm, soft woman in her arms. Reaching over, she placed her hand lightly against Maggie's forehead and grinned. For most of the night Alex had held her, rubbing her back and arms to try to fight off the chills that had ravaged her body. In the early hours of the morning, Maggie had finally fallen asleep, and Alex had quickly followed, and for the next twelve hours, they slept soundly...and fever free.

Stealthily slipping out from under the sheets so as not to wake Maggie, Alex grabbed a pair of sweat pants and crept from the room. Visiting the bathroom first, she emptied her bladder, brushed her teeth courtesy of the packaged toiletries she had found in the cellar, and grabbing a pair of dry socks from the towel bar, covered her feet and shuffled to the kitchen.

Returning to the bedroom a short time later, she was surprised to find Maggie not only awake, but looking better than she had in days. Her skin was no longer a ghostly white, and her eyes were bright and clear.

"Hi there! How you feeling?" Alex said, trying her best to hide her limp as she walked to the bed.

It should have been an easy question to answer. Maggie was clear-headed for the first time in days, and while she felt as if she had run a marathon, her fever was gone. She was thirsty. She was hungry, and her powers of observation were rapidly returning. The fact that Alex wasn't wearing a bra was more than evident, and having a hard time keeping her eyes off of the woman wearing a gauze-thin white t-shirt, Maggie quickly sputtered, "Better...I...I...I think the fever broke."

Totally unaware of her appearance, Alex handed Maggie a bottle of water. "Yeah, it broke last night, but I still think you need to drink this."

Nodding her head, Maggie began to gulp the water until Alex pulled the bottle away.

"Slowly, remember?"

"Sorry," Maggie said, her eyes once again finding their way to Alex's chest.

Watching as she sipped the water, Alex asked, "You hungry?"

"Actually, I am."

"Good. Drink your water. I'll be back in a few minutes."

As Alex headed for the door, Maggie called out, "Alex, can you...um...can you find me something to wear?"

"Oh, right," Alex said with a chuckle, remembering that Maggie was naked under the blankets. "Hold on."

Grabbing a flannel shirt and a pair of sweat pants, Alex placed them on the bed.

"You going to be all right with this?"

"Yeah, I think I can manage."

"Right, well then you get dressed, and I'll scrounge us up some food," Alex said, leaving the room to give Maggie some privacy.

When she came back a short time later, Maggie was not only thankful for the breakfast she was carrying, but also for the fact that the slight chill of the cabin had forced Alex to put on an over-sized corduroy shirt. Sitting quietly as she sipped her tea and ate some peaches, Maggie listened as Alex told her about the root cellar and its contents.

"So we'll be okay, then?" Maggie asked.

"Yeah, we've got food, water, toiletries…all the comforts of home, except home, that is."

Noticing that Maggie seemed to be fidgeting in the bed, Alex grinned, already knowing the question before it was asked. "You need the loo?"

A hint of blush crossed Maggie's cheeks. "Yes, please."

Helping Maggie to her feet, when she began to sway, Alex wrapped her arm around her shoulders and walked her slowly to the bathroom.

"You can handle this yourself now – yes?"

Maggie's cheeks flamed instantly. Alex's words solidifying what she had already assumed, Maggie nodded her head. "I'll be fine."

"I'm going to get some more wood, so if you need me, just shout out."

"I will. Thanks."

Believing that her trip to the wood pile would be brief, between the ice-laden snow drifts, the heavy winds and the intense pain in her thigh, it was nearly an hour before Alex had enough wood stacked on the porch to last them another day. After transferring the pile inside, she slowly limped to the lounge. About to kick off her boots, she looked over and noticed Maggie standing in the hallway staring back at her.

"What's wrong with your leg?" Maggie asked.

"Nothing. Just a bit sore, that's all," Alex said with a shrug.

Even though Maggie felt as if she could crawl back into bed and sleep for a week, her temper was as healthy as ever. Sensing that Alex was hiding something, Maggie glared at the woman as she walked closer. "Don't you dare lie to me, Alex. You've just spent the last four days saving my bloody life, and if there's something wrong with you, if you're *hurt*, then I think I have the right to know."

Letting out a long breath, Alex sat on the arm of the sofa and looked at the woman who had haunted her dreams for over three years. The clothing Maggie wore was wrinkled and several sizes too large, and her hair was tangled and in need of a wash, but as Alex gazed at the auburn-haired Inspector, she couldn't remember ever seeing anyone more beautiful. Captivated, Alex allowed her chivalry to slip a notch.

"I got a few cuts on my leg when we crashed," she said. "One seems to be doing okay, but the other still hurts like a bugger."

"Why don't you let me take a look?"

"Because *you* need to rest."

"Alex—"

"Look, I'll make you a deal. You take a short kip, and when you wake up, I'll let you play doctor. How's that?"

"No," Maggie said firmly.

Raising an eyebrow, Alex said, "Excuse me?"

"I'll take a nap *after* I look at your leg."

"Christ, you're pushy."

"You have no idea," Maggie said with a grin. "Now take off those sweatpants."

***

As she waited for Alex to return with the first-aid supplies, Maggie sat on the sofa taking in her surroundings. Other than the faded Mohican patterned upholstery covering the sofa and chairs, and several fish mounted in various poses of capture hanging from the walls, the main room of the cabin was identical to the bedroom down to the fireplace encompassing one wall. Noticing a bit of sunlight creeping in around the shutters covering the windows, Maggie walked over and removed one of the wooden bars holding them closed. Blinking as sunlight streamed through the frost-covered window, she smiled when she felt the cold radiating through the glass. It was good to be alive.

Hearing a noise, Maggie looked over her shoulder and watched as Alex limped back into the room carrying the first-aid kit and a bottle of what appeared to be liquor.

"What's in the bottle?" Maggie asked.

"Scotch," Alex replied, placing everything on the coffee table.

"Bit early for that, don't you think?"

"There's not much disinfectant left, and if the cut is infected, you might need something else to clean it."

"Well, hopefully it won't come to that," Maggie said, returning to the couch. "You'll need to take off your boots."

"Oh, right," Alex said, easily stepping out of the left one. However, when she tried to do the same with the right, she instantly grimaced.

"Here, let me do that," Maggie said as she reached down, carefully removing the boot.

Sitting on the sofa, Maggie looked up at the tall woman now standing in front of her. Swallowing hard at the beauty staring back at her, Maggie suddenly felt as if the past three years had never happened. All the feelings that she had worked so diligently to bury seemed to have come back in force. Taking a deep breath to clear away her thoughts, she untied the string holding up Alex's loose-fitting sweat pants, and a second later the baggy clothing was puddled around Alex's feet.

Alex's body throbbed in response, and surprised by the intensity of the pulse of awareness between her legs, a small groan slipped from her lips.

Looking up, Maggie asked, "You okay?"

"Um…yeah…yeah, I'm fine. Just wasn't prepared for the draft," Alex quipped, all the while praying that the cool cabin air would help to stifle her overactive libido.

Flashing a quick grin, Maggie returned to the matter at hand, and lifting the hem of Alex's shirt, she examined the small cut on the front of her thigh. Running her finger lightly over the rapidly healing cut, she said, "This doesn't look infected."

"The entrance wound is on the back of my leg. I could never manage to get a good look at it," Alex said as she turned her back to Maggie. Feeling her shirttail being lifted out of the way, Alex waited for Maggie to say something, but when she heard the woman gasp, it confirmed what Alex had already known.

Blanching at the sight of the wound, Maggie asked, "How did this happen?"

"When I woke up after the crash, I found that a piece of metal had gone through my seat…and through my leg."

"Jesus Christ!" Maggie blurted. "Why didn't you say something?"

"If you remember, you weren't in any shape to listen, and once I got myself free, it wasn't too bad."

"Well, it looks bad now."

"Yeah?"

"Alex, it's definitely infected. You need to lie down and let me see what I can do."

Moving off the sofa to allow Alex room, Maggie opened the first-aid kit and examined the contents. Although there seemed to be plenty of gauze, bandages and tape, the only disinfectant was a partially filled bottle of isopropyl rubbing alcohol.

Returning to sit on the edge of the couch, Maggie lifted the tails of the shirt and looked at the gash again. It was less than two inches long, but the entire thing was swollen, and yellow pus appeared to be building just below the surface of the skin. Gently, Maggie ran her finger over the cut, hoping that the slight pressure she was applying would force it to open on its own, but when Alex yelped in pain, Maggie pulled her hand away. Thinking for a moment, she looked around the room, and seeing a cast-iron kettle hanging on a hook over the fire, she asked, "The pot over the fireplace, what's that for?"

"I use it to boil water." Alex answered, looking over her shoulder at Maggie.

"Do we have salt?"

"Yes, in the cellar. Why?"

"Because we need to draw this infection out."

"Is it that bad?"

Grimacing as she glanced at the cut again, Maggie said, "It's worse."

***

After losing the argument deciding who would gather the water, salt and washcloths, Alex sat on the edge of the sofa, trying her best not to put pressure on the back of her leg while Maggie shuffled around the cabin for the supplies. Eyeing the bottle of scotch still sitting on the coffee table, Alex was contemplating having a sip when Maggie came from the kitchen carrying two glasses. Without saying a word, she picked up the bottle and began filling the glasses.

Confused, Alex tilted her head and waited for an explanation.

"I'm not Florence Nightingale," Maggie said, offering Alex a weak grin. "The compresses have to be hot in order to draw out the infection, so I thought that this might help settle our nerves a bit." Handing Alex a glass, Maggie said, "Now you drink it, and I'll check on the water."

Carefully lifting the cast-iron pot from the hook above the fire, Maggie set it on the hearth and poured in an ample amount of salt, followed by several washcloths. Slowly stirring the mixture until the salt was dissolved, Maggie's expression grew pensive. Quietly, she said, "You'd best get comfortable. This is almost ready."

As Alex took another swallow of scotch, she noticed the worried look on Maggie's face. Thinking for a moment, she said, "You know, if this is going to bother you, I'll do it myself. I'm sure I can manage."

Stopping what she was doing, Maggie looked in Alex's direction. Grinning ever so slightly at the woman's continual need to be chivalrous, Maggie said, "I can't remember much about the past few days, but I'm fairly certain that I threw up at least once. Didn't I?"

"Yeah, a few times, but—"

"And you cleaned and dressed the cut on my side. Right?"

"You know I did, but that doesn't mean—"

"And by the comment you made this morning, I'm pretty sure you helped me…you helped me when I needed to use the bathroom. Yes?"

"Okay, sure, but Maggie…"

Pulling two washcloths from the pot, Maggie placed them in a small saucepan and then made her way to the sofa. Sitting on the coffee table, she said, "Alex, I'm not squeamish, but this is going to hurt…a lot. I don't remember much about what you did for me, but I do know that you never hurt me, and I'm about to hurt *you*." Grabbing a towel from the arm of the sofa, Maggie handed it to Alex. "Now, lie down and put this under you. The sooner we get this over with the better."

Nodding her head, Alex stood long enough to cover the sofa with the terrycloth, and then slowly took her position across the couch. Reaching over, she grabbed her glass of scotch from the coffee table and quickly drank it down.

Lifting the tails of Alex's shirt out of the way, Maggie paled at the greenish-yellow lesion on Alex's thigh. Reaching into the saucepan, she removed a washcloth, and folding it in half as quickly as possible, Maggie asked, "You ready?"

Taking a deep breath, Alex replied, "Yeah. I'm good."

"I'm sorry," Maggie said sadly, wincing as she covered the wound with the steaming cloth.

"Christ!" Alex groaned in protest. Feeling as if she was being branded by the heated towel, a long line of expletives entered her thoughts, but holding back her desire to scream them, she took a deep breath and waited for the pain to ease.

Over the next several minutes, Maggie continued to exchange the cool cloths for the ones fresh from the steaming salt water, and while the muscles in Alex's arms and legs tensed, she uttered not a sound.

As Maggie knew they would, the hot compresses eventually did their job. Forcing the infection upward, the gash on Alex's thigh re-opened, and the foulness hidden beneath the surface erupted. Spewing from the break in the skin, the yellow-green pus drained from the wound, and wincing at both the sight and the smell of it, Maggie gingerly wiped the ooze from Alex's leg. After alternating a few more steaming washcloths to make sure that all the infection had leached out, Maggie took a closer look at the puncture wound and swallowed hard. Biting her lip, she reached around and refilled Alex's glass with liquor. Tapping her on the arm, Maggie said, "Here, you might need this."

"Why?" Alex asked, glancing over her shoulder.

Frowning, Maggie replied, "Because I know why it got infected. It looks like there is still some metal in your leg."

"What!"

Nodding her head, Maggie asked, "Do you know if there are any tools around here?"

"Um…there's a tackle box in the basement. Why?"

"I need to find something to get this thing out."

"There are tweezers in the kit. Just use them."

"It's not a splinter, Alex. It's a shard. I don't know if I could grab hold of it with tweezers," Maggie said, handing her the glass of scotch.

Watching as the woman got to her feet, Alex asked, "So now what?"

"Now, you drink, and I try to find something that I can use to get it out."

Before Maggie had disappeared down the hall, Alex had already emptied her glass and without hesitation, filled it again. Her determination had silenced her screams moments before, but her leg was now on fire. Painfully throbbing, with bolts of pain radiating across her thigh, Alex winced at the thought of Maggie touching the wound again. The salt had been bad enough, but soon it would be time to disinfect the cut. Blanching at the thought, Alex took another gulp of her drink. Hissing at the burn of the liquor as it made its way down her throat, she placed the glass on the floor and laid her head on the sofa, waiting for the scotch to take effect.

By the time Maggie came back, Alex was lying with her face toward the back of the couch, and noticing that the bottle of scotch was now half empty, Maggie decided that small talk wasn't needed. With the amount of alcohol Alex had consumed, it was clear to Maggie that the woman had tried her best to prepare herself for whatever pain was to come. Dropping the pair of needle-nose pliers into the boiling water, Maggie quietly walked over and sat on the coffee table, picking up her own glass as she studied the woman lying on the couch.

The cabin was quiet save for the tiny pops and snaps of the fire crackling in the hearth, and both women lost themselves in thought. One, fogged by scotch, studied the weave of the upholstery in front of her eyes, while the other found herself admiring the athletic physique of the woman lying in front of her.

Sipping her drink, Maggie's eyes slowly traveled up Alex's long, lean legs. The muscles in her calves and thighs were toned to perfection, and Maggie couldn't help but admire every well-defined ripple. Unconsciously, her eyes traveled north and immediately flew open wide. Alex's shirt had ridden up, and Maggie found herself staring at a pair of black thong knickers that were doing absolutely nothing to hide Alex's firm, shapely ass.

Realizing that she had been staring, Maggie shook herself from her thoughts and blurted the first thing that came to mind, "Do you work out?"

Whether it was the liquor, or the fact that the wee Detective Inspector had apparently been ogling her, Alex began to giggle. Looking over her shoulder, she asked, "Why, do you see something you like?"

Feeling her cheeks redden, Maggie tried to clarify. "No! I mean...um...I just noticed that you have a lot of muscles."

Wearing a lopsided leer, as Alex retrieved her empty glass from the floor, she asked, "And what else have you noticed?"

Raising an eyebrow at Alex's drunken playfulness, Maggie said, "Nothing, but I think that *you've* had enough to drink."

"Why, because I'm hitting on you?"

"Yes."

"And you don't like it?"

"I didn't say that. I mean...no...no, I don't like it!" Maggie blurted as she went to get the pliers out of the water. "I'm straight!"

"I bet I could bend you if given half the chance," Alex said with a low, throaty chuckle, her eyelids growing heavy from the scotch.

Returning to the sofa, Maggie took the glass from Alex's hand. "Do you want any more before I start?"

Shaking her head, Alex said, "No. No, let's just get this over with."

Nodding in agreement, Maggie picked up the pliers, but when she looked at the wound again, she frowned. When it had gaped open to release the infection, she had seen the sliver of steel, but now the gash was closed. As lightly as she could, she ran her finger down the cut and found that not one millimeter of the shard was near enough to the surface to feel.

"Shit," she said under her breath.

"What's wrong?" Alex asked anxiously.

"It's not through the skin."

"What? But you said that you could see it."

"I could, but I'm…I'm going to have to…."

Stopping mid-sentence, Maggie reached for her drink and took a quick gulp. Returning the glass to the table, she turned around and found Alex staring back at her waiting for an answer. With a sigh, Maggie said, "Alex, I'm…I'm going to have to…I'm afraid that I'm going to have to force the cut open to get to it."

Alex paled. Looking into Maggie's eyes, she could see both worry and compassion, and trying to be brave, she offered Maggie the weakest of grins. Again turning her face away, Alex said, "Go ahead, then. Do what you have to do."

Wasting no time, Maggie moved closer. "I'd hold on to something if I were you," she whispered, biting her lip as she spread open the cut.

"Oh, fuck me!" Alex screamed into the cushions, tensing and arching her body from the pain.

"You have to stay still," Maggie instructed, placing her hand on Alex to push her back to the couch. "Please, just try not to move."

Panting, Alex nodded her head and grabbed the edge of the sofa until her knuckles were white.

Holding her breath, Maggie widened the gash with her fingers, wincing immediately as blood spewed from the gaping wound and covered her fingers. Praying that her churning stomach would not let loose its contents, she moved a finger inside to feel for the sliver, and within seconds, it snagged the steel.

"Oh, Christ! Maggie...please...please...I need a minute. Oh, dear God, please stop," Alex pleaded.

Sitting back, Maggie did what she was asked, grabbing a nearby towel to wipe away the blood covering her hands and running down Alex's leg. Waiting until she heard Alex's breathing come under control, Maggie handed her another glass of scotch, and without hesitation, Alex emptied it in one swallow. Holding it out for a refill, Maggie did as asked, and then watched as Alex guzzled the second just as quickly.

Seeing the glass drop from Alex's hand, Maggie asked, "Are you ready?"

"Yeah," Alex said, her eyes meeting Maggie's for a moment. "But now you need to promise *me* something."

"What?" Maggie asked, grabbing another towel in preparation for the blood that she knew would flow again.

"Don't you dare stop until you get that fucking thing out, okay?"

"I promise," Maggie replied as she picked up the pliers. "Hold on, Alex," she whispered as she reopened the wound, pushing her finger under the flesh until she found the metal shard.

"Sweet Jesus!" Alex howled as a lightning bolt of pain shot down her leg. Grasping the fabric of the sofa, she buried her head in the pillow and wailed, the cushion doing little to muffle her sounds of agony.

Determined, Maggie worked quickly. Disregarding Alex's screams as she tensed against the intrusion, Maggie reached under the skin with the pliers. She tried several times to extract the shard until finally she pulled the two-inch needle of ragged steel from Alex's leg. They had already discussed how she would disinfect the wound, but when she pulled the wad of gauze from the glass filled with rubbing alcohol, she held her breath. Pressing it on the open wound, as Alex shrieked in pain, Maggie wept openly for the woman who was quickly finding a place in her heart…again.

CHAPTER ELEVEN

Alex awoke slowly. She could hear the crackle of the fire and Maggie doing something in the kitchen, but the dull throb between her temples convinced her that opening her eyes to face the light of day might be a mistake. With a groan, she rolled tentatively to one side. Leaning against the back of the sofa, she took several deep breaths thinking that it would clear away the pounding in her head. It didn't.

Noticing that Alex was awake, Maggie came over and sat down on the coffee table. "How's your leg?" she asked quietly.

"Better than my head," Alex muttered.

Chuckling, Maggie tapped Alex on the arm so that she'd open her eyes. Handing her a bottle of water, she said, "Here, drink this. It should help with the headache."

Swallowing a few mouthfuls of water, Alex glanced at Maggie, immediately noticing that her hair was now brushed, and a bit more color had returned to her cheeks.

"How long have I been asleep?"

"Don't you mean passed out?" Maggie said with a snicker.

Smiling, Alex nodded her head, "Yeah, that too."

"Almost eight hours, I think."

"What?"

"Somehow I don't think you've had a lot of sleep since the crash, so between that, the alcohol, and the pain—"

"Yeah, but what about you?"

Rolling her eyes at Alex's worrisome ways, Maggie said, "Relax. As soon as I got you cleaned up, I went and took a kip. I only woke up about an hour ago, and I was just about to fix some tea. Would you like some?"

"Yeah, that would be nice."

Noticing a pained look on Maggie's face when she stood up, Alex reached out and grabbed her hand. "What's wrong?"

Drinking in the feel of Alex's warm hand wrapped around hers, several seconds passed before Maggie replied. "I tried to put some more wood on the fire, but I think I may have pulled open the cut on my side."

Concerned, Alex let go of her hand and lifted Maggie's shirt just far enough to see the bandage. Seeing the spots of blood on the gauze, she frowned as she got to her feet. "You better go lie down, and I'll get the bandages," Alex said, cautiously putting weight on her right leg.

"How is it?" Maggie asked, looking down at Alex's heavily bandaged thigh.

The pounding in her head far outweighing the dull ache in her leg, Alex grinned. "Actually, it's not too bad."

A few minutes later, after getting the antibiotic cream that she had hidden in the bathroom, Alex joined Maggie in the bedroom. Sitting on the edge of the bed, Alex lifted the hem of Maggie's shirt and began to tend to the injury.

"Where'd you get that cream?" Maggie asked, noticing the small tube that Alex had placed on the bed.

"It was in the bathroom."

"I thought you said the only disinfectant we had was the rubbing alcohol?"

"Is that what I said?"

"Alex, why did you let me use the alcohol if we had that?" Maggie said, her Scottish accent becoming very pronounced as her temper flared.

Shrugging her shoulders, Alex looked up. "There isn't enough for both of us, and after what you've been through, there's no way in hell I was going to use the other stuff on you. That shit really stings and I...I couldn't do that to you."

Unsure whether to thank Alex for her concern or scream at her for her stubbornness, Maggie remained silent. Taking a few deep breaths to curb her temper, she thought about the woman whom she had once described as hard and coarse. Maggie already knew that Alex had saved her life, and it was now more than obvious that she had done it while totally disregarding her own pain. Watching as Alex worked on redressing the wound, Maggie asked, "Have you always been gay?"

Laughing out loud, Alex said, "No. One morning I woke up...took a pill, and wham – I was gay!"

Chuckling at the stupidity of her own question, Maggie regrouped. "What I meant to say was, have you never been with...um...have you never been *interested* in men?"

"No, to *both* of your questions."

"Why not?"

"Because I'm a *lesbian*," Alex emphasized lightheartedly.

Smiling, Maggie said, "But how do you know? I mean, if you've never... um...if you've never *been* with a man, how can you be so sure?"

"Are you sure?"

"What?"

"I'm assuming that you've never been with a woman – yes?"

"Of course not!" Maggie blurted, immediately blushing at her quick response.

"Then how do you know you wouldn't like it?"

"That's not the same thing."

"No? Do tell," Alex said with mock surprise.

Her foot now firmly placed in her mouth, Maggie struggled to find a response. "I guess all I'm saying is that women are normally attracted to men, not other women."

"So being a lesbian is not *normal*?"

"I didn't say that."

"It sounded like it to me."

"That's not what I meant," Maggie said with a sigh, well aware that she was making a total tit of herself. "Alex, I don't have a problem with you being gay or anyone being gay. It's just that when I became old enough to date, girls dated boys, not other girls."

"Oh, so you succumbed to peer pressure, did you?"

Pleased to hear the hint of amusement in Alex's voice, Maggie grinned. "Maybe I did, who knows, but as far back as I can remember, I've only ever thought about men in that way."

"That makes one of us."

"But why?"

"I believe I just answered that."

"No, I mean, why do you find men so offensive?"

"I never said I found them offensive," Alex said with a chuckle. "I don't see them as beasts or anything like that; I just don't want them in my bed. I prefer someone a bit softer and with far less hair. I like curves and swells." Unable to resist, Alex quickly glanced at Maggie's chest and when she raised her eyes to see Maggie's wide-eyed look of shock, Alex added in a sultry tone, "And some of them are nothing less than perfect."

"Are you flirting again?"

Maggie's words took a moment to sink in and when they did, Alex's shoulders fell. With a groan, she asked, "Please tell me that I wasn't hitting on you when I was drunk?"

"You did, but just a little, and I've never been hit on by a woman before, so it was interesting."

"Is it that different from when a man does it?"

"Actually, no it wasn't."

"Can I ask what I said, or more importantly, what I *did*?" Alex said cautiously.

Amused by the worried look on Alex's face, Maggie said, "Nothing too terrible. I just said that I was straight, and you said that you could *bend* me, if given the chance."

"Oh, Christ," Alex moaned, a blush creeping across her cheeks. "I'm sorry."

"It's okay. I'm sure it was just the alcohol speaking – right?"

"Well, I definitely don't make a habit of hitting on straight women," Alex said as she finished with the bandages and lowered Maggie's shirt. "All better. It opened up a bit, but it looks okay. Just don't do anymore heavy lifting, and you should be okay."

Insisting that Maggie stay in bed, Alex made them dinner, and even though it was only chicken soup, they both agreed that it was the best they had ever tasted. Within minutes of finishing her dinner, Maggie rested her head on the pillow and fell asleep, and after quietly gathering the bowls, Alex crept from the room.

Having not yet discussed the sleeping arrangements, Alex was relieved that Maggie had fallen asleep before the subject came up. Returning to the sofa, she stretched out across the cushions and sighed. It was happening again.

Most of her department thought that she disliked Maggie Campbell because of her penchant for strictly following the rules, but that was far from the truth. Alex had worked with several partners over the years, and all had different views on how to perform their job. She had worked with men and women, and she had worked with good cops and bad, but she had never worked with anyone as beautiful as Maggie Campbell, and it turned her head around. She couldn't keep her eyes off the attractive Scottish woman with the lyrical accent and the hazel-green eyes. She noticed every detail about her: how she drank her tea, how she unconsciously tucked her auburn hair behind her ear, how she walked, and even how she smelled. The simple fact of the matter was whenever Maggie was around Alex found it impossible to control her hormones. It infuriated her then, and it infuriated her now. The woman was not her type, the woman normally wouldn't give her the time of day, *and* the woman was straight.

As she lay there staring at the fire, Alex ran her fingers through her hair and let out another long breath. It had taken three years to get Maggie Campbell out of her head *and* out of her dreams, but she knew when sleep finally came, Maggie would appear once again.

***

Hearing a log being dropped on the fire, Alex opened one eye and saw Maggie leaning over the hearth.

"I told you, *no* heavy lifting," she mumbled sleepily.

Turning, Maggie smiled. "It was a small log, I swear. How's your leg?"

"It's fine," Alex said as she rolled to her side, but the pain etched on her face was telling different story. Noticing the first-aid kit on the coffee table, Alex paled. "Why's that there?"

"Because you and I both know that the bandages need to be changed."

"Can I at least use the loo and get some bloody coffee first?" Alex grumbled. Standing, she limped to the bathroom with a scowl on her face.

Sleep had eluded Alex for most of the night. Unable to stop her mind from conjuring up images of Maggie in positions mostly of the horizontal variety, she had tossed and turned on the sofa for hours. Finally, well after midnight, she had fallen asleep only to be awoken less than an hour later by a dull throbbing in her leg. Numbing it with the help of some scotch, she drifted off to sleep, knowing that when she awoke, Maggie would mostly likely have to drain out what remained of the infection.

Alex's mood had not improved by the time she walked from the bathroom. With sweatpants in hand, she shuffled to the kitchen with a frown on her face. Taking the cup of coffee Maggie was offering her, Alex quietly said, "Thanks."

"You're welcome," Maggie said, eyeing the woman suspiciously. "Are you okay?"

"Just peachy," Alex said flatly, placing the cup on the counter. "Let's get this over with, shall we?"

Without saying another word, Alex limped to the lounge, and lying across the sofa, waited dutifully to be told what she already knew.

Although curious as to why Alex had woken up on the wrong side of the couch, Maggie knew what it was like to suffer through morning doldrums. After spending months waking up alongside Glenn Shaw, climbing out of bed with a frown on her face had been a daily occurrence. However, remembering that Glenn was no longer sleeping in her bed brought a smile to Maggie's face, and cheerily she padded into the lounge and sat down opposite her crabby patient.

Carefully cutting away the bandage on Alex's thigh, the smile on Maggie's face disappeared. The gash was red and swollen again. Leaning closer, when Maggie saw a small pocket of pus just under the skin, her heart sank. "Shit."

"It's still infected," Alex said matter-of-factly.

"You knew?"

"Yeah, it bothered me most of the night."

"Why the hell didn't you say something?"

"You were asleep, and I figured that it could wait."

Holding on to her temper, Maggie looked at the wound again. "Alex, I'm sorry, but we're going to have to use more compresses to get the rest of this infection out."

"More alcohol, too, I suppose," Alex said with a heavy sigh.

"I can use the cream—"

"No! That's for you."

"Alex—"

"Maggie, just heat the bloody water!"

During the time it had taken her to apply and re-apply several hot washcloths to the back of Alex's leg, Maggie had both pleaded and threatened Alex, trying her best to make her reveal the location of the antiseptic cream, but Alex remained stubbornly mute. Reduced to cleaning the wound with isopropyl alcohol again, while the cut was no longer gaping, the astringent's sting was still as strong.

***

Worn out from the pain of having the wound drained again, Alex fell asleep shortly after having a small breakfast of tea and canned fruit, and with nothing but time on her hands, Maggie decided to investigate the larder. Oil lamp in hand, she descended the ladder and her eyes opened wide at the sight of the shelves stocked with food. For the next hour, she happily read every package of the freeze-dried assortment, and convinced more than ever that they could easily last until spring if need be, she was about to return upstairs when she noticed a variety of toiletries on a shelf. Grabbing a few, she made her way up the ladder, and quietly closing the bathroom door behind her, she sat on the edge of the tub and stared down at the water that was once snow.

Removing a small piece of gauze still floating in the tub, she reached in, pulled the plug, and watched as the dirty water circled down the drain. While she had never used one herself, she was familiar with the concept of pitcher pumps, so grabbing hold of the cast-iron handle attached to the tub, Maggie began working the pump. After ten minutes, she was about to give up when she heard a gurgle, followed by a belch of air, and with one more push of the handle, a gush of rusty water spewed into the tub.

Smiling at her success, Maggie continued until the water ran clear, and replacing the drain plug, filled the tub with several inches of cold, clean water. Quietly returning to the front room to retrieve the cast-iron kettle hanging over the fire, Maggie dumped the heated water into the bathtub and then left the room in search of clean clothes. Returning a few minutes later, she quickly stripped and immersed herself into the lukewarm water, and while it was far from the temperature she preferred, it was still a bath, and it felt bloody marvelous.

Maggie loved long baths. She adored soaking in a tub filled with steaming water and overflowing with bubbles that would quietly pop and snap as they disappeared, but tepid water makes for a quick bath. Less than ten minutes later, as a shiver ran down her spine, Maggie hastily climbed out of the tub and looked around for her towel...and then she looked again.

Tickled by her own stupidity, Maggie began to giggle. "Oh, you've got to be kidding," she said, glancing around the room for the third time. More concerned with returning to the tub before the water had cooled, than thinking through her list of things to bring, she had remembered clean clothes, shampoo and even a razor, but a towel apparently had slipped her mind. Soaking wet and covered in goose bumps, when she saw the closet in the corner, she rushed over and opened the door. Grinning as she spied a towel on the top shelf, she quickly pulled it down and when she did, her grin transformed into a wide smile. Out of the folds fell the tube of antibiotic cream which Alex had been hiding from her.

Feeling more human than she had in quite a while, Maggie took her time getting dressed, adoring the feel of the clean clothes on her skin and the fact her hair was shining and knot-free. It wasn't until it came time to remove the soggy bandage still taped to her side, when she hesitated for a moment. Having never seen the wound before, Maggie held her breath as she carefully removed the tape, and then let it out just as quickly, seeing that the cut was almost entirely healed over. Deciding that it no longer needed a bandage, she dabbed a bit of cream over the thin, red welt and buttoned her shirt. Gathering her dirty clothes, she went to the kitchen, dropped them on the floor and then crept to the hearth. Without giving it a second thought, she tossed the soggy bandage into the fire.

The immediate hiss from the waterlogged gauze caused Alex to stir, and taking a long, deep breath, she rolled to her side and opened her eyes. As Maggie came into focus, Alex noticed her wet hair and immediately went ballistic.

"What the fuck do you think you're doing!" she yelled, struggling to sit up.

Startled by the unprovoked outburst, Maggie asked, "What?"

"Are you insane?" Alex shouted. "You just got over having a fever that almost *killed* you, and you went *outside!* Are you crazy?"

Chuckling at the assumption, Maggie grinned and calmly explained, "I didn't go outside. I took a bath."

"What?"

"I took a bath."

"You took a bath?"

"Yes."

"In that freezing, dirty water...you took a bath?"

"No, I took one in clean, semi-warm water, and I highly recommend that you do the same."

"I'm confused," Alex sighed, running her fingers through her hair.

"I got the pump to work."

"You got the pump to work?"

Laughing out loud, Maggie said, "This is going to be a very boring co-existence if you keep repeating everything I say."

Taking a deep breath, Alex relaxed against the sofa and stared at the woman smiling back at her. "Sorry, I guess I'm still a bit fuzzy, but a bath sounds really nice."

"I thought it would," Maggie grinned as she carefully removed the pot of water from the hearth. "But it gets cool rather quickly, so once I add this, you'd better hop to it."

***

After washing away four days of grime and sweat, Alex emerged from the bathroom with her black hair shining, and her legs, once again, silky smooth. Assuming that Maggie would want to replace the bandage around her leg, wearing only a green and brown flannel shirt and a clean pair of black bikini knickers, Alex padded to the kitchen carrying an armful of dirty clothes.

"I'll take those," Maggie said, grabbing the wadded up clothing and adding them to the clothes already piled in the sink. "We're running out, so I thought I'd wash a few."

"Sounds good to me," Alex said. "Need any help?"

Shaking her head, Maggie added some more soap and swished around the clothes. Glancing in Alex's direction, and making a concerted effort not to allow her eyes to wander lower than the scantily-clad woman's shoulders, Maggie asked, "How's the leg?"

Deciding that her bravado was no longer necessary, Alex replied, "It hurts a bit. More sore than anything else."

"Why don't you go lie down, and I'll change that wet bandage," Maggie said softly, appreciating the woman's honesty.

A few minutes later, Alex lay on the sofa and waited in silence to hear Maggie's prognosis. After what seemed like forever, her patience finally ran out, and she blurted, "Well? How is it?"

Her intention had only been to examine the wound, but Maggie found herself, again, marveling at the sight of Alex's body. Jumping slightly when Alex's words interrupted her thoughts, Maggie stammered, "Oh…um…it…it looks good."

Grinning, Alex let out the breath she had been holding. Feeling something cool being applied to her thigh, she looked over her shoulder.

"What the hell are you doing?"

Smiling, Maggie held up the small tube of antibiotic cream. Alex's expression morphed from curiosity to anger in a split-second, but before she could say a word, Maggie quickly said, "I found it in the bathroom. My cut is healing fine, and there's no way I can put back in the tube what I just put on your leg, so just shut up and let me finish."

***

Later that night, as Alex set about making some tea, Maggie began draping the clean clothes around the cabin to dry, but when she pulled a black bra from the pile, she stopped in her tracks. Plunging low in the front with underwire to add lift, it was obvious that the shimmering spandex was meant to make an impression, and it had. Feeling like silk between her fingers, as much as Maggie tried not to, she couldn't help but imagine what the brassiere's owner would look like wearing it, and the more she thought, the longer she stared.

Several feet away, Alex stood silent, thoroughly amused at the expression on Maggie's face. Appearing to be mesmerized by the high-end undergarment, Maggie hadn't moved a muscle in well over a minute. Pleasantly intrigued by the woman's apparent infatuation with her bra, Alex debated whether to interrupt the love affair unfolding before her eyes. Finally, unable to control her mirth any longer, a snort of laughter escaped as she called out, "I think that one's mine." It was all Alex could do not to laugh even louder when she saw Maggie's cheeks flame crimson.

Her trance broken, Maggie dropped the bra as if it was on fire and then instantly winced at her own reaction. Embarrassed, and blushing like she had never blushed before, she angrily snatched it from the floor, trying her best to ignore Alex's non-stop cackling. Rummaging around the pile of clothes until she found the matching knickers, as well as her own set in white, Maggie stomped down the hall to hang them in the bathroom. Closing the door behind her, she sat on the edge of the tub and put her head in her hands.

Maggie had never been attracted to a woman before, but that changed the minute she had met Alex Blake. The introduction was simple and standard; one Detective Inspector meeting another in the middle of a police station as phones were ringing and officers were bantering back and forth over their coffee and donuts. No one took notice of the casual handshake or the smile that Alex offered Maggie upon meeting her, but in that moment, in that flicker of newness and coalition, Maggie became enamored with Alex Blake. She had never met anyone as confident as the tall, dark and handsome Detective Inspector, nor as sexy. From her long-legged swagger to her expressive eyes, Alex exuded charm and Maggie found it impossible to keep her eyes or her mind off of the woman.

It was well known that they approached their police duties from opposite ends of the spectrum; however, both were determined to find the little boy who had been kidnapped from a neighborhood park, and their doggedness had not gone unnoticed. Peers and supervisors alike recognized how well the two women worked together, and the station scuttlebutt suggested that after the case was closed, Maggie Campbell and Alex Blake would become partners...permanently.

On the day of the kidnapper's arrest, Maggie spent almost the entire afternoon sitting in a parked car outside the suspect's home with Alex by her side. Their conversation was light and friendly, but when Alex smiled or lightly touched her arm to get her attention, Maggie felt her body react. Thoroughly annoyed by her body's refusal to listen to the orders her brain was screaming, by the time they climbed out of the car, Maggie was livid. She was straight. She wanted a husband. She wanted a house full of children. She did *not* want Alex Blake. Subject closed!

In Maggie's opinion, the method of interrogation that Alex used that night was excessive, but when the man broke under the intimidating pressure which Alex had applied, Maggie was duly impressed. As they walked from the kitchen after learning the location of the boy, Maggie found herself being pulled into Alex's arms. It was a hug of friendship and of a job well done, but when Maggie felt her body betray her again, she knew that if she wanted to live the life she had planned for herself, she needed to get as far away from Alex Blake as possible. They could never be partners. They could never even be friends.

Standing on the sidewalk, Maggie did the only thing she could think of to ensure they would never become partners. She criticized Alex's police work, fully aware that if there was one thing that Alex Blake took pride in, it was how she did her job.

CHAPTER TWELVE

After sequestering herself in the bathroom for almost thirty minutes, by the time Maggie went back to the kitchen for her tea, it was barely tepid. With a sigh, she gulped it down, and then noticing a new bottle of scotch sitting on the coffee table, she walked over and poured herself a healthy splash. Sitting on the chair by the fireplace, she lazily propped her legs on the ottoman and stared into the flames. Lost in the same thoughts that had kept her locked in the bathroom, Maggie sipped her drink, totally unaware that the woman sitting on the sofa was staring at her.

In the shimmering light of the fire, Maggie's auburn hair had turned golden, and watching as she pushed a few strands of hair behind her ear, Alex grinned. It was something that she had grown accustomed to seeing Maggie do when they had worked together, and Alex was convinced that the unconscious habit could never possibly grow old. Captivated, she wondered if Maggie had any idea how beautiful she was…any idea at all.

Startled from her thoughts when Alex stood up, Maggie watched as she grabbed her coat and walked toward the door. Having already brought in enough firewood to last the night, Maggie asked, "What are you doing?"

Guiltily, Alex reached into her pocket and pulled out her cigarettes, holding them up so Maggie could see.

"You don't have to go outside. You can smoke in here," Maggie said. Seeing Alex raise an eyebrow and tilt her head, Maggie grinned. "There's no *law* against smoking in *here*."

"Oh, I see," Alex said with a smile, tossing her coat on the chair. Getting another cup from the kitchen to use as an ashtray, she returned to her spot on the sofa. Noticing that Maggie was again staring into the fire, Alex said, "Can I ask what you're thinking about?"

Taking a deep breath, Maggie took a sip of scotch. "My father. He probably thinks I'm dead."

"Maggie, you can't think like that."

"No?"

"We've both been on cases where a person's gone missing. The parents never give up. It's not in their nature. Until someone can bring him concrete proof that you're dead, he'll keep thinking you're alive. He doesn't have a choice. He's your dad."

"I suppose you're right. He is quite stubborn."

Amused that the daughter apparently didn't fall far from the father's tree, Alex took a quick drag of her cigarette to hide her grin before asking, "What about your mother?"

"She died when I was born."

"Oh, sorry," Alex said quietly. "That must have been tough. Not knowing her, I mean."

Whether it was the scotch heating her blood, the fireplace warming her body, or the comfort she felt being alone with Alex Blake, Maggie took another sip of her drink and then began to talk.

"I never knew her, but I know everything about her. I don't think a day went by when my dad didn't tell me a story about her, or how she did things a certain way. I know how she looked, how she folded clothes. I know her favorite color and flower, her favorite book. I know that she liked simple things, and hated fancy clothes and makeup, and all she ever wanted to be was a good wife and mother.

"My dad was in the Royal Air Force, and we moved around quite a bit when I was young. I had just turned thirteen when we moved to Leuchars, and while my father was at work, I started unpacking some of the boxes. I came across one that was all dusty and beat up, like it had been moved around a lot. Well, being quite the inquisitive teenager, I opened it, and inside I found a collection of books on how to raise a child. On the very top was one called *Naming Your Baby*, and on the cover the name *Margaret* was written in big, loopy letters. When my dad came home, I asked him about the books, and he said that my mum had bought all of them the day she found out she was pregnant with me. She wanted to make sure that she did everything right, even down to my name. It had to be perfect.

"He told me that she had spent hours reading the books, learning everything she could, but up until the day I was born, she couldn't decide on a name." Stopping to take a sip of her drink, Maggie went quiet for a moment. Finally, she said in a whisper, "Dad said that she picked it out minutes before they left for the hospital. It was the last word she ever wrote."

Seeing the sad look on Maggie's face, Alex said, "Sorry, I didn't mean to bring up something painful."

"It's not…not really. It was a long time ago, and I never knew her, but I know I have the name she wanted me to have, even though I never go by Margaret."

"Why not?"

"Because my dad hates it," Maggie said, laughing out loud. "He loved my mum, and wanted to abide by her wishes, but apparently he thought the name was too formal for a little girl, so he always called me Maggie. Actually, he called me Magpie when I was a kid, but when I reached puberty, he changed it to Maggie."

"Magpie, eh?"

"Don't go there," Maggie warned playfully.

"It sounds like you and he have a great relationship."

"We do. I'm sure it was tough on him raising me – *a girl* – alone, but it never seemed that way. He was a Group Captain, and I used to watch him through the window at school shouting orders at his men, but when we came home at night, he'd lie on the floor with me and play with my dolls. I can't remember a time when he ever raised his voice to me…or his hand. It's funny. I didn't have many friends growing up since we moved so much, but the ones I did have always thought that he was so strict, but to me, he was just my dad. If he wanted me in bed by eight, then I was in bed. If I had chores to do, I did them."

"It sounds like he was very…formidable."

"No, not at all, it's just that whenever he talked about my mum, he'd get this big smile on his face. He would absolutely light up, but then he'd get sad. I never liked seeing him like that, so following his rules seemed a small price to pay to make him happy. That was, until I told him that I wanted to go to university."

Puzzled, Alex asked, "Why?"

"I think he wanted me to be like my mum, content with just getting married and having children, but I wanted more. Don't get me wrong, he never stood in my way, but the day I left home, even though he tried to hide it, I could see that same sadness in his eyes like after he would talk about Mum, but luckily, he came around," Maggie said with a grin.

"How'd you manage that?"

"I was always a good student, and university wasn't any different. Before too long, I was top in my class, and his sadness disappeared. One of his greatest worries was that I hadn't chosen a career when I had first entered school, but all that changed after I took a class in law. I was hooked. So, after I graduated, I applied to the Met, and by that time he was used to me making my own decisions. He wasn't thrilled with the idea of me living so far away, but he never tried to stop me."

"So he still lives in Scotland?"

Nodding her head, Maggie said, "Yeah. He's retired now, *and* remarried. Her name is Jean, and they met shortly after I left for school. It was funny, every time I went home for a visit she'd be around, and Dad would insist they were just friends. I don't know *who* he thought he was kidding," Maggie said with a laugh.

"That must have been odd though. I mean, all those years it was just you and him."

"Yeah, a bit, but it was clear they were in love."

"Then why'd he try to hide it?"

"I think he was just worried that I'd be jealous or angry, and to tell you the truth, at first I was, but the more I saw them together and how happy she made him, the less threatened I felt. I guess I realized that he'd always love me, and he'd always be there for me, and so would she." Pausing to pour more scotch in her cup, Maggie said, "And right now, I'm glad that Jean's there for him, because I'm sure he's crazy with worry."

Since the moment she had seen Maggie in the airport, there had been a question nibbling at the back of Alex's brain, and Maggie had just unknowingly opened the door to ask it. Halfway between wanting to know the answer, and dreading what it might be, Alex asked quietly, "So, is there a boyfriend or a husband crazy with worry back in London, too?"

"There was a boyfriend up until the day I met you at the airport, but I broke up with him that morning," Maggie said. Thinking about all the time she wasted with Glenn, Maggie let out a sigh. "It was probably one of the worst mistakes I've ever made."

Holding back a scowl, Alex offered halfheartedly, "I'm sure you can get him back if you want to."

Maggie shook her head and grinned. "No, the mistake was asking him to move into my flat in the first place. I was trying to be a friend and got myself into a relationship that was never going to go anywhere."

Although a smile didn't appear on Alex's face, a large one blossomed in her heart. Mustering up her most sympathetic tone, she said, "Oh, that's too bad."

Shrugging her shoulders, Maggie said, "You know how they say that women are attracted to men who remind them of their fathers?"

When Alex's only response came in the form of a raised eyebrow, Maggie realized what she had said. "Okay, *most* women," Maggie said with a snort. "Anyway, Glenn seemed to be a lot like my father, unassuming and good-natured, but it wasn't enough. I just didn't love him."

"Have you ever been in love?"

Without thinking, Maggie replied, "Not that I care to admit."

"What do you mean?"

Inwardly, Maggie cringed. Truths, loosened by alcohol, were beginning to slip through her barriers. "Oh, um…what I meant to say was no, I've never been in love. I thought I was with Glenn. He's very polite and attentive, but then I started feeling more like a servant and less like a girlfriend. I realized that what we had wasn't love, it was just convenience. Someone to go out with, someone to hold my hand, someone to warm my bed…but love should be more than that. It should be passion and caring, a willingness to give your all to someone because they're the reason you breathe…and Glenn wasn't that person for me." Focusing on the flames dancing in the hearth, Maggie took a sip of her drink. She didn't want to talk about love anymore.

"What's wrong?" Alex asked, noticing that Maggie had gone quiet.

Looking back at the woman whose eyes seemed filled with concern, Maggie said, "I'm thirty-two years old, and I have no idea where my life is going or *where* I want it to go. I have a good job, which I'm more than capable of doing, but I want to get my law degree, and that means spending lots of time studying. How can you start a relationship when you don't have the time?"

"You should just stop worrying about it and let whatever happens, happen."

"Is that what you do, or do you have a boy…um… *girl*friend back home?"

"Nope, just Sandy."

"A dog doesn't really qualify as a life partner, does it?"

"I don't know. We normally sleep together, she eats from my plate when I allow her to, and she gives me lots of kisses."

Chuckling, Maggie said, "And it sounds like you love her very much."

"I do."

"But no *real* girlfriend?"

"No, I swore off of them a few years back."

"Can I ask why?"

Leaning back on the sofa, Alex propped her feet on the coffee table and took a drink of scotch. "I met a woman named Debra while I was attending a conference in Brighton. She was the concierge at the hotel where I was staying. She was tall, blonde, blue-eyed and gorgeous, totally my type, and eventually we hooked up. We were together for just over two years."

"You were partners?"

"No, not exactly," Alex said. "I offered to transfer down to Brighton a dozen times, but she kept telling me that she didn't want me to change my life for her, and every time I suggested that she move to London, she'd come up with some excuse. I didn't understand why she was so against the idea until I decided to surprise her on Valentine's Day with a visit. It was on a Friday, so I took the day off so that we'd have the entire weekend together."

Stopping to light a cigarette, Alex slowly emptied her lungs of the smoke. Letting out a low, throaty chuckle, she shook her head. "It was a typical Hollywood scene. You know the one? I show up with candy and flowers, and find her in bed with someone else. I honestly think I could have handled it, except for the fact that it was a man. She told me that she loved being with me, but she didn't love the life. She said that she needed *normal*...and I was totally gutted. I can't even remember driving back home that day, but later that night, sitting alone in my flat, I decided that I'd never allow myself to be hurt like that again. It just isn't worth it."

Pausing to take another drag of her cigarette, Alex let out a snort, remembering how completely boorish she had been during that time in her life. With a smirk, she said, "I walked around with a fairly large chip on my shoulder for weeks. My life consisted of nothing more than work, food and sleep. I even blew off my best friend for our weekly dinners out just so I could wallow in my self-pity. I was a complete mess, and it went on for months, until one day, Paige showed up at my flat with a gift."

"Paige? She's your best friend?"

"Yeah," Alex said, nodding her head. "Paige knows me better than I know myself at times. Anyway, she walked in the door and placed a small paper sack in my hand, the kind you'd put a sandwich in – you know?"

"Yeah."

"I had no idea what she was up to and when the bloody bag began to move, I almost dropped it. Inside was a little black and brown puppy no bigger than a tea cup, with the saddest brown eyes I had ever seen...and with one blink, she stole my heart."

"Sandy, I presume?"

With a wide smile, Alex said, "Paige knew I needed something more to care about than just my work, because it would force me to live again, and Sandy did the trick. So, for the past few years, it's just been Sandy and me, and I think I can speak for her in saying that we're both quite happy with the arrangement."

"Sounds a bit...um...lonely."

Laughing out loud at Maggie's assumption, Alex cheerfully corrected the error. "I'm not saying that I haven't had sex since Debra, I just haven't had it with anyone whom I wanted to have a relationship with beyond a night or two."

The conversation was heading in a direction that Maggie did *not* want to travel. Finding the thought of Alex having sex with another woman somewhat annoying, Maggie quickly changed the subject. "Do you think someone will find us?"

"I'm sure they will, but not until the weather improves. I think you and I are in for a long winter's nap in this place."

Nodding, Maggie stood and stretched, and Alex took a second to admire the small amount of skin peeking out from under the woman's shirt as her arms rose in the air.

"I think I'm going to get some sleep," Maggie announced. "Are you...I mean, did you..." she stuttered as she motioned toward the bedroom.

"No," Alex replied, "I think I'll stay out here."

"Are you sure?"

"I'm fine, Maggie. Good night."

"Good night, Alex."

CHAPTER THIRTEEN

After a breakfast of freeze-dried eggs and sausage, they sat in the lounge sipping their tea as snow floated past the window panes.

"So, what about you?" Maggie asked.

"Huh?"

"Tell me about your family."

A wide smile appeared on Alex's face. "Well, let's see. I have two brothers. James is the oldest. He's married, has two children and teaches adult education. Kevin is four years younger than me. He's single and manages a large book store in Soho. My mother is a book editor, and my father is an author."

"An author?" Maggie asked, "What types of books does he write?"

Chuckling, Alex pointed to the shelf over the fireplace.

Following her eyes, Maggie saw the remains of a paperback book on the mantle. "Oh, you're kidding!" she exclaimed, jumping up to grab the book. Scanning the cover, her eyes grew wide. "Your father is G. A. Blake?"

Nodding her head, Alex replied, "Yep. Mystery writer extraordinaire, that's my dad."

Realizing that Alex had used the book as kindling, Maggie blurted, "And you *burned* one of his books?"

Laughing out loud, Alex said, "I didn't read the author's name, Maggie. At the time, I was more worried about the frostbite forming on my tits!"

Giggling, Maggie sat down, holding the book in her hands. "Do they know? I mean, about you?"

"You mean do they know I'm gay? Yeah, I told them years back," Alex said. "Just like most, I knew early on, but kept it a secret for years, but by the time I was twenty I was tired of living in the proverbial closet, so I told them. My father got really quiet. My mother started to cry. James was shocked and Kevin…well, Kevin thought it was cool."

"So, what happened?"

"I went back to school, worried and confused, and I stayed away until spring break. I remember walking into the house that night, wondering if I was still welcome. It was quite late, so after a few unusually stiff hugs, we all went to bed. The next morning when I woke up my father was standing in the doorway of my bedroom staring back at me. He came in, sat down without saying a word, and then he took my hand and told me that he and my mum had done a lot of talking, and they realized the fact I was gay didn't really bother them."

"No?"

Shaking her head, Alex said, "No, he said that they were more worried about what other people would think of it…of me…and it wasn't *my* problem, it was theirs. He told me that they loved me, and I was their daughter, and nothing would or *could* ever change that."

Smiling, her voice soft and retrospective, Alex continued, "At the end of the week, we all went to dinner and there was this waitress, a very attractive girl, and I guess my father saw me checking her out. He proceeded to lean over and suggest that I get her number. Christ, I almost spit out my coffee! And if that wasn't bad enough, every time I came home from school to spend a few days, my mother would try to arrange blind dates for me with the daughters of her best friends. It was *so* embarrassing."

"I bet," Maggie said with a laugh.

"Luckily, it didn't take long for them to realize that they had no clue how to be matchmakers for their lesbian daughter, thank God, and things went back to normal. They're quite used to it now, and James is no longer shocked, and Kevin..." Stopping to let out a laugh, Alex finally said, "Kevin still thinks it's cool."

***

With nothing to occupy their time, it wasn't long before Alex stretched out on the sofa and Maggie curled up in the chair. With their bellies full, sleep came easily for both, and it wasn't until Maggie heard the sound of a log being dropped on the fire that she finally opened her eyes. Normally a person who preferred to ease themselves into consciousness, when she saw Alex standing in the firelight wearing only a flannel shirt and knickers, closing her eyes to catch a few more minutes of sleep was no longer on Maggie's mind.

Alex had awoken with a dull pain in her thigh. Grimacing at the possibility that the infection had returned, she had crept to the bathroom and debated on whether to tell Maggie. Weighing her options, and coming to the conclusion that she didn't have any, she found the medical kit and waited patiently for Maggie to wake up.

"Hiya," Maggie mumbled softly as she stretched. "What are you doing?"

"Keeping us warm," Alex said with a grin, looking over at the woman with rumpled hair and wrinkled clothes. "And once you're awake, if you don't mind looking at my leg again? It's still a bit sore."

"No, of course not," Maggie said, getting to her feet and walking toward the bathroom. "Just let me get cleaned up, and I'll take a look."

When she came back a few minutes later, Maggie couldn't help but smile at the sight of Alex lying on her belly across the sofa, being the perfect patient. Kneeling next to her, Maggie began to cut away the bandage, but noticing that the muscles in Alex's legs had suddenly tightened, she stopped. Assuming that she was in pain, Maggie said, "I'm sorry. I didn't mean to hurt you."

The discomfort Alex was feeling had absolutely nothing to do with the wound on her leg. Maggie's tender touch had flamed Alex's passion, and stunned by the surge of desire between her legs, Alex had tensed against it. Wishing that she had more injuries for Maggie to attend to, Alex took a deep breath, letting it out slowly as she regained control of her body. Thankful that Maggie couldn't see her heated cheeks, Alex said, "You didn't. It's just a bit sore."

"Oh, okay," Maggie said as she removed the rest of the wrapping. Examining the cut, she said, "It looks all right, but it was fairly deep, so that's probably why it still hurts. I think in another day or so, we won't need to do this again."

"That's good to know."

"Yeah, I guess it is," Maggie said, somewhat disappointed that she would no longer be able to peruse Alex's semi-naked form. Replacing the bandage, she sat back and announced, "All done."

Rolling on her side, Alex smiled back. "Thanks. You've got a nice touch."

Feeling her cheeks begin to redden, Maggie flashed Alex a quick smile. "Thanks…um…so do you."

You have no idea, Alex thought with an invisible leer. Seeing no need to move from the sofa just yet, she watched in silence as Maggie fluttered about the room, packing up the first-aid kit and gathering the morning coffee cups, seemingly unaware that she was being watched, or rather ogled.

Alex appreciated fine art. She appreciated good books, classical music and gourmet cuisine, but as her eyes followed Maggie around the room, her appreciation for natural beauty had never been so keen. Maggie was stunning, and Alex was in trouble.

Little by little, everything that had kept Alex's mind off of her feelings for Maggie was disappearing. Maggie's fever was gone, and the wound on Alex's thigh was almost healed. The cabin was warm, and the woodpile still held enough firewood to last until spring. The larder had ample food, the pitcher-pumps now easily produced water, and although the clothes they wore were borrowed and baggy, they'd do. With no books to read, nor a radio or television to fill the silence of the cabin, Alex was left with only her thoughts, and her thoughts were becoming less and less pure. The nature of the beast called love.

Startled from her daydream when Maggie walked into the room, Alex blurted, "Do you play cards?"

"Sure. Why?"

Godsends can come in all shapes and sizes. They can be as important as a heart finally found for a patient awaiting a transplant, as welcomed as a root cellar stocked with food, or as simple as a box of playing cards.

Alex had found them at the bottom of one of the totes filled with towels several days earlier. At the time, more concerned with Maggie's fever than a deck of cards, she had tossed them aside without giving them another thought, but thoughts had now become the issue. In hopes of keeping her mind occupied with something other than lascivious fantasies involving Maggie Campbell, Alex suggested that they play cards to pass the time. Maggie eagerly agreed, and for the next two days, they filled their time with endless games of gin.

**

As the fire crackled in the hearth, Alex took a deep drag of her cigarette and then blew the smoke above her head in disgust. She hated solitaire. She hated the fact that she couldn't sleep, and she hated that her hormones were about to reign supreme.

In the privacy of her home, Alex had no issue with taking matters into her own hands. A drawer full of toys in her bedroom proved that, and as far as she was concerned, masturbation served a purpose. It relieved tension. It released endorphins, and it felt bloody marvelous. The only problem was tonight her thoughts weren't of some nameless woman, or an actress she had just seen on the television. Tonight, her body's demanding throb had been caused by the woman sleeping in the next room, and Alex knew that if she didn't answer its call, she was in for a long, uncomfortable night.

Climbing off the sofa, she crept down the hall, carefully stepping over the squeaky floorboards until she reached the bedroom door. Listening intently, she smiled at the sound of Maggie's soft snore, and with the knowledge that she was sound asleep, Alex headed back to the kitchen to get a drink. Filling a cup with scotch, she dimmed the oil lamp sitting on the counter and returned to the sofa. Gulping down the liquor, she relaxed across the cushions, and knowing that relief was minutes away, she let out a long breath as she closed her eyes and loosened the tie on her sweatpants. Shifting slightly, she pushed her hand underneath, and as her fingers threaded through her shortened curls, she sighed again. She was so ready for this.

Drenched with desire that had been building for days, Alex purred softly as she slid her fingers through her thickening folds. Rubbing here and rubbing there, she smiled in the darkness as more passion flowed from her core, and shifting a bit, she opened her legs wider. Without hesitation, she dipped a finger inside, and arching her body, she filled herself completely.

"Yes," Alex said in a breath, clenching her walls around her finger. "Oh, yes."

Enjoying the solitary foreplay, Alex took her time as she pleasured herself with skilled fingers, adding a second when the need demanded. Again and again, she stroked herself, arching and relaxing as she drew them in and out. At last, turning her attention to her rapidly hardening clit, she massaged lazy figure eights over the nub, changing her tempo from fast to slow and back again, relishing the feel of the orgasm building within her.

Her imagination soared as thoughts of Maggie filled her mind, and as each flash of the Scottish temptress appeared in her head, Alex's fingers moved faster. Biting her lip as she increased the tempo even more, she slipped her other hand into her sweatpants. Sliding a finger inside herself, she curled it upward, and with one hand pleasuring her core and the other ravishing her clit, it only took a few more seconds before there was no turning back. It was the most primitive of needs, and Alex gave herself to it totally.

As she knew it would be, the orgasm was intense, and a low, throaty groan escaped her lips as it crashed over her. Stilling one hand, she clenched her legs around the other and felt each tremor as it ebbed and flowed inside of her. Several minutes passed before she raised herself to an elbow, and drinking what remained of her scotch, Alex lit a cigarette and relaxed again. Sleep would come soon.

***

The next morning, after breakfast and a few games of gin, Alex announced that she was going for a walk. Forced to stay close to the cabin for the past few days because of the wound on her leg, with the infection now gone and the gash healed over, she could finally put some much-needed distance between Maggie and herself. Grabbing her coat and boots, she left the cabin without saying another word. The cards had helped for a few days, but fifty-two pieces of plastic-coated paper weren't enough to keep her mind off of Maggie Campbell for long.

Breathing in the frosty air, Alex pulled her collar up against the wind and walked in the direction of a stand of trees in the distance. Trudging through the drifts, she mentally scolded herself for what she had done the night before, and frowned because it hadn't worked. While the orgasm had relaxed her enough to get some sleep, it had done absolutely nothing to cleanse her dreams. She had woken up even more frustrated, and as she plodded through the snow, her annoyance level was building with each step. She needed space. She needed time. She needed cold.

She wasn't alone.

In her early twenties, Maggie had quit smoking by following three simple rules. Remove the temptation, keep busy, and don't lose focus on the goal. Cigarettes, she discovered, were a piece of cake compared to Alex Blake.

With the help of an argument which had escalated into a shouting match, Maggie had been able to push Alex from her life, and by doing so, all temptation had been removed. Between her career, and a few night courses she had managed to cram into her schedule, along with the neediness of Glenn Shaw, keeping busy had not been a problem. However, love is like iron, strong and unyielding. Absence and chaos had only bought her a little bit of time. Forgetting Alex Blake was like forgetting how to breathe.

Inside the cabin, Maggie walked from one end to the other and back again, cursing the fact that she hadn't followed her superior's directives. Her ankle-high boots had been made more for fashion than for snow, and the trek from the plane had nearly destroyed them. With one missing a heel and the other ripped at a seam, she had no choice but to stay inside. At first, she had tried to remain lighthearted about her quarantine, jokingly ordering Alex out the door when they needed more wood, but in truth, it was beginning to wear on her. Not only did she want to get some fresh air and stretch her legs, but after spending a week with the woman who now haunted her thoughts, Maggie was looking for something - *anything* - to get her mind off of Alex Blake.

Peering through a window and seeing Alex slowly plodding back to the cabin, Maggie shrugged her shoulders and decided to fix some lunch. Grabbing the oil lamp, she carefully climbed down into the root cellar, only to return a few minutes later with more than just lunch in her hands.

***

Stomping her feet on the porch to rid them of snow, Alex opened the door and walked inside. Tossing her coat on the last remaining chair in the dining room, she was about to kick off her boots when she saw Maggie striding from the bedroom with her coat in one hand, and a pair of old rubber galoshes in the other.

"Two questions," Alex said, staring at the black rubber shoes in Maggie's hand. "One, where did you find those, and two, what are you planning to do with them?"

"I found them in the cellar," Maggie said, sitting on the arm of the sofa. "And I'm planning to go outside, get some fresh air and gather some firewood. No need for you to do all the work."

"No, I don't think so," Alex said firmly, trying to grab the boots from her hand.

Pulling them away, Maggie smiled, "Before you even suggest that I might catch cold, colds come from germs not temperature, so I'm going outside and there's nothing you can do to stop me."

With a grin, Alex held her hands up in mock surrender. Debating for only a second, she retrieved her coat and put it back on.

"What are you doing?" Maggie asked.

"It'll be faster with two, and besides, the snow's fairly deep, and the wind has drifted over wherever I've walked. Don't want you to get stuck."

"I'll be fine," Maggie said, fastening the buttons on her coat. Stomping to the door, she opened it and was instantly blinded by the whiteness of the landscape. Blinking several times to clear the spots from in front of her eyes, she hunched her shoulders against the arctic gusts and stepped onto the porch. Shuffling to the stairs in the oversized boots, she saw that Alex was telling the truth. Other than a few impressions at the bottom of the stairs, all of Alex's footprints had already disappeared.

"I told you so," Alex offered, seeing the look of surprise on Maggie's face. "It's windy as shit out here."

"I can see that," Maggie replied. Taking a deep breath of the fresh air, she squinted as she looked up into the sky. Rays of sunshine split the clouds, and she smiled at the feel of the heat on her face.

"So, where's the wood pile?"

Forgetting that Maggie hadn't yet been outside since they had arrived, Alex pointed to the side of the house. "It's around there."

Playfully saluting, Maggie stomped down the stairs and headed toward the side of the house, making sure that when she pulled her foot from the snow, the oversized galoshes followed.

Alex stood on the porch, snickering as she watched Maggie's wobbly attempt to circumvent tumbling into a drift. Debating on whether to assist, she noticed that Maggie had come to a sudden stop halfway between the cord of wood and the porch. Shouting over the wind, Alex called out, "You doing okay, Detective Inspector Campbell?"

Maggie could feel her cheeks heat with embarrassment. She was up to her thighs in snow and couldn't move. Knowing she had only one way out, she shouted, "I'm stuck."

Unable to resist, Alex yelled back, "I told you so."

Looking over her shoulder, Maggie couldn't help but smile seeing the look of delight on Alex's face. Shaking her head at her predicament, she called out, "Well, are you going to help me, or should I just assume a pose and become a winter statue?"

Laughing out loud, Alex pulled on her gloves and high-stepped through the snow, getting to Maggie's side in a flash. Towering over the woman six inches shorter than herself, Alex grinned from ear-to-ear. "Technically, you'd be more a statuette, don't you think?"

With a playful scowl, Maggie said, "Look, are you going to help or just keep making jokes about my height?"

"What exactly would you like me to do?"

"I have no idea," Maggie said as she once again tried to extract her leg from the drift.

"Hold on, let me try something."

Alex reached down and began digging through the snow with her hands, and a few minutes later she lifted Maggie out of the drift and aimed her in the direction of the stairs. Dusting the snow from her gloves, Alex said, "Now, why don't you go back to the porch like a good little girl and let the *big* girl gather the firewood?" Without waiting for a response, Alex walked to the woodpile. Removing the tarp, she was about to fill her arms with logs when she was thwacked in the back of the head by a wickedly thrown snowball.

Standing several feet away, Maggie giggled at her direct hit, but the longer Alex stood motionless, the more Maggie began to worry.

Alex slowly turned to face her attacker, and when Maggie saw the payback look on her face, she let out a squeal and tried to run to the porch. Two steps away from the stairs, Maggie found herself being grabbed from behind, and as she was tackled into a drift, she let out a shriek.

Laughing, Alex began shoving snow down Maggie's coat, totally ignoring the woman's girly screams and giggles as she tried to fight off the attack.

"You give up?" Alex said, forcing more snow down Maggie's collar.

"No, never!" Maggie said, trying unsuccessfully to push Alex away.

Managing to grab Maggie by the wrists, Alex forced her hands over her head and pushed them into the snow. Struggling to catch her breath, she smiled down at the woman who had yet to stop giggling.

With her eyes filled with tears of laughter, Maggie gasped for air as she grinned back at Alex. Although she was covered in snow and the temperature was frigid, Maggie had never felt so warm or so happy, but when her eyes met Alex's, *warm* didn't begin to describe what Maggie was feeling.

Neither moved as the playful moment became intimate, their breath intermingling in cloudy puffs as they gazed at each other. Entranced in each other's eyes, both became lost in something neither had ever experienced before.

Alex's hormones raged with the knowledge that she was within inches of tasting the lips of the woman who had captured her interest years before. She had never been so turned on by simply the possibility of a kiss. Her body pulsed and her breathing had grown ragged, and inside her leather gloves, her palms were sweating as if she was in the Sahara. With her eyes locked on Maggie's, Alex moved slowly closer to her goal.

Spellbound, Maggie didn't move. The desire in Alex's eyes was palpable, and there was no doubt as to what was about to happen. Years before she had done everything in her power to prevent it, but as she lay in the snow, straddled by the most stunning woman she had ever met, Maggie could no longer deny what she wanted. When she felt Alex's breath on her face, Maggie closed her eyes in anticipation only to open them a second later when Alex let go of her wrists and scrambled to her feet. Confused, Maggie looked up at the woman, and where just seconds before she had seen passion, Alex's eyes now held only sadness.

Fighting to control her emotions, Alex said shakily, "You should go inside and get dried off. I'll get the firewood." Turning on her heel, she disappeared around the side of the cabin before Maggie could say a word.

CHAPTER FOURTEEN

Maggie knew exactly how many timbers supported the roof in the bedroom, and how many stones were embedded in the mortar surrounding the hearth. She could do her multiplication tables up to twenty times twenty, and had even managed to make it through the alphabet backward more than once. It didn't help. She was worried, and sleep no longer came easily.

Since their romp in the snow, Alex had become withdrawn and somber. Content, it seemed, with gathering firewood, dozing on the sofa, or taking walks around the cabin, although Alex had never ventured far, she had also never invited Maggie to join her. Their bantering had all but ceased, and the only card game being played was solitaire.

***

For the better part of forty-eight hours, Alex had silently chastised herself for becoming infatuated with a woman she could never have, at least not in the way she wanted. By the look she had seen in Maggie's eyes, Alex knew that she could have easily taken what she wanted, tasting Maggie's lips in the snow, and her body in the cabin, but that wasn't enough. Lust between the sheets to feed animal urgency would have satisfied her physical hunger, but Alex wanted more. She had fallen in love with Maggie, and Alex didn't just want her in her bed. She wanted Maggie in her life…forever.

Just as she had done for the previous two nights, Alex lounged on the sofa, sipping watered-down scotch hoping it would dilute her anger. Although starting as self-loathing for being so stupid, over the past two days it had gradually grown to volcanic proportions. Mad at herself, her circumstances, and the pain caused by a woman named Debra, silence was Alex's only option. She knew that her words would be laced with rage, and Maggie didn't deserve it. She hadn't done anything wrong. The gaping wound in Alex's heart was self-inflicted, and that fact continued to feed her fury like gasoline to a flame. Setting her jaw, Alex took another swallow of scotch and prayed that Maggie would go to bed soon.

Sitting by the fire, Maggie gathered the cards from the ottoman and shuffled them again. She hadn't won a hand yet, but then again, her mind wasn't exactly on the cards. Even though Alex continued to ignore her, Maggie found it impossible to do the same. She couldn't help but stare at Alex and wonder what she was thinking. Why had she gone so quiet, and why did she look so angry? As the questions ran through Maggie's mind, she felt her annoyance growing, and having had enough of the silent treatment, she blurted, "I think we should talk."

Jarred from her thoughts by Maggie's remark, Alex glared back for a moment. "And what exactly do you want to talk about?" she snapped. "I know! How about the weather, or better yet, how about…let's see…how would you feel about redecorating this place in the spring? You know, get rid of all the dead fish and hang up some watercolors."

Confused by Alex's flippant response, Maggie asked softly, "Why are you so angry at me?"

"I'm *not* angry at you," Alex barked.

"Yes, you are."

"*No*, I'm not!"

"Then *why* won't you talk to me!"

"Fine!" Alex growled, swinging her long legs off the sofa. Sitting up, she stared angrily back at Maggie. "You've got my undivided attention. Now, what the *fuck* do you want to talk about?"

Inwardly, Maggie smiled. Psychology courses had always been her favorite. They had taught her about the strengths and weaknesses of human behavior, and the fact that the easiest way to avoid answering a question was to start an argument. Alex was trying to do just that, but Maggie refused to take the bait.

Relaxing back in her chair, Maggie placed her feet across the ottoman and crossed them at the ankles. "How about what happened outside the other day in the snow? Let's talk about that."

Stunned that Maggie would bring up the subject, it took Alex several seconds to gather her thoughts. Rubbing her neck to ease the tension building under her skin, Alex said, "Look, Maggie, you and I have been through quite a bit in the past...what, two weeks? It's only natural that...that an *attraction* could develop between us, but it's only because things have been so traumatic. Christ, we could have been killed in the crash, or in the snow, and you almost died from that fever. It was just a fleeting thought...heat of the moment and all that. Nothing more, nothing less, so there isn't anything *to* talk about."

With the minutes of her day no longer taken up by endless games of gin or conversation, the deafening silence had afforded Maggie the time to think, and it had been time well spent. She had come to terms with how she felt about the woman whose smile lit up a room, and whose eyes spoke more truth than Maggie had ever thought possible. Somewhere between *hello* and *you're not dying on my watch,* Maggie had fallen in love with Alex, and as she looked across the room into those dark-brown eyes, Maggie knew that she wasn't hearing words of truth, only ones spoken to hide fear and insecurity.

"That's a bunch of crap, and you know it," Maggie said, sitting up in her chair. "Don't lie to me, Alex. Not after we've been through so much. Don't hide behind walls."

Clenching her teeth, Alex took a deep breath and ran her fingers through her hair. Confused as to why Maggie would continue to press the subject, she said in a whisper, "Why are you doing this?"

"I want to know the truth."

Exasperated at the woman's doggedness, Alex drank the rest of her scotch in one swallow, and slammed the cup down on the coffee table.

"All right!" Alex yelled. "I'm attracted to you! Is that what you want to know? Damn it, Maggie, you're gorgeous, and there's nothing more that I'd like than to take you into that bedroom back there and discover what you keep hidden under that staunch exterior of yours. But eventually, they're going to find us. We're going to go back to the real world. To our jobs, to our friends *and* to our families, and I'm still going to be an out-and-proud lesbian who doesn't hide behind doors, or closets, or *walls*! I was a straight woman's experiment once, and I won't let that happen again…because it hurts, Maggie. It hurts too damn much!"

Another smile formed, but again, Maggie kept it hidden. Without saying a word, she stood and walked to the pile of wood by the door. Picking up a few of the logs, she padded down the hall to the bedroom.

Convinced that the subject was now closed, Alex took a deep breath, emptying her lungs slowly as she went to the kitchen. Foregoing any water, she filled her cup with scotch in hopes that the straight alcohol would numb not only her brain, but her body as well. Turning to return to the sofa, Alex jumped when she found Maggie standing directly behind her.

"Fuck, you scared me," Alex said.

"Sorry," Maggie replied, taking the cup from Alex's hand. With her eyes locked on Alex's, Maggie took a sip of the scotch before placing the cup on the counter. Grinning slightly at the confused expression on Alex's face, Maggie took her hand and led her down the hallway.

Caught up in the feeling of her fingers interlaced with Maggie's, it wasn't until they were standing in front of the fireplace in the bedroom when Alex finally found her voice. In a whisper, she asked, "What are you doing, Maggie? Why are we back here?"

"I'm trying to tell you...*show* you how I feel," Maggie said calmly as she reached up and opened the first button on Alex's flannel shirt.

Instantly, Alex pulled away her hand. "No. Don't do this...I don't want—"

"Sshhh," Maggie said in a breath, placing a finger on Alex's lips. Marveling at the silky softness of Alex's lips, several seconds passed before Maggie spoke again.

"What I feel for you didn't happen yesterday...or last week," she confessed, unbuttoning the next in the row on Alex's shirt. "These feelings...these feelings began the day I met you. I tried to deny them. I did everything in my power to push them away...to push *you* away," Maggie said as she undid the next button. "I became involved with a man I didn't even want, hoping...*praying* that he could somehow change what I felt for you, but he couldn't. And now I know that no one can."

As the last button opened, Maggie's eyes traveled downward, momentarily allowing herself the pleasure to view what lay beneath the borrowed flannel. And while the shirt and bra still partially hid what Maggie desired, she unconsciously licked her lips in anticipation.

Raising her eyes to meet Alex's, Maggie said, "These feelings I have for you, they burn inside of me, and I don't want to hide them anymore. I *can't* hide them anymore." Slowly, her hands traveled up to Alex's shoulders, and lightly grasping the fabric of the shirt, Maggie said in a breathy whisper, "I want you, Alex. Please...please let this happen. Please let me love you."

Alex's jaw fell open, and the sound of her ragged breathing filled the room. She had told herself a dozen times that she would not let this happen, but in Maggie's eyes, Alex saw nothing but the truth. Swallowing hard, she closed her eyes and nodded her head a fraction of an inch, and a rush of air escaped her lungs as she felt Maggie push the shirt from her shoulders. As it floated to the floor, Alex said in a whisper, "Oh, God."

Maggie's heart was pounding, but there was no hesitation in her movements. Tracing the straps of the black bra with her fingers, Maggie reached around and as her eyes locked with Alex's, she released the clasp, and both women sucked in a quick breath as the brassiere loosened. Drawing the straps down Alex's arms, Maggie allowed it to fall to the floor, and as her breathing became shallow, Maggie lowered her eyes.

She had never admired another woman's body. Through the years, in the locker room of her local gym or on a movie screen in a darkened cinema, she had seen her fair share, but had never paid them any mind. They were women just like her, with all the curves and attributes that came with being female, but Maggie hadn't been in love with any of them.

Love had changed everything, and now, Maggie couldn't look away.

Alex was beautiful. In the flickering light of the fire, her skin appeared bronze. Maggie could see the tightened ripples of muscles across her toned stomach, but it was Alex's breasts that caught Maggie's attention and held it. Firm and full, with darkened centers pebbled with anticipation, the mere sight of them caused Maggie's libido to lurch.

Reaching out, she placed her hand between them and momentarily marveled at the thumping of Alex's heart beneath her palm. Spreading her fingers, she slowly drew her hand down between Alex's breasts, her thumb and pinkie casually feeling the roundness of both until it settled under one. Cupping the fullness of it in her hand for the first time, the tiniest of grins appeared on Maggie's face. She had never felt something so wonderful in her entire life.

Heavy and round, soft and feminine, the plump mound filled her hand, and as she caressed it, Maggie watched as the nipple, craving for attention, became even more pronounced. She quickly answered its call by gently rolling it between her fingertips, and hearing the grunt of pleasure escape Alex's lips, Maggie grew bold. Lowering her head, she covered the rosy center with her mouth and sucked hard against the tip.

Desire rushed through Alex's body like a wave, and as her juices flowed thick, drenching her knickers in seconds, she threaded her fingers through Maggie's hair. "Oh, Jesus," she said in a breath.

The sound of Alex's throaty reply drove Maggie onward. Continuing to suckle against the peaked tip, enjoying how it filled her mouth and pleasured her senses, Maggie began kneading Alex's other breast in her hand. Caressing the plumpness and rolling the taut tip between her fingers, Maggie didn't stop until Alex pushed her away. Momentarily confused, when she saw Alex lean toward her, Maggie swallowed hard and waited for their lips to meet.

As the distance between them closed, their breathing became labored and the sound of their anticipation filled the room. Touching for the first time, the kiss was tentative, feathery and soft, and both moaned as their bodies began to blaze hotter than the flames in the hearth.

Again and again their lips met, and the flavors of scotch, cigarettes, and essences intrinsically their own swirled together to make a recipe worth dying for. No longer able to deny her want of the woman, Alex let her tongue travel across Maggie's lips, and the response was immediate. Opening her mouth, Maggie allowed the kiss to deepen, and minutes passed while they savored the sweetness of their kiss, the softness of their lips and the warm, smooth texture of their tongues.

Coming up for air, Alex gazed into Maggie's eyes for only a moment before her hands traveled to the buttons on Maggie's shirt. Just as Maggie had done, Alex took her time opening each, and her eyes never left Maggie's until her shirt and bra were on the floor. Pulling her into her arms, Alex kissed her hungrily. Allowing her hands to travel over breasts, creamy and ample, Alex cupped, kneaded and tweaked as their appetite for each other grew ravenous.

Nothing could have prepared Maggie for the feelings coursing through her veins. Her knickers were soaked through with want, and the throbbing in her center was hard, urgent and demanding. Maggie's entire body was pounding for release, and the more Alex took, the more Maggie wanted to give. Hands ran over skin, warmed by fire and need, and nipples were tasted, pinched and pleasured as both became intoxicated on the headiest drug of all...love.

They slowly made their way across the room, the dreamy dance of lovers about to be. Gently lowering Maggie to the bed, Alex moved over her. Pressing her thigh against Maggie's sex, Alex continued to plunder her mouth in an assault that left Maggie gasping for air.

Arching her hips against the pressure Alex was applying, and feeling as if her body was about to explode, Maggie begged in a whisper, "Please...please, Alex, touch me."

Alex smiled knowingly. Placing the lightest of kisses on Maggie's lips, she worked loose the knot of her sweatpants. Climbing off the bed, Alex wasted no time in ridding the woman of what remained of her clothes, and pushing her own pants and knickers to the floor, she quickly returned to cover Maggie like she had done before. Pressing her hardened thigh against Maggie's center, Alex slowly began to rock.

Alex had never been so wet. Her rapture coated her thighs, dripping and mixing with Maggie's as she rubbed against her. The smell of their want filled the air, and breathing in the musky, erotic scent, Alex rocked harder. After capturing Maggie's mouth in another devastating kiss, Alex let her kisses continue down Maggie's neck, across her throat and toward her breasts.

"Please...Alex...oh, God...please," Maggie begged. The force building inside of her craved release, and when Alex moved slowly down her body, leaving a trail of kisses behind, Maggie trembled at the prospect of what was to come as she opened her legs wider. She could feel Alex's breath against her sex, the wispy currents carrying with them the promise of ecstasy, and when she felt Alex's tongue lap against her folds, Maggie cried out, "Oh...dear...God!"

Arching her hips toward Alex's tongue, Maggie grabbed fistfuls of the quilt as an orgasm quickly rocked her body. Shaking and moaning from its power, Maggie struggled for air as the waves crashed over her again and again.

Alex knew exactly what had happened. Stunned, albeit pleasantly, she stilled her movements and rested her head on Maggie's thigh, waiting for her lover's breathing to slow. Hearing a soft whimper, Alex moved up the bed and noticed a tear rolling down Maggie's flushed face.

"Hey, what's this?" she asked quietly, wiping it away with her finger.

"I'm sorry," Maggie replied, her voice cracking with emotion.

Alex pushed a strand of hair from Maggie's forehead. "You have nothing to be sorry for."

"Yes, I do. I just…I just…oh, crap!"

Unable to stop a laugh from escaping, Alex smiled at Maggie as she cupped her chin in her hand. "Darling, it's okay. Trust me, I know."

Wide-eyed, Maggie said, "Are you saying that you…I mean…did you?"

"No, not yet," Alex said, grinning.

"I feel stupid," Maggie said, her cheeks flaming with embarrassment.

"Don't," Alex said, placing a kiss on her lips. "There's nothing to feel stupid about."

Blushing even more, Maggie said, "I just wish—"

Stopping Maggie's words with a kiss, Alex placed her hand between Maggie's legs. Sliding through her wet folds gingerly, Alex whispered, "Touch me, Maggie. Touch me like this and I promise you'll get your wish."

Maggie gazed into Alex's eyes. The color she once thought as cinnamon had darkened to almost black, and in those eyes, she saw love and passion. Alex's confident fingers had already begun to ignite Maggie's desire again, and slithering her hand down Alex's body, Maggie let it settle between her lover's legs. The warmth and wetness she found there took her breath away.

The petals were soft, slick and thickened with want, and Maggie took her time tenderly drawing her finger through each. Alex's breathing turned strained instantly, and when Alex slipped a finger inside, Maggie did the same. In unison, they gasped at the sensation of being inside the woman they loved.

When Alex increased the tempo, Maggie did the same, and within minutes, their bodies were covered in the sheen of sweat. Their breathing came in short gulps, sighs and moans, and their movements became a dance that neither had ever danced so perfectly before. They were one.

Alex slipped another finger inside of Maggie, but when Maggie mimicked her, a low, hungry, sexy sound rose from Alex's throat. "Oh, Jesus," Alex said in a breath, feeling her climax approaching. "Oh, don't stop, Maggie. Please...please, don't stop."

Maggie had no intention of stopping. Plunging into Alex, she pillaged her tight, wet opening with fervor. In and out, Maggie worked her fingers as Alex did the same to her, and when she felt Alex curl her fingers, pressing them against the soft bundle of nerves that would send her over the edge, Maggie mirrored the movement. The result was immediate, and Alex began to buck wildly against Maggie's hand.

Out of control, and with release seconds away, Alex's thrusts grew frantic. With every stroke, her need announced itself in the form of guttural sounds of pleasure until, with one final push, Maggie sent Alex over the precipice.

Crying out, Alex buried her head in Maggie's shoulder as the pulsating waves of splendor washed over her. Flexing her hips as nectar spilled from her body, she tightened her legs around Maggie's hand, arching and relaxing as each spasm exploded within her.

The feel of the pulsing orgasm around her fingers was amazing, and Alex's sounds of pleasure filled Maggie's ears. Her body now throbbing once again, she clamped her legs tightly around Alex's hand. Unabashedly, Maggie squeezed her walls around the stilled fingers inside of her and with only a few more thrusts of her hips, she drove herself over the edge.

CHAPTER FIFTEEN

Maggie wanted nothing more than to stay wrapped in Alex's embrace, but the need to use the bathroom forced her to extract herself from the sleeping woman's hold. Grabbing some clothes from the floor, she softly padded from the room, visiting the bathroom first before heading to the kitchen to make some tea. After filling the kettle with water and placing it over the fire, Maggie relaxed on the sofa and gazed into the flames. Exhaling a sigh of contentment, she closed her eyes and in an instant, the memories of the night came flooding back.

It had been a sensual thrust and parry of want and need. With tender words, gentle caresses and whispers of encouragement, they had awakened things in each other that neither had believed possible. A passion so urgent that sleep took a back seat to desire, and a thirst that could only be quenched by the nectar that flowed from their centers; they had feasted on each other until exhaustion finally won out. Smelling of sex and with bodies dampened by sweat, they slumbered safe and sated; their minds empty of dreams for reality had become so much sweeter.

Maggie let out a low, sexy chuckle as she opened her eyes. She was totally in love with Alex, and it felt bloody wonderful. The sound of the water boiling brought her to her feet, and as she went about making the tea, another smile graced her face. Her life would never be the same…and she was looking forward to every single minute of it.

Alex sighed as she stretched across the bed to pull Maggie back into her arms, but when she came up empty, she opened her eyes and frowned. She was alone. For a split-second, memories of Debra came rushing back. Quickly pushing them away, Alex swung her legs over the edge of the bed and instantly wished she hadn't. It had been a long time since she had made love through the night, and chuckling to herself at the soreness in her muscles, she slowly got to her feet. Reaching for the ceiling, Alex worked out the kinks and listened as a series of soft little pops worked their way down her spine. Flexing her neck and shoulders, she quickly donned her shirt and socks and strolled to the bathroom.

A few minutes later, with teeth cleaned and hair combed, Alex padded down the hallway in search of Maggie. Coming around the corner, she spotted the object of her desire standing in the kitchen wearing only an oversized shirt and socks that matched her own. Silently, Alex stood there and admired the view.

Feeling as if she was being watched, Maggie glanced over her shoulder and when she saw Alex's lecherous look, she smiled. "Good morning, sweetheart."

Instantly, Alex's smile widened, the simple term of endearment squelching any anxieties about the possible awkwardness of the morning.

"Good morning," Alex replied, her voice low and sultry.

Turning around, Maggie stood her ground as she took in the view. Able to ogle without the fear of getting caught, she took her time and allowed her eyes to travel, and travel they did. Appreciating Alex's beauty from her narrow calves to her muscled thighs, Maggie's gaze paused at hips barely hidden by plaid fabric, and then again, at the roundness of breasts visible through the gape in the shirt before raising her eyes to meet Alex's. Curious as to why the woman was continuing to stare back at her with an impish grin, Maggie said, "What?"

"I want to kiss you," Alex admitted, taking a step closer.

"I was kind of wondering what was taking you so long," Maggie said, an eager smile spreading across her face.

Two quick steps and they were in each other's arms, and the good morning kiss soon became so much more. At first slow, almost tentative, as feelings stirred, lips opened and tongues explored. A few minutes passed before they finally pulled apart, and a slight blush appeared on Maggie's cheeks as she felt the need between her legs.

"I made tea," she whispered, trying to regain her composure.

"I see that," Alex responded, glancing at the mugs on the counter before leaning in to kiss Maggie's neck.

With a sigh, Maggie relaxed in her arms. Delighting in the feel of the wet kisses on her skin, when she felt Alex push the shirt aside to expose even more skin, Maggie said weakly, "You don't...don't want any tea then?"

Tracing Maggie's ear with her tongue, Alex smiled at the question. "Erm...not just yet," she said as she found the buttons on Maggie's flannel top. "Maybe in a while."

"Oh..." Maggie breathed, moaning softly as Alex cupped her breast.

On the verge of making love standing in the kitchen, Alex pulled away. By the heated expression on Maggie's face, Alex was well aware of the answer before she asked the question, but she asked it nevertheless. "You wouldn't consider returning to the bedroom, would you?"

Taking Alex's hand, Maggie grinned and nodded her head, unable to deny what they both already knew. Leading Alex down the hall, as they got to the bed, Alex sat on the edge and pulled Maggie between her legs.

"I want to look at you," Alex confessed in a whisper. Not waiting for a response, Alex unfastened the remaining buttons of Maggie's shirt and pushed it from her body.

Maggie blushed immediately, totally unaccustomed to this kind of perusal from a lover. The ones in the past had always seemed to be in a rush to get her into bed, rather than admire what they had before them. Maggie was quickly finding out that Alex Blake was like no other lover.

Unhurried, Alex took in every freckle, line and curve of Maggie's body. Although they had spent the night together, it was in the shadows of firelight. With the shutters now open to allow in the natural light, the sun's rays streamed through the frosted panes and lit up the room.

For a few moments, Alex remained spellbound by Maggie's beauty, and when she finally moved, it was slow and deliberate. Placing her hands lightly on Maggie's hips, Alex pulled her close, and leaning forward, began placing tender kisses across Maggie's belly.

Maggie closed her eyes, running her fingers through Alex's hair as she savored each caress. Never before had a lover ignited her passion so skillfully. In the past, utterances were rare to pass her lips, but it was impossible for Maggie to stop her deep, throaty sounds of pleasure from filling the room.

Slowly, Alex moved her kisses north. Covering the roundness of one breast and then the other, she revisited the first and nibbled at the taut peak. Inwardly smiling at the feel of Maggie squirming in her arms, Alex continued to feast on the nipple until Maggie grabbed her by the hair and forced her to look up. Finding herself consumed by a kiss filled with animal urgency, when Alex felt Maggie push her to the bed, she went more than willingly.

Wasting no time, Maggie straddled Alex and after practically ripping the shirt from her body, she captured Alex's lips in another voracious kiss. Unable to hold back the words that had haunted her though the night, when their lips parted for an instant, Maggie looked into Alex's eyes, exhaling the words, "I love you," before they became lost in the passion of the morning.

***

Their day had been filled like their night, and neither found a need to venture from the bedroom until their stomachs began to growl, and the hearths held only ash. As Alex gathered more wood, Maggie prepared dinner, and shortly after the fireplaces were stocked and their appetites satisfied, they returned to the bedroom in search of sleep.

Under the quilt, naked and warm, Maggie appeared to have nodded off almost instantly, but Alex remained awake, thinking about the past two weeks. As she looked down at the woman in her arms, she noticed Maggie's crucifix, and ever so gently, Alex reached over and ran her finger over the gold cross.

Without opening her eyes, Maggie asked with a grin, "Admiring my jewelry?"

"Amongst other things," Alex quipped at her sleepy partner.

Chuckling, Maggie rolled to her side, finally opening her eyes and smiling up at Alex. Noticing the pensive look on Alex's face, she asked, "What are you thinking about?"

Smiling softly, Alex replied, "I was thinking that I never thanked you for saving our lives."

"I think you've got that backward, sweetheart. *You* saved our lives, not me."

Shaking her head, Alex smiled softly as she pushed a few strands of hair behind Maggie's ear. "How much do you remember about the crash and finding this place?"

Thinking for a moment, Maggie said, "Just bits and pieces, I'm afraid. I remember being in the plane, and then everything started to spin, and the next thing I knew you were yelling at me to wake up. I honestly don't remember much after that other than it was really cold, and I was…I was sure I was going to die."

"I know how you feel."

"What do you mean?"

"After I got you out of the plane, we headed north like Busby told us to do. I have no idea how long we walked, but it felt like hours. When I finally found this place, I thought that everything was going to be okay, but when we got here, all the windows and doors were locked."

"What?"

"It's true. Every bloody one of them was padlocked," Alex said, nodding her head. "I was so angry. We survived a plane crash and found a cabin in the middle of a blizzard, but without a key, we were going to die. I searched everywhere. I can't tell you how many times I walked around this place…and then…and then I lost hope. There was nothing else to do, so I came back around front, pulled you up onto the porch and waited to die." Seeing Maggie's shocked expression, Alex offered her a weak grin. "I was so tired, darling. We had walked for so long, and when you couldn't, I carried you. I was thirsty. I was hurt, and I was so bloody cold. I couldn't think anymore. It was like ice invaded my brain, numbing my will to live. All I wanted to do was fall asleep, and even though I knew I wasn't going to wake up, it…it didn't seem to matter anymore."

The memories of that night came flooding back, and Alex frowned. The taste of defeat hadn't been pleasant. Taking a ragged breath, she said, "As I was sitting there waiting for the inevitable, I propped the flashlight between us, so we wouldn't have to die in the dark, and that's when I saw this," Alex said, pointing to the tiny gold cross. "I hadn't noticed it before, but as I sat there with you in my arms, it shined brightly in the light. To tell you the truth, at first I thought it was a sign for me to make peace with God, you know? One final prayer to be said before sleep took us both, but then I remembered something."

Engrossed in Alex's story, Maggie blurted anxiously, "What?"

Smiling at Maggie's impatience, Alex explained. "I notice things, things that other people miss sometimes. I guess that's part of what makes me a good cop, I don't know, but as I stared at your necklace, I remembered seeing something that I thought seemed a bit out of place."

"Such as?"

"A crucifix."

"I don't understand. Why would that be out of place?"

"Even with the limited light I had that night, it was fairly easy to see that this place is quite rustic. Log walls, wood railings and all the hardware *except* for the padlocks was black iron."

"So?"

"When I trudged around the cabin the first time, I noticed that there was a white cross hanging over the door to the small storage shed. I thought it was a bit odd that it was there and not over the front door, but at the time I was more concerned with finding a way inside, so I paid it no mind. It wasn't until I saw your necklace when I remembered the crucifix, and the fact that it didn't belong...at least not there. So, I went back and took it down, and that's where I found the key." Lightly fingering Maggie's necklace, Alex said, "So you see, you saved our lives, because if you weren't wearing this, we wouldn't be here."

Processing what Alex had just told her, Maggie said, "By what you've said, you believe in God – yes?"

"Yes, I do. There's been a few times in my life when I found it hard to believe that there was one, but I just can't grasp that there's nothing or no one out there. Why?"

"Maybe God saved our lives, so we could finally be together."

With a snort, Alex said, "Nice thought, but there are a lot of homophobes in the world that would dispute your theory, vehemently."

"I don't care about them."

Raising an eyebrow in disbelief, Alex asked, "What happens when we get back to London?"

"What do you mean?"

"Maggie, I don't live behind doors anymore."

"I know that, and I don't want you to."

"So what happens when we go out on a date and some creep says something, or we run into an old friend of yours? How are you going to handle that?"

"To tell you the truth, I haven't thought about it," Maggie said, relaxing against a pillow. "If someone says something stupid, I don't know how I'll react, but *when* we run into someone I know, I'll introduce you as my partner. Why wouldn't I?"

"Some wouldn't," Alex said, thinking back to a time when another woman broke her heart.

"Sweetheart, do you really think that I'd be here with you like this and say the things I've said to you, and then return home and act like none of this has happened? I'm not going to pretend that I don't feel the way I feel about you, Alex. It's taken me three years *and* a plane crash to finally come to terms with this, and I have no intention of changing my mind. You're stuck with me, so you sure as hell better get used to it!" Maggie said, flashing Alex a toothy smile.

Surprised at Maggie's tenacity, Alex couldn't help but laugh. "That's not all I need to get used to. I seem to keep forgetting that you have a temper."

"And it's a Scottish one at that," Maggie replied in her best Scottish brogue.

The thickened accent brought a smile to Alex's face. They hadn't spent a lot of time talking about their return to London, but now that the subject had been brought up, Alex had a few other things on her mind. "Okay, so I have another question."

"Jeez, I think I liked you better when you *weren't* talking." Although Maggie had meant it as a joke, when Alex's face fell, she quickly added, "I was just kidding, sweetheart. What do you want to know?"

"What about your father and…and your boyfriend?"

"*Ex*-boyfriend," Maggie said firmly. "Remember?"

With a nod, Alex said, "Right, I stand corrected, but what about your dad? How do you plan to hide this from him?"

"I don't."

"What?"

"When we get home, I'll tell him," Maggie said matter-of-factly.

"Darling, look…um…this isn't like you found a new dress or got a new puppy—"

"You think I'm moving too fast, don't you?" Maggie asked, hearing the hint of worry in Alex's tone.

"Maybe…well…yeah, I do."

"I thought you liked it when I moved fast," Maggie said with a twinkle in her eye.

Rolling her eyes at the innuendo, Alex said, "I do, but you've got to be sure—"

"Why do you keep thinking I'm not?" Maggie asked as she sat up and faced Alex. "Sweetheart, I've been in love with you since the day we first met. Yes, we've only just found each other, but I don't see a point in denying what I feel anymore. I've wasted enough time, and when we get back home, I have every intention of telling my father about us." Cupping Alex's chin in her hand, Maggie continued, "Look, I'm not stupid. I know he'll be upset, and probably worried that I'm making some huge mistake, but if I tried to hide this, which I wouldn't, that would hurt him more than anything. For so long, it was only just him and me, and we've never had secrets, and I'm not going to start now. I can't do that to him. He loves me and I love him, and he'll be okay with this. I promise."

Unable to come up with a counterpoint, Alex leaned over, and kissed Maggie lightly on the lips. "I hope you're right."

"I am, sweetheart, trust me," Maggie replied, followed quickly by a tremendously long yawn.

"I think someone needs some sleep," Alex said, reaching over to turn down the wick of the oil lamp.

Alex had no way of knowing that sleep was the last thing on Maggie's mind until she rolled onto her back and found herself being quickly straddled by the naked Scot. Laughing at Maggie's playfulness, Alex said, "Hey, I thought you were tired. What the hell are you doing?"

"I think it's called making up for lost time," Maggie whispered as her hands traveled south.

***

The next morning, Maggie shuffled into the kitchen to find Alex up to her elbows in sudsy water. "Whatcha doing?"

"Thought I'd clean up some," Alex replied, looking over her shoulder at the sleepy-eyed woman. "I've been a bit lax in the housekeeping duties for the past few days. It seems as if someone wouldn't let me leave the bedroom."

Maggie's cheeks reddened instantly. Turning on her heel, she went to get dressed, her blush getting another shade darker when she walked in and saw the state of the bedroom.

Socks and shirts were thrown about the room, empty mugs balanced precariously on night stands, and the quilt and pillows were everywhere *except* on the bed.

Giggling at the mess, Maggie quickly straightened the room and got dressed. Grabbing all the empty cups, she went back to the kitchen and plopped them in the soapy water. "You forgot some," she said, flashing Alex a smile.

"Yeah, well, I knew they were there, but I feared if I returned, you'd accost me again," Alex said, rinsing another dish and stacking it on the counter.

"Correct me if I'm wrong, but I didn't hear any argument a few hours ago," Maggie said as she grabbed a towel and began drying the dishes piled by the sink.

"What can I say, you give great head."

Unbreakable dinnerware comes in handy when you have children, clumsy partners or when words are spoken that you're not expecting. Slipping from Maggie's fingers, the plate fell to the floor and then, as if trying to escape, rolled out of the room. Coming to a stop in the lounge, it wound down on its rim until still.

Snickering at the embarrassment burning Maggie's cheeks, Alex glanced at the dish now several feet away. "I suppose you're going to want me to wash that one again – eh?"

Pursing her lips, Maggie glared back at Alex, but the merriment in Alex's eyes was Maggie's undoing. Shaking her head at the woman's playfulness, Maggie retrieved the plate and dropped it in the sink.

"Let's try this again, shall we?" she said, snatching another plate to dry. "And no more comments from you."

Working in silence, casting only winks, grins and the occasional peck on the cheek, before too long, the kitchen was clean. As Alex was putting the remaining dishes in the cabinet, Maggie leaned against the counter, twirling the wet towel in her hands and playfully flicking it in the direction of Alex's ass.

"You'd best not do that," Alex warned, glancing over her shoulder at the woman threatening her bum with a rat tail.

"No worries, sweetheart, I've never mastered the technique."

When Alex turned back to finish, Maggie twirled the towel tight, and one last time, flicked it hard in the air. When she heard the loud, wet crack, Maggie's eyes went wide and in an instant, the only sound that could be heard were the remaining bubbles in the sink, fizzing as they disappeared. The few seconds that passed seemed like an eternity to Maggie, but when Alex finally spun around, the look on her face said it all. Maggie was in *big* trouble.

"Shit!" Maggie shrieked, running from the room.

"Oh, no you don't!" Alex called out. Grabbing the wet towel, she chased Maggie down the hall with a smile in her eyes. "You are *so* mine right now!"

Laughing, Maggie fell on the bed, quickly followed by Alex, who decided that her punishment would come in the form of tickling. The days and nights of lovemaking had given Alex the opportunity to discover quite a few places on Maggie that were ticklish, so undaunted by Maggie's giggles and squeals, Alex began attacking each and every one.

"No...no...Alex...please stop," Maggie sputtered between fits of laughter. "Sweetheart, I will not be held responsible for my actions if you keep this up!"

"You started it," Alex said, mercilessly allowing her fingers to dance lightly over Maggie's sides, belly and the backs of her knees. "This'll teach you to flick me with a wet towel!"

Laughing so hard that she thought her bladder was going to release any minute, Maggie fought against the tickle barrage until she couldn't take anymore. Using all the strength she had left, she brought her knee up to fend off the attack and met Alex's face straight on.

"Fuck!" Alex yelled as the force knocked her to the side. Holding her hand to her face, Alex rolled over without thinking and promptly fell off the bed, landing with a thud against the hard wooden floor.

"Shit!" Maggie exclaimed, scrambling off the bed. Running to the other side, she found Alex curled up in a ball with her hand firmly pressed over her eye, moaning softly.

"Oh, Christ, are you okay," Maggie said with a snicker, believing that Alex was playing on her sympathies. "I *did* tell you I wouldn't be held responsible if you kept tickling me."

"I didn't think you'd try to knock my bloody head off!"

Amused, Maggie reached over, urging Alex to roll onto her back. "Come on, let me see."

Refusing to remove her hand from the pounding in her cheek and eye, Alex moved from her fetal position to her back and instantly heard Maggie gasp.

"Oh shit," Maggie said, seeing the blood covering Alex's face. "I'll be right back."

As Maggie ran from the room, Alex tasted something metallic in her mouth, and tentatively opening her eyes, she saw the blood now covering her hand. "Oh, crap. I think you broke my bloody nose!"

Returning with some wet towels, Maggie fell to her knees and tried to stop the blood from flowing from Alex's nose. "Sweetheart, I'm so, so sorry," she said, still unable to hide a small grin from appearing. "But I did tell you—"

"Well, I didn't think you'd try to fucking kill me!"

Laughing, Maggie said, "Move your hand, sweetheart. Let me see."

"Why? So you can laugh some more?"

"I promise if you let me see, I'll kiss it and make it all better. Now come on, move your hand."

Slowly, Alex did as asked, blinking several times before her eye finally focused. "Well?"

Noticing that the bleeding had already stopped, Maggie ran her finger down the bridge of Alex's nose. "It doesn't feel broken and it's definitely not crooked, but your cheek is bruised. It must have been a glancing blow."

"Trust me, there was nothing glancing about it!"

Frowning at the damage she had inflicted, Maggie lightly touched Alex's bruised cheek.

"Oi!" Alex exclaimed. "What? You want to make sure it hurts or something?"

With a giggle, Maggie shook her head. Leaning forward, she placed a feathery kiss on Alex's lips. "Say you forgive me."

"I'm not sure I should."

"It was an accident."

"You could have killed me."

"But I didn't, so that's a plus," Maggie said with a smile.

Sitting up, Alex said, "Yeah, I suppose it is."

"So, do you forgive me?"

"That depends."

"On?"

"On whether you're lying to me about my nose still being straight."

Placing the softest of kisses on Alex's cheek, Maggie whispered, "It's straight, and as soon as you're feeling better, I promise to take very good care of you, in a very non-straight way. How's that?"

Waggling her eyebrows at Maggie's offer, Alex got to her feet. "I'm feeling better already."

"Why don't we get some breakfast first? I have a feeling that we're both going to need our strength for what I have in store."

Alex's body pulsed at the possibilities. Letting out a groan, she nodded her head. "Fine, food first, but after that *you* have a lot of *apologizing* to do."

Beaming, Maggie took Alex's hand and they walked from the bedroom. Halfway up the hallway, their progress stopped when the door to the cabin swung open with such force that it crashed against the wall.

Hands held in love turned into those gripped in fear, and frozen in the hallway, Maggie and Alex suddenly became afraid. While they had talked endlessly about being found, as the imposing figures blocked the sunlight coming into the cabin, it was impossible not to feel terror.

Wearing identical bulky white parkas and their faces hidden behind black ski masks, the two men were absolutely menacing, and both women quickly glanced around the room for something to protect themselves with. There was nothing.

Stomping their feet on the porch, the strangers walked inside. Seconds ticked by before one of the intruders pushed back the fur-lined hood of his jacket and pulled the mask from his face.

Seeing the bruise on Alex's face, John Harper said with a scowl, "Well, it looks like we got here just in time."

CHAPTER SIXTEEN

His conversations with their fathers had echoed in his head for days, and he had read the women's files a dozen times, studying them like criminals even though they weren't. John Harper knew that Campbell followed rules and Blake bent them. He knew that both, regardless of their methods, were good police officers, and he knew that one night, three years earlier, they had come to blows. Assuming that the bruise on Alex's cheek was the result of another heated argument between the two Detective Inspectors, John Harper did the only thing he could. He looked the other way. The two women had been through enough. Neither deserved a mark on their record, so instead of questioning them about who or what had caused the injury, he decided to give them a few degrees of separation.

With another winter storm on its way, within minutes of his arrival, Maggie and Alex were ushered from the cabin and placed on the back of separate snowmobiles parked at the edge of the forest. Taken to an awaiting helicopter near where their plane had crashed, they were given seats on the opposite sides of the chopper and whisked to an airport where a small jet was waiting to take them back to England.

Upon boarding the plane, Harper instructed the onboard medic to take care of Alex's swollen cheek, and for the rest of their journey, he monopolized Maggie's time with endless questions about their adventure, never once bringing up her partner's bruised face. Both women had stolen glances at each other when they could, and a couple of times Alex had managed to send a flirtatious wink in Maggie's direction, causing her to blush, but other than a few words spoken during the noisy helicopter ride, the women hadn't been able to talk for hours.

Their arrival in London was as secretive as their departure. The damp English weather filled the air with misty rain, and the lights streaming from the many hangars cast an eerie glow across the tarmac. When the plane finally taxied to its destination, it was near a hangar far from prying eyes.

Harper, running interference as he had done the entire trip, escorted Maggie from the plane with Alex following closely behind. Stopping for a moment on the stairs, Alex breathed in the crisp English air. She was home.

Smiling, she trotted down the steps and the minute her feet landed on English soil, the quiet of the night was split by the sound of Paige Harrison's squeals of delight. Chuckling at the loud whoops and hollers traveling across the tarmac, Alex quickly glanced in Maggie's direction to let her know that she'd be right back, but Maggie wasn't paying attention, at least not to Alex.

Two men with outstretched arms ran from the hangar in Maggie's direction, and even though she had never met them, Alex knew who they were. The quicker of the two, sprinting as if for position, was Glenn Shaw, the ex-boyfriend. He was taller than Alex had imagined, and as he galloped across the airstrip, he reminded her of a newborn colt, all legs and wobbly. His floppy hair bouncing with every step he took, Alex rolled her eyes at his comical appearance and focused on the other man.

At a slow jog that comes from age, Douglas Campbell was of medium height, but broad-shouldered and barrel-chested, he still looked like a force to be reckoned with. Even in the shadows, Alex could see his wide smile, and she smiled too. A father's prayers had been answered, and his daughter had come home.

Unfortunately, Alex's smile didn't last long for when she looked in Maggie's direction and saw her in the arms of Glenn Shaw, her shoulders fell. Watching as the man covered Maggie's face with an endless amount of sloppy kisses, Alex pulled the collar up on her coat and shook her head. *So much for returning to civilization and telling the truth*, she thought. *Old habits die hard.*

Out of the darkness her name was called, and instantly she grinned. Running to the people standing under an overhang to stay out of the rain, Alex fell into the arms of her parents and her best friend. Tears were shed, and kisses were exchanged. Hugs were bear-like and smiles were wide, and for a few moments, Alex's disappointment was gone.

***

"What the hell is this?" Maggie exclaimed as she walked into her house to find it overflowing with empty take-away containers, soda cans and long forgotten tea cups.

"I guess I should have cleaned up a bit," Glenn whimpered. "But Mags, I've been so worried about you. I couldn't focus on anything else."

"Glenn, unless I'm mistaken, I asked you to move out *two* weeks ago!"

"Yeah, but the next day your boss called and told me that your plane went missing. I didn't know if you were dead or alive, so I thought—"

"What?" Maggie said. "Did you think you'd just squat here until they pulled my corpse from the bloody lake!"

"Of course not, darling."

Maggie's eyes filled with fury. Marching up the stairs, she entered her bedroom like a tornado on steroids. Seeing dirty clothing draped over almost every piece of furniture, as well as partially covering the floor, her anger increased tenfold.

Snatching it all up, she emptied drawers and hangers and stomped to the stairs, tossing the lot over the railing without giving it a second thought, and then returned to the bedroom for round two. Stripping a pillow of its case, she filled it with anything even remotely hinting that it belonged to Glenn and carried it down the stairs. With her Scottish temper now hotter than the fever that almost killed her, she shoved the bundle so hard against Glenn's chest that he stumbled back a step.

"I'm going upstairs to take a shower," Maggie said through gritted teeth. "Don't be here when I get out, and if there is *one* thing left in this house that belongs to you, consider it *gone*!"

"Maggie—"

"This *isn't* up for debate!"

It had worked many times before, so inwardly grinning as he assumed the outcome, Glenn played his sympathy trump card. "Maggie, you know that I've had a stretch of bad luck—"

"Well, it's *about* to get worse!" she shouted. "Glenn, I don't love you. Hell, I don't even bloody like you anymore."

"Mags, you don't mean that."

"Oh, but I do!" she said defiantly. "Glenn, let me make this crystal clear, shall I? I don't want you in *my* house. I don't want you in my bed, and I don't want you in my *bloody life*!"

***

"Thanks for driving me home," Alex said flatly. "My folks looked wiped out."

"What do you expect? We were all told you were dead."

When Alex didn't respond, Paige looked over and saw her staring aimlessly out the window, tracing a drop of rain with her finger as it made its way down the glass.

While the reunion at the airport was filled with laughter and smiles, Paige had sensed that something was wrong. Alex's answers to their questions had been clipped, and when everyone asked about the bruise on her cheek, she had shrugged it off and changed the subject. The last time Paige had seen her friend this withdrawn, a woman named Debra had been the cause. Debating for only a moment, Paige pulled off the road and parked in front of a small coffee shop with a green neon 'Open' sign flickering in the window.

Brought back to now by the car's lack of movement, Alex looked around. "What's wrong? Why'd you stop here?"

"Because *I* need a cup of coffee, and *you* need to talk to me."

"Paige, I'm tired and I just want to go home."

"Really?"

"Yeah, so please, can we just go?"

"And there's nothing bothering you? Nothing on your mind?"

"No, I told you, I'm tired!"

"Bollocks!"

"Paige—"

"Alex, just who the hell do you think you're talking to? I may be blonde, but I'm not stupid!"

"I don't know what the fuck you're talking about," Alex grumbled, slumping in her seat.

"No?" Paige asked as she stepped out of the sedan.

"No!"

Leaning back into the car, Paige grinned at her friend. "Well, then riddle me this, Alex. How can a woman who claims that nothing is wrong, explain the fact that she's been back in London for almost two hours and not *once* has she asked about her beloved dog?"

Seeing the mortified look on Alex's face, brought a smile to Paige's face. "I love it when I'm right," she said with a chuckle. "And I'll be inside when you're ready to talk."

***

There are those that only appreciate the finer things in life. Without fancy cars, expensive jewelry, the newest technology or a house larger than their neighbors, they simply aren't happy. Maggie Campbell was not one of those people. She didn't need towels embroidered with her initials, or a marble-lined shower large enough to fit six to put a smile on her face. All she needed was hot water…lots and lots of hot water.

Forty minutes after arriving home, Maggie stepped out of her shower with her skin rosy, her fingers pruned and her smile wide. Pulling on a pair of track pants and a blue vest, she jogged down the stairs with purpose. She had a house to clean, a pantry to stock and a woman to call.

Stepping around empty soda cans and paper plates holding remnants of pizza crust, Maggie made her way to the phone, but as she started to dial the number, she stopped.

"Shit!" she said, shaking her head. "I don't have her bloody number!"

Pausing for only a moment, Maggie called work, and a few minutes later, she was punching in Alex's mobile number. Sighing when it went to voice mail, she left a quick, perky message telling Alex that she was home, Glenn was gone, and the house would take hours to clean. Rattling off both her home and mobile numbers, Maggie smiled wide as she said, "I love you" and then hung up the phone.

Although she had every intention of telling her father and stepmother about Alex, the airport hadn't been the place. It was late, everyone was tired, and Glenn had attached himself to her like a leech. So instead, Maggie invited her family to brunch, where they could talk in private. Unfortunately, she didn't know at the time that Glenn had turned her house into a dorm room.

Looking around at her disheveled home, Maggie chuckled and flicked on the stereo. Adjusting the volume one decibel below waking up the neighbors, she headed to the kitchen to make a shopping list. Stunned to find the pantry nearly empty, she jotted down the necessities and then opened the fridge. Scrunching up her face at the foulness inside, she grabbed a rubbish bag and began removing any remaining evidence that Glenn Shaw ever existed.

Three hours later, Maggie climbed the stairs, stripped out of her clothes and fell into bed. Smiling at the smell of the clean sheets, she let out a long breath and closed her eyes. Alex hadn't called, but Maggie wasn't worried. There's a lot to do when you return from the dead.

*****

"How's Sandy?" Alex asked, sliding into the booth.

Pushing a cup of coffee in Alex's direction, Paige said, "Oh, so you *do* remember her."

"Is she okay? What about the pups?"

"Sandy's fine and so are the puppies," Paige said with a smile. "She had them the morning after you left. Two adorable little girls, but Jesus Christ, Alex, they were so tiny. I almost shit myself!"

Laughing at Paige's bug-eyed expression, Alex asked, "And they're okay?"

"They're fine. I called the vet and had them checked out. Sandy is keeping them fed, and Amy and I are keeping them in newspaper, which, I might add, we had to beg, borrow and steal."

"What? I was saving it for weeks. I had stacks."

"Yeah, well apparently puppies spend all their time sleeping, nursing and peeing, with an emphasis on peeing."

"I owe you one."

"I'm just...I'm just happy that you're all right," Paige replied, her eyes filling with tears. "When your dad called to tell me what had happened, I fell apart. If it hadn't been for Amy, I...I don't know what...what I would have done."

Reaching across the table, Alex took Paige's hand. "I'm all right, and it sounds like I owe you and Amy a night out on the town."

Wiping the tears from her face, Paige snickered. "You owe us at least two."

"Two it is then," Alex said, smiling. Motioning to the waitress, she ordered more coffee, and then leaned back in the booth and looked at her friend. "Thank you, by the way. I don't know what I did to deserve a friend like you."

Grinning back, Paige said, "More importantly, what did *you* do to deserve that bruise you've got on your face?"

"It was an accident, nothing more than that," Alex said quietly. Staring at the coffee cup in her hand, she ran her finger around the edge as she became lost in her thoughts.

Eyeing the woman across the table, Paige leaned over and asked, "So, are you in love with Campbell as much as I *think* you are?"

Continually impressed with Paige's perceptive ways, Alex raised her eyes. "Yeah, I am."

"And she doesn't feel the same way?"

"No, she does."

Confused, Paige leaned back in the booth. "Wait, let me get this straight. You love her, and she feels the same way. Right?"

"Yep."

"And those men who greeted her at the airport were—"

"Her father and her boyfriend."

"Boyfriend?"

"Sorry...*ex*-boyfriend."

"And you were angry because?"

"I'm afraid she's going to do what Debra did," Alex said quietly.

"And you told Campbell that?"

"No, of course not!"

"Oh...sorry, I thought that's why she hit you."

"Who?"

"Campbell."

"Maggie didn't hit me!"

"She didn't?"

"No, she kicked me."

"*What!*"

Laughing at Paige's outrage, Alex quickly filled in the blanks. "We were playing around on the bed. I was tickling her and she *accidentally* hit me in the face with her knee."

"You were playing around on the *bed*?"

Smiling, Alex replied, "Yes...to both your questions."

"I only asked one."

"You asked one. You thought the other."

Nodding in agreement, Paige smiled. "So, you love her and she loves you. The sex is great, but you're here with me. I'm confused."

"Everything was fine when we were in the cabin, but apparently she's changed her mind. As soon as her feet hit the tarmac, she was back in that prick's arms."

"Is Campbell gay?"

"What?"

"Is she gay? You know, out and proud like you and I?"

"No, and her name is Maggie."

"So, before *Maggie* met you—"

"She dated only men."

Thinking for a moment, Paige said, "So, with that being said, you expected her to shove her tongue down your throat in front of the ex and the father after all of us have spent the last two weeks worried sick about you two? In an airport, I might add."

"Of course not!" Alex snapped. Glaring back at Paige, Alex watched as her friend simply raised an eyebrow and cocked her head to the side without saying a word. Suddenly, Alex knew words weren't necessary. "Oh, crap," Alex moaned. "I'm being a daft cow, aren't I?"

"The only thing missing is a moo," Paige replied with a laugh. "So why don't just call her and see what her plans are?"

Alex smiled, reaching into her pocket for her mobile. "Shit! My battery's dead."

"Use mine," Paige said, sliding it across the table.

"Thanks," Alex said, flipping it open. Staring at the keypad for only a second, she exclaimed, "Fuck!"

"Oh, my God! Please don't tell me that the great Alex Blake forgot to get her bloody number!"

***

While Maggie went about making a new pot of coffee, Douglas and Jean Campbell relaxed in the lounge, doing their best to digest the enormous brunch they had all just devoured.

"This place looks a lot better than the last time we saw it," Douglas whispered to his wife.

"Yes, and I don't see anything of Glenn's around," she replied.

"That's because I told him to leave," Maggie chimed in, carrying a tray of coffee and biscuits into the room.

"That's a bit sudden, isn't it?" her father said, taking the coffee he was being offered.

Plopping down in her favorite chair, Maggie swung her legs onto the ottoman, crossing them at the ankles as she sipped her coffee. Smiling at the familiar comfort, she said, "I actually asked him to leave before I went on assignment, but apparently he thought he'd just hang around in case I didn't come back."

"Maggie, I hope you don't mind me saying this, but he was quite the arse. I honestly never knew what you saw in him," Jean said.

It was one of the many things Maggie adored about Jean, and the woman's honesty put an even larger smile on Maggie's face. "Well, shall we make it unanimous?"

Both women looked at Douglas Campbell, and a low chuckle escaped his lips. "Okay, I'll admit it. I thought the man was a daft prick."

"Why didn't you tell me how you felt?" Maggie said.

"Because I've always stood by your decisions, and I thought if I gave him enough time, he'd grow on me."

"Are you saying that I should call him back? Maybe give him more time?" Maggie said, jokingly.

"Not if you value our relationship, you won't," Douglas said with a grin. Taking a sip of coffee, he said, "By the way, I'd like to meet that woman who saved your life. Alex, wasn't it?"

Maggie beamed, unable to control her smile. "Yes, Alex Blake."

Jean was thankful that no one was looking in her direction, because as hard as she tried, she could not suppress her knowing smile. Ever since greeting Maggie at the airport, she had noticed that something had changed about her stepdaughter. Maggie seemed happier, almost animated in her cheerfulness, and now, seeing the gleam in Maggie's eye as she spoke a woman's name, two and two finally equaled four.

"Well, I'd like to thank her for all that she did. By what you've told me, she put herself at risk. I'm impressed with both her fortitude and determination to save not only herself, but you as well. Strangers aren't always that noble."

"Dad, we weren't exactly strangers," Maggie began. "We worked together a few years ago on that kidnapping case that I told you about. Remember?"

Silent for a moment, suddenly Douglas' eyes flew open wide. "She's the one that got you suspended!"

"Alex didn't get me suspended, Dad. I did."

"What in the world are you talking about? You told me that she was some sort of bully and goaded you into it."

"That's not exactly what happened," Maggie said, finishing her coffee in a gulp.

Crossing his arms, and more than a little disappointed that his daughter had lied to him, Douglas leaned back on the sofa. "Care to tell me the truth, and why you felt the need to lie to me?"

Chewing on her lip, Maggie gathered her thoughts. "Dad, I coerced her into getting angry. I knew if I criticized her police work, she'd lose her temper."

"And why the hell would you do that?"

"Because...because I found myself feeling things, and everyone was saying that after the case was closed, they were going to make us partners...and I was scared."

"Maggie, you're not making any sense," Douglas said, frowning. "What do you mean you were scared?"

"Fuck," Maggie muttered under breath. Realizing that all the words she had practiced the night before had become a muddled mess of nouns, verbs and adjectives, she got to her feet and strode to the window. Sometime during the night, the rain had changed to snow. While the sun had melted most, the shrubs and trees were still draped in white, and placing her hand on the cold glass, she remembered the cabin and the passion that had been ignited inside its walls.

Turning around, she faced her father's stare. "Dad, three years ago, when I first met Alex, I found myself feeling things that, at the time, I didn't think I should feel. I was confused, and I was scared."

"Maggie—"

"Let her finish, Doug," Jean said, placing her hand on her husband's arm.

"Thanks," Maggie said, smiling weakly at her stepmother. "Anyway, after that night, I made it a point to stay as far away from Alex Blake as I could, but then we got this assignment. I hadn't spoken a word to her in over three years, and I thought I was okay. I mean, I was with Glenn, and I seemed to be heading in the right direction, but honestly, Dad, I never loved Glenn. I just used him to keep…to keep myself in check."

Seeing her father's confused look, Maggie swallowed hard, realizing she had reached the moment of truth. Taking a deep breath, she said, "Dad, I'm in love with Alex."

The world stood still for a moment. Other than the tick of the clock on the mantle, not a sound could be heard as Douglas Campbell replayed his daughter's words in his head. Placing his cup on the table, he said quietly, "You're what?"

"I'm in love with her, Dad, and I have been since the day I met her."

Getting to his feet, Douglas angrily ran his fingers through his hair, his face getting redder as his anger continued to build. Glancing at his wife and then back at his daughter, he walked over and grabbed his jacket from the hook on the wall. As he opened the front door, he said, "I'm going to get some fresh air and clear my head."

"Dad," Maggie called out as she tried to run after her father.

"No, let him go," Jean said, blocking her way.

"But—"

"Give him some time, Maggie," Jean said as she took Maggie's hand and gave it a squeeze. "He needs to think things through. He'll talk when he's ready."

A moment later, Maggie's mobile rang and her eyes lit up. Running into the kitchen, she yanked it from the charger.

In the lounge, Jean could hear the happy lilt in Maggie's voice and instantly knew that she had to be speaking to Alex. Slowly gathering the cups and plates, Jean tidied the lounge, and it wasn't until she heard Maggie say good-bye, that she walked into the kitchen and found her stepdaughter wearing an amazingly large smile.

"I'm assuming that was Alex," Jean said with a grin, placing the dirty dishes in the sink.

"Yeah, she doesn't have a land line. I left a message on her mobile last night, but she didn't get it until this morning."

Noticing something written on a pad of paper on the table, Jean asked, "What's that?"

"Oh, it's her address. She wanted me to come over, but until I talk to Dad—"

"I think you should go see her."

"Jean, I can't leave now. What about Dad?"

"Your father needs some space right now. That was quite a bombshell you dropped a minute ago, and we both know him well enough to know that he's going to take some time to put his thoughts in order before he talks to you. So, why spend the afternoon with me when you can spend it with her?"

"You're taking this very well."

"I know love when I see it," Jean said. "Go see your lady, Maggie, and I'll wait for your father. It'll give him and me a chance to talk, too."

"Are you sure?"

"I've lived with the man for a few years. I think I know him by now," Jean said, pointing to the stairs. "Now go get changed. She's waiting."

"Thanks," Maggie said, flashing a toothy grin. After giving her stepmother a hug, she ran up the stairs.

"Maggie," Jean called out.

Turning on the landing, Maggie said, "Yeah?"

"Just don't put on one of those power suits of yours," Jean said. "They are truly awful."

"Why doesn't anyone like my clothes?" Maggie mumbled, walking into her bedroom.

CHAPTER SEVENTEEN

After hanging up the phone, Alex ran around her flat like a madwoman. Tossing the hoard of Sandy's toys back into the small plastic crate in the corner of the lounge, she straightened magazines, fluffed pillows and made sure everything was perfect. It had to be perfect. Maggie was coming over.

Satisfied that she had nothing left to primp, Alex grabbed a quick shower and then pulled on her favorite black jeans, a red tank top and an oversized black silk shirt. Fastening the buttons on the cuffs, she knelt by the makeshift pen in the corner of the room and peeked inside.

Instantly, Sandy sprang to her feet, covering Alex's face with endless licks of love. Laughing at the dog's enthusiasm, Alex rubbed her behind the ears, and as she knew she would, Sandy tilted her head further, encouraging the friendly massage to continue.

"You're quite the lover, aren't you?" Alex said, scratching the dog's head. "And speaking of lovers, you and I need to have a talk. I've met someone, and I've invited her over. She's really special to me, Sandy. She's the one…so I want you to be on your best behavior today, okay? I know you don't like strangers, and you'll no doubt run the other way, but I love her, Sandy, and I want you to love her too."

Smiling over at the two tiny black lumps curled up asleep in the middle of a pink blanket, Alex reached out and gently touched their heads. "And you two," she began, grinning at their newness. "The sooner I get you house-trained, the better."

Gathering the wet paper, Alex jogged to the kitchen, threw it away and then returned to the bedroom with a fresh supply. Just as she finished arranging the shredded newsprint around the sleeping puppies, the doorbell rang.

Practically sprinting to the door, Alex jerked it open so quickly that the velocity caused Maggie to jump.

Chuckling at Alex's apparent anxiousness, Maggie grinned. "Hiya, Alex."

"Sorry, I didn't mean to scare you," Alex said, a hint of blush creeping across her cheeks.

Several seconds ticked by as they stared at each other before Maggie finally asked, "Can I come in?"

"Oh, yeah," Alex said with a snort, standing back to allow Maggie to enter. Closing the door, she turned around and looked down into Maggie's hazel-green eyes. Grinning, she leaned over and placed a light kiss on Maggie's lips. "Hi," Alex whispered.

Maggie took a deep breath, smiling back at the woman she loved, but as she moved to extend the kiss, Alex pulled away. Confused, Maggie said, "What? What is it?"

Shaking her head, Alex held up her hands and explained, "I was just cleaning up some puppy piddle papers. Give me a second to wash my hands, okay?"

"Sure, sweetheart," Maggie said as her eyes followed the sway of Alex's hips as she walked down the hall. "Take your time."

Placing her coat and handbag on a chair, Maggie looked around the flat and wasn't at all surprised by the simplistic décor.

A lacquered ebony entertainment unit filled one wall, the center holding a flat-screen television while the surrounding cubicles displayed photographs and knickknacks. On the opposite wall, a matching bookcase stood practically overflowing with volumes stacked in every direction. The tables in the room were glass-topped, and Maggie smiled when she saw the bronzed female forms that created their bases. Foregoing a large couch, Alex had used a small loveseat and two overstuffed chairs to form the seating area, making the room appear much larger than it actually was. It was comfortable, just like Alex.

Unbeknownst to Maggie, Alex stood silently in the hallway admiring the woman as she perused the flat. Having only ever seen Maggie in business suits or the borrowed clothing in the cabin, Alex couldn't help but smile at the woman wearing form-fitting blue jeans and a crimson sweater that dipped just low enough to make Alex's mouth water.

Walking around the small sofa, Maggie laughed when she saw a little crate in the corner filled to the top with dog toys of every color, shape and size. Picking up one that Alex had missed, as she tossed it into the box, Maggie said, "Strong and tough, eh?"

"Sure," Alex said from the hallway. "Except when it comes to Yorkshire terriers and a beautiful Scottish woman with a body to die for."

Amused at the comment, Maggie slowly sauntered over to stand in front of Alex. Lightly placing her hands on Alex's hips, Maggie gazed into her eyes. No other words were necessary.

Alex dipped her head, their lips meeting softly for a moment before want and passion took over. They drank in each other's essence, hungrily kissing until the need for air became too great. Separating for only a moment, they filled their lungs and moved close again, but as their lips were about to meet, Maggie felt something scratching at her leg and pulled away.

Looking down and eyeing the black and tan terrier at her ankle, she grinned back at Alex. "Sandy, I presume?"

Smiling, Alex reached down and scooped up the tiny dog. "Maggie, I'd like you to meet the other love of my life," Alex said as she held the dog up to her cheek. Without missing a beat, Sandy proceeded to coat her mum in loving licks.

"She's adorable," Maggie said, watching as Sandy continued to bestow affection on her owner.

"Yeah, she can give quite the tongue bath if you're not careful."

"Must take after her mother," Maggie quipped, giggling as she saw Alex blush. "Can I hold her?"

"Well, you can try, but don't take offense when she squirms away," Alex said, placing Sandy in Maggie's outstretched hands. "Other than me, Paige and Amy are the only other people she allows—" Alex's words died in her throat. Slack-jawed, she watched as her dog snuggled against Maggie's neck, honoring her with a dozen quick licks as Maggie giggled and cooed at the affection.

Smiling at the stunned woman, Maggie said, "You were saying?"

"What a tart!"

"Are you talking about me or the dog?"

"*Both* of you," Alex said, her voice raising an octave in mock outrage.

Carefully placing the terrier back on the floor, Maggie said, "Sweetheart, what can I say? I have a way with animals."

Raising an eyebrow, Alex asked, "Are you talking about the dog...or me?"

Laughing, Maggie leaned in and placed a light kiss on Alex's lips. "The dog," she whispered. "And speaking of dogs, can I see the puppies?"

Beaming, Alex said, "Yeah, sure, but you've got to be quiet, they're sleeping."

Leading Maggie down the hall, they crept into the bedroom, and Alex nodded toward the corner. Before leaving on their assignment, Alex had prepared an area for Sandy and the pups, but Paige and Amy had taken it upon themselves to upgrade the surroundings. While Alex had planned to use boxes to block the youngsters in, her friends had fashioned a few sections of short garden fencing together, wrapping each in old towels before covering everything in a clear plastic shower curtain. Even though Alex appreciated what they had done, it wasn't until she had to clean up the papers that she truly understood their actions. The plastic prevented anything from soaking through to the carpet, and the fencing was short enough for Sandy to jump over easily, but tall enough to prevent the pups from wandering.

As Sandy pranced to the corner, easily bouncing over the small fence, Maggie tentatively walked over and peered inside. Several seconds passed before she finally realized that what she thought were just two more toys, were, in fact, the infants curled up in balls.

"Oh my God, Alex, they're so small," she whispered.

Carefully, Maggie reached down and gently touched the tiny black heads, both puppies sniffing at her touch but unwilling to open their eyes. "They're beautiful."

"So are you," Alex said in a whisper, walking up behind Maggie and placing a soft kiss on the back of her neck. The sound of Maggie's sigh was all Alex needed to hear. Continuing her journey, her tongue traveled over the softness of Maggie's neck, and nibbling on her earlobe, Alex's hands slipped under her sweater.

Leaning back, Maggie allowed the foreplay to continue, sighing again when Alex playfully sucked on her neck, and whispered words of love in her ear. Alex's breath was warm, but her scent had changed. Gone was the smell of the generic soap of the cabin. It had been replaced by something crisp and fresh, and Maggie breathed it in. It was as familiar as it was new.

As Alex's hands covered her breasts, a bolt of desire rushed through Maggie's body, and turning in Alex's arms, Maggie captured Alex in a kiss that took both their breaths away. Fingers ran through hair, now silky and conditioned, and tongues played while fingers danced over skin rapidly turning heated. The sound of their ragged breathing filled the room, and when they parted, jaws dropped open to pull in more air.

Gazing at each other for only a second, Alex lifted the sweater from Maggie's body and swallowed hard at the sight of the red bra, trimmed in lace. Mesmerized by the swells held captive by silken cups, several seconds passed before Maggie finally broke the silence. Amused by Alex's overt stare, Maggie said, "I take it, you like?"

Shaken from her thoughts, none of which were pure, Alex nodded her head as she looked up. "I like it a lot. Did you wear that for me?"

"What do you think?"

"I think you need to get out of your clothes."

Smiling at the huskiness in Alex's voice, Maggie was about to say something when Alex walked to the bed and quickly began to remove her own clothes.

"A bit anxious, aren't you?" Maggie joked, watching as Alex tossed her black shirt aside and unzipped her jeans.

"You have no idea," Alex said, stepping out of her denim. The night before Alex had lain awake in bed thinking about Maggie, and when sleep finally took hold, her dreams had been filled with images of carnal pleasure. She had awoken frustrated, wet and in need of release, and while in the past, she would have serviced herself, something had stopped her that morning. She didn't want her fingers or her toys; she wanted Maggie. She wanted her lips, her tongue, her body and her scent. And in a few minutes, she was about to have it all. Pulling the tank top over her head, Alex dropped it to the floor. "Besides, you still owe me a promise."

"A promise?" Maggie asked, casually pushing her jeans down her legs. "What promise?"

Leering at the sight of Maggie dressed only in her ruby-red underwear, Alex replied, "If I'm not mistaken, I believe what you promised me in the cabin was that you'd take care of me in a very non-straight way."

Amused by Alex's recollection, Maggie said, "You have a good memory."

"I'm a cop. It's part of the job."

"Yes, it is," Maggie said, reaching around to unclasp her bra.

"Don't do that," Alex said quickly. "I'd like it on for a while."

"Well, that's a first," Maggie joked. "Anything else you'd like?"

Their eyes met and as Maggie watched, Alex stripped out of her undergarments and tossed them aside. Amidst the rays of sunlight streaming through the window, Alex stood in all her glory, smiling back at the woman she loved.

Taking in the vision that was Alex Blake, Maggie noticed something that made her grin. Tickled by the fact that she already knew the woman's body so well, Maggie lowered her eyes and raised them again. "You trimmed," she said, nonchalantly.

With a snort, Alex nodded her head. "Yes, I did. I hope you don't mind. I prefer *all* of my hair to be short."

Shaking her head, Maggie walked over and pushed Alex onto the bed. Running her hands over Alex's hips and thighs, Maggie said, "I'll let you know how I prefer it in a minute."

A rush of air escaped Alex's lungs. Grabbing a pillow, she propped it under her head and relaxed across the bed. Her heart was already racing, and her breathing shallow, and when she felt Maggie's fingers stroke the inside of her thighs, silently urging her legs farther apart, Alex's body turned liquid.

"Oh, God," Alex gasped, stunned at the flood of need flowing from her center. "Oh, God."

Somewhat tickled by the throaty response, Maggie continued to massage Alex's thighs, her fingers sliding toward the inside of her legs and then back out again, each dip closer to the goal. "You okay?" Maggie asked, running her thumbs through Alex's newly shortened curls.

"Yes," Alex said in a breath. "But I suddenly don't think slow is an option here."

"Good, neither do I," Maggie said. Pushing Alex's legs farther apart, Maggie knelt on the floor. "Closer, sweetheart."

Eagerly sliding to the edge of the bed, Alex raised her head, and swallowing hard, placed one leg over Maggie's shoulder. Taking full advantage of the position, Maggie swept her tongue through the silky furrows, and as she began to taste, Alex began to moan.

Alex's nectar was thick and salty, and both had already discovered that Maggie liked the flavor. In the cabin, an entire night had been spent giving oral satisfaction to each other, and Maggie had relished every minute of the lessons she had been given. Taking her time, she slid her tongue down each puckered crease, pausing to probe and tickle while Alex writhed on the bed, urgently lifting her hips when Maggie teased a bit too much.

The heady musk of Alex's desire invaded Maggie's senses like a euphoric drug. In the past, there had been times with other lovers when Maggie had felt awkward, but love has a way of changing everything. With Alex, Maggie's shyness and insecurities had been replaced by the need to give pleasure; to give love to someone who gave it back so deliciously, and Maggie did not falter. Burying her face between Alex's legs, she suckled and licked every tender spot, avoiding only one as she led her lover down the path of sexual destruction. Unrelenting, Maggie continued until Alex's movements became frenzied, and parting the thickened folds, Maggie pushed her tongue against her entrance.

"Oh, Jesus," Alex moaned, lifting her hips as she grabbed fistfuls of sheets. "Oh, darling, yes."

Urged on by the sounds of Alex's pleasure, Maggie moved her attention to Alex's swollen labia, gently suckling it as she placed a finger at Alex's center. Barely pushing it inside, she pulled it out and started again, each plunge slightly deeper, but only just slightly. It was excruciatingly slow and erotic, and the result was immediate.

"Maggie...Maggie, please," Alex begged. "I need more...give me more."

Smiling at the request, Maggie answered it by sliding two fingers deep inside, and when Alex placed her other leg over Maggie's shoulder, demanding even more, Maggie finally gave her what she wanted. Uncovering Alex's clit, Maggie circled the swollen button with her tongue, flicking over the sensitive organ while her fingers worked the woman's wet opening again and again. Hearing the deep, guttural growl rise from Alex's throat, Maggie knew she was close to release, and curling her fingers, she pressed against the bundle of nerves as she gently sucked Alex's engorged clit.

Alex's body released in an endless wave of spasms as the orgasm claimed her. Tremors of ecstasy flowed through her being, and she gave herself to each one whole-heartedly. The sounds she made were garbled, throaty trills born from the most exquisite pleasure known to women, and it took Alex a while before she finally relaxed enough to move her legs from Maggie's shoulders.

Pulling air into her lungs, she lay on the bed, stunned by the power of what Maggie had created. It had never been like this. So true and right, and taking a deep breath, Alex smiled to herself. It was time to turn the tables, and turn them, she would.

Opening her eyes, Alex raised herself on her elbows and grinned at the woman standing at the edge of the bed. Maggie's face was flushed, heated by passion and need, and as she panted for air, she pushed a few strands of dampened hair behind her ear. Alex smiled again.

Taking the pillow from behind her head, Alex placed it atop another at the head of the bed. Sliding across the sheets, she rested against the stack and curled her finger at Maggie. "Come here, and take those off," Alex said, pointing to Maggie's bikini briefs.

A resounding thud of awareness settled in Maggie's core when she heard Alex's directive, and as she hooked her fingers in the band of her silk knickers, Maggie coyly asked, "All…or just these?"

Lowering her eyes, Alex said, "Just those. They'd definitely be in the way, and it would be a shame for me to have to rip them off, wouldn't you agree?"

Chuckling at the woman's cockiness, Maggie stepped out of her damp underwear. Only a few weeks earlier, standing nude in front of someone had felt uncomfortable, but now Maggie was invigorated. Free of worry and insecurities, she rejoiced in the freedom that her love for Alex gave her. It felt good to be naked. It felt good to be naked for Alex.

Maggie climbed on the bed, but as she began to lie down, Alex stopped her. "Not there," she said, grinning as she pointed to her waist. "I want you over me."

Raising an eyebrow, Maggie straddled Alex. "Like this?"

Enamored, Alex simply stared back, entranced by a goddess wearing a red bra and nothing else. She could feel the slippery wetness of Maggie's want against her belly, and the aroma of her need filled the air. Reaching out, she cupped breasts still trapped behind dark-red spandex, running her thumbs over erect nipples, desperate to be free. Tweaking one and then the other, Alex grinned at the sound of Maggie's deep murmur of approval. The erotic massage went on for several minutes, but when Maggie began to grind herself against Alex's stomach, Alex dropped her hands to Maggie's hips.

Maggie's eyes fluttered open, disappointed that the caresses had stopped. "Why'd you stop? It felt good."

"Because what I'm about to do is going to feel so much better," Alex said, reaching around to adjust the pillows behind her head. "Now, come up here."

All the air in Maggie's lungs emptied in one whoosh as the reality of what Alex was suggesting hit home. "Up there?"

Alex smiled. Even though there was a modicum of nervousness in Maggie's question, the look on her face said quite the opposite. She was thoroughly aroused by what Alex was offering, but Alex decided to give her an option just in case. "Unless you don't want to, that is."

"Oh my," Maggie said with a sigh. "I've…um…I've just never quite been in that position before."

"Is that a no?"

Taking a few deep breaths, Maggie shook her head, and slowly made her way up Alex's body until she was practically sitting on Alex's breasts. "I feel like I'm going to crush you," Maggie admitted.

"You won't," Alex said. "And you can lose the bra."

Looking down, Maggie grinned. "You're quite bossy today."

"In a few minutes, you'll be the one shouting instructions. Now take off your bra, darling. I want to feel your tits," Alex said with a twinkle in her eye.

Alex's playfulness did the trick. Relaxed, amused and most certainly aroused, Maggie undid her bra and tossed it over her shoulder. "Better?" she asked with a smile.

"Getting there," Alex said, reaching up to fondle Maggie's breasts. Mounds of creamy flesh filled Alex's hands, and she wasted no time in kneading them until the tips were hard pebbles, and Maggie's breathing became ragged.

Like all women, Maggie had erogenous zones, but her list had grown under the ministrations of Alex's mouth, tongue and hands. It seemed to her that Alex had uncovered several more in only the past week, and lost in the feel of sensual rubdown, when Alex urged her backward, Maggie willingly rested her hands on the mattress behind her.

With Maggie arched above her, Alex had the best of all worlds. Her hands covered Maggie's breasts, her fingers pinching and pulling at her taut nipples, while within a mere inch or two, feminine pleats of pink, glistening with want, lay waiting to be tasted.

Entranced by Alex's hands, it wasn't until Maggie felt warm breath between her legs that her eyes flew open wide. Filling her lungs with air, they emptied just as quickly when she felt Alex's tongue lap against her sex. Instincts told Maggie to move forward, and forward she moved, brazenly offering herself to Alex to do with what she wanted, and Alex did just that.

Running her tongue from Maggie's center to her clit and back again, Alex was almost nonchalant in her approach. Wanting to delay the inevitable for as long as possible, she casually licked the folds, wiggling and darting her tongue into every crevice. Suckling on engorged flesh, she nuzzled and burrowed her face into Maggie's most secret places, feasting on the delights of the woman she loved.

As Alex plundered, Maggie undulated above her. Matching the ebb and flow of Alex's mouth with that of her hips, Maggie rocked against Alex's tongue, and with each probe, Maggie moaned a breathy, "Yes."

Things primitive and feral had invaded Maggie's soul, and her body moved like a wave, rising and falling in sheer abandon as Alex took her to nirvana. As Alex had predicted, Maggie gave instructions when Alex moved too quickly past a spot needing attention, and reaching down, Maggie guided her back. "There...I need you there," she said in a whisper. "Oh, sweetheart...please go...please go deeper."

With one final pinch of nipples, distended and hard, Alex brought her fingers to Maggie's lower lips and spread them wide. Exposing her center, dripping with want, Alex flicked her tongue at the opening, and Maggie promptly lost control.

Pushing herself off the mattress, Maggie sat up for barely a second before she leaned forward and grabbed the iron rail of the bed. Grinding her sex against Alex's tongue, her legs began to tremble as her orgasm started to build. "I want you inside, Alex...please...please...oh, God, now."

Maggie had expected fingers, twin probes that would take her to ecstasy, but when she felt Alex's tongue push into her, she almost came on the spot. "Oh, my God," she screamed, grabbing Alex by the hair to keep her in place. "Oh, you're...you're...amazing."

Gluttonous in her assault, Alex moved her tongue in and out, and then circled the opening before starting again. Maggie's gyrations grew more uninhibited as Alex pushed her tongue as far as she could. Knowing that Maggie needed it deeper, Alex replaced her tongue with two fingers, and Maggie's groans of pleasure grew louder.

Thrusting into Maggie, Alex buried her fingers to the hilt and then began stroking Maggie with fervor, twisting her fingers with every plunge she made. Over and over, Alex pushed into her and Maggie matched Alex's tempo, raising and lowering her body, and taking all that Alex could give until her legs began to quiver. Feeling the trembling, Alex slowed her fingers for only a moment, the pause giving her time to uncover Maggie's clit, and as she sank her fingers again, she flicked her tongue over the swollen button, and seconds later, the room was filled with the sound of Maggie's orgasm.

CHAPTER EIGHTEEN

Jean Campbell glanced at the clock on the wall again. Letting out a sigh, she heard the coffeemaker finally go quiet, and pouring herself a cup of the steaming brew, she walked to the kitchen table. She had barely slumped into a chair when she heard the front door open. Going to investigate, she let out a breath of relief seeing that her husband had finally returned.

"How was your walk?" she asked, watching as he removed his jacket. "I was starting to worry. It's been a few hours."

"Sorry. I lost track of time."

"Apparently."

"I just needed some time to think," Douglas said quietly, walking to the kitchen.

"Coffee is made, but if you prefer tea, I'll make you some."

"No, coffee's fine. Thanks," he said, grabbing the pot and quickly filling a mug. Wrapping his hands around the ceramic to warm them, he sat at the table and looked up at his wife. "Where's Maggie?"

"Alex called. She went over to see her."

"So much for worrying about me."

"It was my idea. I thought it would give us some time to talk."

"Oh."

"So, do you want to talk?"

"What's there to talk about?" Douglas said, running his fingers through his hair. "My daughter *thinks* she's in love with a woman. I've never tried to run her life, so until she comes to her senses, I've just got to stand by and watch her make a total fool of herself!"

Sitting down next to her husband, Jean reached across and took his hand. "Doug, she's in love with Alex. This isn't some...some experiment. It's the real thing."

"Oh, you're daft!" he blurted. "And how in the hell would you know that anyway?"

Amused by her husband's incredulous expression, Jean said, "Because when Maggie says Alex's name, she gets a certain look in her eye. It's the same one that, over the years, I've grown accustomed to seeing in her father's eyes."

"Jean—"

"Let me finish, Doug," she said, giving his hand a squeeze. "I know that you love me, but the look I see in Maggie's eyes when she talks about Alex is the same look you get...when you talk about her mother."

Instantly, Douglas' head snapped up, his green eyes staring back at his wife in shock as the color drained from his face. "Jean—"

"It's all right, darling," she said, offering her husband a soft smile. "Like I said, I've had years to get used to it."

"I do love you, Jean," he whispered, holding her hand tightly. "You've got to know that."

"I do, but I'm not the love of your life."

"And you think this...this *woman* is Maggie's?"

"I know she is," Jean said. "Doug, surely you noticed how jovial Maggie was at the airport. She almost died up in that cabin, yet she steps off a plane as if she just came back from her honeymoon. She's walking on air, and that smile that she wears was put there by a woman. A woman named Alex Blake. All you need to do is see her eyes when she talks about Alex, and you'll know I'm right."

"She's only ever dated men," Douglas said flatly. "Why did she keep this a secret?"

"I don't think she did, at least not consciously."

"I know that your views have always been open about things like this, but this is my daughter we're talking about. I'm just worried that…that…damn it, Jean, the world can be a cruel place at times."

"I agree, so I don't think that parents should add to the cruelty, do you?"

His eyes filled with tears, and he nodded his head. Leaning back in his chair, he finished what remained of his coffee and then looked at his wife. "I love you."

"I love you, too."

"It'll take some time getting used to."

"I would think so."

"So what now?"

"Well, I think that you and I should go out and get some take-away, and then go over to Alex's flat and get to know her."

"What!"

"Doug, it took a great deal of courage for Maggie to tell us about this, and I think we should take the next step."

"That's one hell of a step, don't you think?" he grumbled, all the while knowing that his wife was smarter than him in so many ways.

"Not if we take it together."

***

They had dozed, then showered, then dozed again, and the afternoon was lost to love and dreams. Sandy had visited once or twice, scampering up for attention as her pups slept soundly in the pen, and both women had cooed at her kisses and giggled at her insistence to receive more scratches behind the ears.

Returning from the kitchen with two bottles of water, Alex slid between the sheets and handed one to Maggie. "So let me get this straight. You got rid of Glenn *and* told your father about us?"

Quickly taking a gulp from the bottle, Maggie placed it on the nightstand and rolled on top of Alex. "If there's one thing you need to learn about me, sweetheart, it's that when I make up my mind to do something, I do it."

"Yeah," Alex said, leering at Maggie's breasts pressed against her own. "I seem to remember a night not too long ago when you did exactly the same thing."

A sexy chuckle slipped from Maggie's lips as she shifted a bit, and when her leg made it between Alex's, Alex said, "You'd best be careful, darling, or you're going to start something, that I'm going to finish...again."

Smiling, Maggie rolled to the side. "Better?"

"Not exactly, but it'll do for now," Alex said. Thinking for a moment, she asked, "Do you think there's a need for us to have two flats?"

Maggie's eyes opened wide. "Are you asking me to move in with you?"

"I'd actually like to ask you to marry me, but I realize that may be a bit presumptuous. So, I thought that living together might be a less scary proposition."

"Are you serious?"

"About shacking up or getting married?"

"Both."

"Yes."

Sitting up, Maggie stared back at Alex. "Now who's moving fast?"

"Me," Alex said with a grin. "Look, I know that there is a plethora of lesbian jokes out there about bringing a moving van on the first date, but this isn't a joke. This is real. This is how I feel and what I want. You're not the only one that fell in love three years ago – remember? But if you want to wait, that's fine. I understand."

"I didn't say that."

"Okay?"

"Do you want children?"

Laughing out loud, Alex said, "I can't tell you how many jokes there are about *that* subject in the lesbian journals of comedy."

"I'm serious. I want to know," Maggie said cautiously.

Hearing a hint of worry in Maggie's tone, Alex sat up. Studying her face, Alex reached over and held Maggie's hand. "Yes, I do…as long as they're yours."

Maggie's face lit up, and leaning over, their lips met in a slow, tender kiss. "Ask me again," Maggie said as she pulled away.

"Ask you about moving in…or getting married?"

"Actually, it doesn't matter."

"No?"

"The answer will be yes to both."

Smiling wide, Alex leaned back against the pillow, gazing at the woman she loved. The sheet had dropped enough that Maggie's chest was exposed, and Alex unconsciously licked her lips at the sight of nipples in desperate need of a nibble.

"You're incorrigible," Maggie said, covering her chest with the sheet.

"No, I'm not. I'm horny, and in case you're wondering, I so want to have you again like I had you earlier."

Maggie's mouth dropped open and laughing, Alex said, "What? I'm just being honest."

"Yes, and your honesty can be quite unnerving at times. I just need to get used to you speaking your mind."

"Does it bother you?"

"No, it's just...it's just...I need to get dressed," Maggie said, fighting the urge to give Alex what she wanted.

After placing a quick kiss on Alex's lips and successfully avoiding her wandering hands, Maggie jumped out of bed. Grabbing Alex's knickers from the floor, she tossed them into her outstretched hands, and then proceeded to gather her own clothes from around the room.

Paying no attention to Alex, Maggie stepped into her knickers and took her bra from the chair. Pulling the straps over her shoulders, she looked up to see that Alex was now wearing knickers, but absolutely nothing else. Stretched across the sheets, her arms folded behind her head, Alex seemed quite comfortable in ogling Maggie as she got dressed. Their eyes met for a moment, and Maggie instantly blushed. Alex didn't need to say a word; the intensity of her glare said it all.

Noticing Maggie's heated cheeks, Alex asked, "Am I embarrassing you?"

"Yes...I mean no," Maggie stuttered, fumbling with the clasp. "I just keep thinking that by the time I get this thing on, *you'll* be taking it off."

Laughing, Alex swung her legs off the bed and strode over to Maggie. Spinning her around, Alex fastened the clasp. "The thought had crossed my mind," she admitted as she spun Maggie back around. "But I could use some food, and I really need to take Sandy for a walk."

Giving Maggie a quick peck on the cheek, Alex grabbed her clothes and got dressed, looking up to see that Maggie was now leering in her direction.

"Hey, when I get back, what say you and I go out and get something to eat?" Alex asked, pulling on her boots.

"Sounds like a plan."

Trying her best not to step on the tiny terrier dancing around her ankles, Alex walked out of the room, and a few seconds later, Maggie chuckled, hearing the non-stop yapping coming from the front room. "Demanding like your mother, I see," Maggie said to herself, zipping up her jeans.

Tidying the bedroom, she checked on the pups and then made her way to the kitchen to find something to quiet her growling stomach. Opening the fridge, she snorted at its emptiness. Unless she wanted dog food or a beer, she was out of luck. Opening a few cabinets, she continued to come up empty, and when she heard the doorbell ring, she smiled. Believing that Alex had forgotten her key, Maggie padded to the door. Deciding to pay back Alex for earlier, Maggie yanked the door open as fast as she could, and her jaw nearly hit the floor.

"Dad! Jean! What are you doing here?" she exclaimed.

"Well, your father and I were getting a bit hungry, so we picked up some Chinese take-away," Jean said, glancing at her husband to see if he wanted to join in the conversation. Seeing that his eyes were focused solely on the floor, Jean continued, "And we thought what better time to invite ourselves over to meet Alex than now. I hope you don't mind."

"What? How—"

"You left her address on the paper in the kitchen," Jean explained. "Can we come in?"

"Oh, sorry," Maggie said sheepishly, stepping out of the way. "Of course."

Jean stopped in the entryway to remove her coat while Doug took a few extra steps toward the lounge, distancing himself from his daughter. With the box of food still in his hands, he stood silent, hoping that his wife would keep up the conversation. Unfortunately, Jean had other ideas.

Sensing the tension in the room, Jean took the box from his hands. Giving him a quick wink and a knowing smile, she walked in the direction of what she assumed was the kitchen without saying a word. Whatever needed to be said, Doug would have to say it.

Dumbfounded and nervous, Maggie walked into the lounge. Looking at her father, she had no idea what to say. Other than the shocked look on his face when she had opened the door so swiftly, her father's expression had been nothing short of brooding.

"Tell me about her," Douglas said, removing his coat and placing it over a chair.

Jerked from her thoughts, Maggie said, "What?"

"*Tell* me about her," he repeated as he sat on the arm of the chair and crossed his arms.

"She'll be back in a minute and—"

"No, Maggie," he said, intently watching his daughter's eyes. "Tell me something about the woman who's supposedly stolen your heart."

Feeling as if she was being tested, Maggie cocked her head to one side and smiled. "What would you like to know?"

Douglas shrugged his shoulders. If his wife was right, once Maggie began to talk about Alex, she wouldn't be able to stop. Thinking for a moment, he asked the simplest of questions, "What does she look like?"

In the blink of an eye, a smile appeared on Maggie's face that was the widest and happiest he had ever seen on his daughter.

"She's beautiful," Maggie said in a breath, "She's tall and has black hair, and the most amazing brown eyes. Not just ordinary brown, but more like cinnamon…dark cinnamon. She's funny and smart, and a bit cocky at times, and when she puts her mind to it, she can be *unbelievably* stubborn," Maggie said, laughing out loud. "She's strong, but you wouldn't know it by looking at her, and she likes to laugh. With one look, she can make me smile, and with the next, she can make me blush. I've never met anyone as courageous as

Alex, nor as determined, but that's only a small part of who she is. She cares, Dad. She cares about people and the fate of the world. She doesn't just want to sit back and watch it go by. She wants to help change it for the better, for the future…for our kids. When I look at her…" Pausing for a moment, Maggie closed her eyes and took a deep breath. "When I look at her, I see in her eyes a love that's pure and true, and I know that she'll love me until the day I die. She'll be my champion when I need one. She'll be my nurse when I fall ill. She'll be the person who stands by me no matter what, and the one that I'll no doubt argue with more than any other person on the face of this planet. And honestly, I look forward to those arguments. I love her intensity. I love her passion for what's right and what's wrong, and I can't imagine living another day if Alex isn't by my side. I love her, Dad. I love her more than words can say."

Standing in the doorway of the kitchen, Jean wiped a tear from her cheek as she glanced at her husband. Looking back, he smiled and nodded his head in silent agreement. There was no more doubt. His daughter was truly in love with a woman named Alex Blake.

"Well," he said with a smile, his voice bringing Maggie back to reality, "Then I can't wait to meet her."

Shocked at her father's apparent quick acceptance of her new lifestyle, Maggie said, "How come I feel like I've just missed something really important?"

With a hearty chuckle, Douglas pulled his daughter into his arms. Kissing her on the top of the head, he said, "You're my daughter, and I love you, and *that's* what's important. If she's who you want, Magpie, I'll be in your corner, just like always."

Looking up with tears in her eyes, Maggie said, "Thanks, Dad."

Sniffling back a few tears of his own, he smiled. "Now, let's go give Jean a hand, shall we? We can't be sniveling like children when your lady gets back. What kind of impression would that make?"

***

A short time later, containers of Chinese food were spread across the counter with plates at the ready, awaiting Alex's return. As Jean filled glasses with wine, Maggie heard the front door open and smiled, but before she could make it out of the kitchen, Alex called out, "You'd best not still be naked!"

If she could have fit into one of the kitchen cabinets, Maggie would have crawled inside and latched the door. With her face vivid scarlet and her eyes as wide as saucers, several seconds passed before she forced herself to look in Jean and Doug's direction. Mortified, she whispered, "I'll be right back."

"There you are," Alex said, seeing Maggie come from the kitchen. "Oh, I could have told you there's nothing in there. I haven't had time to shop yet. Sorry."

"That's where you're wrong," Maggie said with a weak grin as Sandy scampered past her and headed for the bedroom.

Leaning over for a kiss, Alex said, "What do you mean?"

"My *father* is in the kitchen," Maggie whispered, trying her best not to smile.

"What!" Alex said, wincing as she realized that he had no doubt heard her jovial greeting.

"Oh, and my stepmother, too."

"Oh, Christ," Alex whispered angrily. "You could have warned me."

"How was I supposed to know that you were going to come in the door and ask if I was naked?"

"Good point."

"Thanks."

"What are the chances that I can leave before he sees me?" Alex asked quietly.

"Not very good, I'm afraid," Douglas Campbell replied as he stood in the kitchen doorway eyeing the attractive dark-haired woman whose cheeks were as red as the tank top she was wearing.

Smiling, Maggie winked at Alex, took her hand and led her to the man and woman standing near the kitchen.

"Alex, this is my father and stepmother, Douglas and Jean Campbell."

Holding her breath, Alex held out her hand. "Very nice to meet you, Mr. Campbell," she said politely with her cheeks still blazing red.

Briefly glancing at his wife, Douglas smiled and took Alex's hand. "Nice to meet you, too."

EPILOGUE

"You need any help with that?" Alex asked, walking into the kitchen to find Jean basting the turkey.

Glancing over her shoulder, Jean smiled. "No, dear, I'm fine. Why don't you sit down, and I'll make you some tea."

"Thanks," Alex said, sinking into a chair.

"Did you have a good rest?"

"Yes," Alex said, looking around. "Where's Maggie?"

"Oh, we ran out of milk, so I sent her to the store. She should be back in a few minutes."

"And the boys?"

With a grin, Jean nodded toward the window. "They're in the backyard with their grandfather, trying to make a snowman."

Pushing herself out of the chair, Alex walked over and peered through the frosted glass. Laughing, she watched as Douglas Campbell tried to keep up with his three-year-old grandsons. Merrily running through the snow, the little boys filled their tiny hands with the white powder and then dashed back to their grandfather, who piled it atop the small snowman, before playfully demanding that they run and get more.

"He adores them," Jean said with a grin, looking at her daughter-in-law.

"*They* adore him," Alex said, opening the refrigerator to look for a snack.

Taking a package of biscuits from the cabinet, Jean motioned for Alex to sit. Filling a plate, she placed it in front of her hungry daughter-in-law, along with a cup of tea. Joining Alex at the table, Jean took a sip of tea and said, "It's a shame that Maggie couldn't have any more."

"Yeah, she wanted more, but with the fevers, it's just too risky for her to try again."

"And how about you?"

Laughing, Alex looked down at her enormous belly, rubbing it gently as she smiled at the concerned grandparent, "I'm fit as a fiddle, as they say."

Debating for a moment, Jean said, "I have to tell you, Doug and I were a bit concerned when Maggie told us that you were going to do this."

"Why, because I'm contrary, stubborn and don't always think before I act?"

Laughing out loud, Jean nodded her head. "Yes, basically," she replied wiping the tears of laughter from her eyes.

"Well, if we're speaking truths, I should tell you that I was scared shitless."

"Really?"

"Yeah," Alex said, nodding her head. "I mean, it's one thing to watch someone else carry a child, or in our case, two, but to go through it myself? I can't tell you how many times I tried to talk myself out of it."

"So what changed your mind?"

"Maggie and the boys."

"How so?"

"Maggie went through a lot to get pregnant, you know? All the tests and procedures, and after each attempt failed, she became more and more depressed...and then finally it happened. I remember how she cried that morning. Crying because she was pregnant, crying because she was happy, crying just because she could cry. You know how they say that women glow when they're pregnant? Well, Maggie's light was damn near blinding," Alex said with a smile.

"It wasn't long after that when the morning sickness started. I remember thinking how stupid it was to call it that because for Maggie, it lasted most of the day. And then the cravings began, and each time she asked for something, I'd run out to the store for it. You can't imagine the looks that you get when you're buying pickled herring, sardines and ice cream at one in the morning, but then she started to bleed and was put on bed rest, and things got scary."

"Yes, I remember that," Jean said. "We were all worried sick about her."

Nodding her head, Alex said, "But do you know what? Through it all, she never once complained. Not once! Through the morning sickness and the cravings, through the bloating and four months bed rest, and even though those two little boys out there did their best to kick the shit out of her, she never said a word. Not one bloody word!" Alex said, shaking her head in amazement.

"And then they were born," Alex said, her voice cracking with emotion as she remembered that night. "Maggie was in so much pain and they got all twisted up inside, and then the doctors had to...had to cut her..." Choked by emotion, Alex stopped and took a deep breath. Wiping the tears from her face, she offered Jean the weakest of grins and sniffled back another tear. "When they had to cut her, she took my hand and tried to calm *me* down. Me! Can you imagine? My wife is lying on a table with her belly cut open, and she's trying to console *me*."

Shaking her head in disbelief, Alex took a sip of tea. "And then, there they were. All bloody and wrinkled, and next to their mother, they were the most beautiful things I had ever seen. I remember looking down at Maggie, both of us crying and laughing, and then she said *thank you*. Thank you? I don't know that I've ever felt so small in my life as I did at that moment. There I was, standing in complete awe of her and all that she went through, and she's thanking me…for what? For holding her hand or going for groceries?"

Raising her eyes to meet Jean's, Alex said, "You asked what changed my mind. I love Maggie and I'll do anything for her, and that's the reason I'm carrying her babies inside of me."

"And you never found out what she was thanking you for?"

"No, I just figured it was the drugs talking," Alex said with a laugh.

"It wasn't the drugs," Maggie said, standing in the doorway to the kitchen. Surprised, both women turned in their chairs as she walked over and smiled down at Alex. "I was thanking you for pulling me out of a plane against my will. I was thanking you for carrying me when I couldn't walk, and for not allowing me to die in that cabin. I was thanking you for all the laughs that we've shared and the love that we've made, and I was thanking *you* for allowing me to be *your* wife."

Placing the grocery bag on the table, Maggie leaned down and kissed Alex on the mouth. Although Jean was quite used to their displays of affection, she found herself needing to look away as the kiss deepened. Finally, they pulled apart, and Maggie slid the bag in Jean's direction as she removed her coat and sat down.

"How you feeling?" she asked, her eyes dropping to Alex's extremely large baby bump.

"I feel enormous, and like I'm carrying sumo wrestlers instead of two girls."

"You should try boys," Maggie said with a wink, rubbing Alex's belly. "Did you get a nap?"

"Yes, dear," Alex answered in a sarcastic twang.

"None of that, Blake, or no ice cream and pickles for you tonight."

"Ouch."

"What's wrong, sweetheart?"

"Nothing, just a stitch," Alex said, rubbing her side. Struggling to stand, she said, "And I need to use the loo...*again*. Be right back."

As Alex waddled up the stairs, she quickly moved to one side as Sandy and Peaches bounded down the stairs, with the littlest, Tulip, in quick pursuit. Scooping her up before she could pass, Alex laughed as the teacup terrier wiggled in her hand, licking and nipping as she tried to get away and catch up with those that had stolen her toy.

"I love Doug and Jean to death," Alex said to the pup. "But I would never have given you a handle like Tulip."

Placing the fur ball on the stairs, she laughed again as Tulip bounced, rolled and thumped her way to the bottom, all the while yapping at her sister and mother.

***

"Is there anything I can do?" Maggie asked, pouring herself a cup of tea.

"No, I've got it all under control, dear," Jean said as she checked a pot on the stove. "The reason we invited you up was so that you and Alex could relax. In a few weeks, you're going to have your hands full."

"Isn't that the truth," Maggie said, rolling her eyes. "But you're still planning to come down and stay with us for a while, aren't you?"

Smiling, Jean said, "Don't worry, Maggie, I doubt that you could keep us away even if you tried. Thank God you bought that huge house."

"It's not that big."

With a snort, Jean said, "It's not that small either."

"Maggie, could you come up here for a minute please," Alex called from upstairs.

"Probably can't get off the toilet," Maggie said with a giggle, winking at Jean as she left the room and jogged up the stairs. Entering their bedroom, she walked up to the bathroom door. Snickering, she said loudly, "What is it, sweetheart? Need help getting up?"

"Um, can you come in here for a minute?"

Maggie's heart dropped. Quickly opening the door, she rushed inside and found Alex sitting on the edge of the tub, surrounded by a puddle of water on the floor. Confused, Maggie asked, "What happened?"

Raising an eyebrow, Alex stared back and watched as the penny dropped.

"Your water broke!"

"No! You think!" Alex shouted, still quite flustered at the gush of water that had soaked through her trousers.

Chuckling, Maggie tiptoed to the tub. "Sweetheart, you knew that this was going to happen."

"It didn't happen to you!"

Tickled by the fact that her normally unflappable wife was freaking out, it was all Maggie could do not to laugh. Sitting on the edge of the tub, she patted Alex's knee. "No, it didn't happen to me, but you knew there was a chance. What's wrong, sweetheart? You seem almost angry?"

"I just had a pain that made me see stars, for Christ's sake. I thought I had to pee, and then suddenly – whoosh – I'm a two-year-old again! My trousers are soaked through, not to mention my knickers, and I can't stand wet knickers!"

"Since when?" Maggie joked, laughing out loud when Alex gave her a dirty look. Pulling a towel from the rod, Maggie covered the puddle on the floor. "Let's get you to hospital, okay?" she said, taking Alex by the arm and helping her stand.

"Not until I change my trousers."

"Alex—"

"Margaret, this is not up for debate. I'm not going anywhere until I'm wearing dry knickers!"

Biting her lip, Maggie tried her best to hide her grin as she guided Alex into the bedroom and helped her changed her clothes. A few minutes later, as they were about to leave the room, another labor pain rocked Alex, forcing her to stop in her tracks and grab hold of the door jamb until it passed.

"Are you all right?" Maggie asked in a whisper, the amusement she had felt a few minutes earlier having disappeared at the sight of Alex in pain.

"Yeah," Alex replied, taking a few deep breaths to clear her head. "But that one was worse than before."

"How much worse?"

"A lot."

"Are you timing them?"

Nodding her head, Alex looked at her watch. "Four minutes."

Maggie's eyes flew open. "Four minutes! Alex, that's fast."

"Yeah, well you know me. I've never been known for my patience."

"Well, you're about to *be* a patient. We need to get you to hospital. Come on."

Hearing voices, Jean came to the landing. When she saw Maggie holding the small overnight case for the hospital in her hand as she carefully guided Alex down the steps, Jean rushed outside and called for her husband. Gathering his grandsons in his arms, Douglas rushed into the house, depositing them in the kitchen, before hurrying to the front hall.

"Oh, Christ. Is it time?" he asked, helping Alex down the last two steps.

Before Maggie or Alex could answer, another pain ripped through Alex and this time, she couldn't stop herself from crying out. Grabbing hold of the railing, she began taking rapid breaths as she waited for it to pass.

Grabbing his keys from the table, he forced them into Maggie's hand. "Take these and go start my car."

"Dad, our car—"

"Maggie, it's snowing and mine is safer, so stop arguing and do what I ask!"

Taking the keys, Maggie ran out the door. Jumping into her father's SUV, she started the ignition, adjusting the seat and mirrors while she waited for the defogger to clear the windows. Turning the heater on full blast, she scrambled out and ran to the house. Halfway up the walk, she stopped in her tracks when the front door flew open, and her father came out with Alex in his arms.

"She just had another contraction and almost hit the floor," he explained, carefully walking down the snow-covered path. Gingerly placing Alex in the front seat of the car, he waited while Maggie climbed back into the driver's seat.

"I'll stay with the boys, and Jean is going with you," he said.

"Dad—"

"Don't worry sweetheart, I'll call Jean's sister, and I'll be there as soon as I can."

Kissing Alex on the cheek, he winked at his daughter and shut the door, quickly jogging into the house in search of his wife. Seconds later, Jean ran down the path and got into the car.

"Maggie, I'm scared," Alex said quietly as Maggie carefully backed out of the driveway.

"I know, sweetheart, but it will be okay. I promise."

"But what if it's not?"

"Since when do you think like that?" Maggie snapped, stopping the car and putting the gearshift into park.

"Maggie, dear, I really don't think you should stop," Jean chimed in from the back seat.

"I'll move when I'm damn well ready," Maggie growled, her temper thickening her accent like it always did.

She had read all the books. She had been with Maggie from conception through birth, yet nothing could have prepared Alex for the emotions now coursing through her body. In a short time, two little girls would emerge from her, and she was terrified.

Glaring back at the woman with a deer-in-the-headlights look on her face, Maggie said, "What's wrong, Alex?"

"I guess I'm just scared."

"Of what?"

"Of not being as strong as you."

"What?"

"You know, how you went through all of this with the boys like a champ."

Rolling her eyes, Maggie said, "Sweetheart, this isn't some fucking competition! If you want to scream and swear, or rant and rave, have at it! It's totally understandable given the circumstances."

"Really?" Alex said, wincing as she could feel another contraction starting.

"Really," Maggie replied with a smile.

"Well, with that being said," Alex said, stopping to take a few quick breaths. "Could you do me a favor?"

"Anything, sweetheart, just name it."

"Could you please drive me to the fucking hospital? I'm dying here!"

Laughing, Maggie leaned over and kissed Alex on the cheek. Casting a quick wink at Jean, who was smiling in the back seat, Maggie slipped the car into drive and carefully took her wife, now swearing like a sailor, to the hospital.

***

"Let's get you out of these wet clothes while we wait for your Aunt Janet," Douglas said to his grandsons as he began removing the multiple layers of clothing that Maggie had dressed them in.

"Where's Mum and Mummy?" DJ asked as his grandfather tugged off his soaked mittens.

"They've gone to the hospital to get your sisters."

"I want to go, too!" John stated emphatically as he fought with the zipper on his jacket.

"No, not tonight, but maybe tomorrow."

"I want to see my mum!" DJ shouted, pulling away from his grandfather.

"Hey, what's this?" Douglas said, grinning as he pulled the boy into a hug. "Mummy told you that Mum would be away for a day or two. You know that."

"But Mum was crying! Mum was hurt! I want to see my mum! I want to see Mum now!" DJ screamed.

Totally forgetting that the children were in the kitchen when Alex had cried out in pain, Douglas sighed and knelt down beside them. Pulling them into his arms, he tried to find the words.

"Sweethearts," he began, looking into their dark-brown eyes. "When a woman has a baby, it sometimes hurts a little."

"Like when I fall down?" John asked.

"Exactly," Douglas said, nodding his head. "But once Mummy gets Mum to the hospital, the doctors have something that will make the pain go away. I promise. They know what to do."

With all the force that a three-year-old could muster, DJ wiggled out of Douglas' grip. "I know what to do!" he shrieked, running to the door. "I know how to fix Mum!"

Before Douglas had a chance to stop him, he watched in shock as DJ opened the back door and ran out into the snow. Jumping to his feet, he strode to the door. "Douglas Jarrod Campbell-Blake, you get in here this minute!" he bellowed, seeing his grandson dart about the snow in his stocking feet.

Having kicked off his boots after coming back inside, Douglas frantically looked around the kitchen, but just as he spotted them in the hallway, his other grandson rushed past him. "Oh, me, too! Me, too!" John yelled, dashing through the snow to meet up with his brother.

"Jesus Christ!" Douglas muttered as he looked up at the ceiling. "Thank you God for giving me a girl. Boys are a pain in the arse!"

The sound of their shrieks of joy changed his focus, and standing in the doorway, he screamed again. This time, adding a bit more emphasis to get their attention. "John Ethan and Douglas Jarrod, get in this house *now*!"

His booming voice finally did the trick, and out of breath, but smiling, the two youngsters scampered back to their grandfather, giggling all the way. Ushering them into the house, he ran his fingers through their black hair to dislodge the snow, and then pulling off their socks, rubbed their cold, tiny feet until they were warm.

Exasperated and confused, he said, "What the hell...um...what in the world did you think you'd find outside that could help your mum?"

"This," DJ said proudly, as both he and his brother held out their hands.

Feeling as if he had been sucker-punched, Douglas sank to the floor. Unable to stop the tears from forming in his eyes, he wrapped his arms around his grandsons and held them close. Placing a kiss on each of their cheeks, he held out his hands...and they filled them with ice.

The End

ABOUT THE AUTHOR

Lyn Gardner began her career writing fan fiction. In 2009, she sat down and wrote a story with no expectations other than to entertain. Three years later, at the insistence of her readers, and after listening to their praise as well as their prods, she published her first book - Ice.

Now a multi-published author, Lyn lives in the sunny state of Florida where she enjoys playing a round of golf every now and then...that is, when her muse isn't whispering in her ear.

You can find out more about the author by visiting her website or her blog, or feel free to follow her on Twitter or Facebook...and by all means, say hello if you'd like.

Blog: www.lyngardner.blogspot.com
Website: www.lyngardner.net
Facebook: https://www.facebook.com/#!/lyn.gardner.587
Twitter: @LynGardner227

Other Works by Lyn Gardner

Mistletoe

Give Me A Reason

Printed in Great Britain
by Amazon